THE LIVES

OF

NOTORIOUS HIGHWAYMEN.

THE LIVES

OF

NOTORIOUS AND DARING

HIGHWAYMEN,

AND

ROBBERS.

COMPILED FROM AUTHENTIC SOURCES,

BY G. THOMPSON.

LONDON:

PUBLISHED BY J. S. PRATT.

MDCCCXLIII.

CONTENTS.

THE LIVES

OF

HIGHWAYMEN & ROBBERS.

WILLIAM NEVISON.

THE advancement of the arts and sciences is not more rapid than the progress of folly and vice. In the following memoir it will be fully demonstrated, that the best education may be perverted by vicious dispositions.

William Nevison was born at Pontefract in Yorkshire, about the year 1630, and his parents, being in good circumstances, conferred on him a decent education. He remained at school until he was about thirteen years of age. During that period, his expanding talents promised a luxurious harvest; but the bent of his character, and the ruling motive of all his actions, were exhibited at that time. He commenced his depredations by stealing a silver spoon from his own father. The too indulgent pa·rent, instead of chastising him for the crime, transferred the unpleasant work to the schoolmaster. The father who resigns authority over his own children, may expect either to lose them altogether, or to have his heart grieved and his family dishonoured by their conduct. The schoolmaster having punished young Nevison for the theft, he spent a

sleepless night in meditating a revenge. He knew
that the pedagogue had a favourite horse, which
grazed in an adjacent paddock. William rose early
in the morning, moved quietly into his father's closet, stole his keys, and supplied himself with cash,
to the amount of ten pounds; then, taking a saddle
and bridle from his father's stable, he hastened to
the paddock in which the schoolmaster's horse was
accustomed to feed; and, having saddled and bri-
dled the animal, with all haste rode towards London.
About a mile or two from the capital, he cut the
throat of the poor horse, for fear of detection. Arrived in London, he changed his name and clothes,
and then hired himself to a brewer. Although circumstances compelled him to be for a while industrious, in order to obtain the necessaries of life,
his mind was always upon the stretch to invent
some more expeditious mode of acquiring money,
than the slow return of annual pay, accordingly he
often ineffectually attempted to rob his master.
One evening, however, the clerk happening to use
his glass too freely, Nevison followed him into the
counting house, and, while he was enjoying a recruiting nap, stole the keys of the desks, and re-
lieved them of their burden, to the amount of about
two hundred pounds. Without waiting to discover
whether the clerk, or the servant would be blamed
for the cash, he sailed for Holland.

But change of climate had no effect in changing
his nature. Through his instigation, the daughter
of a respectable citizen robbed her father of a large
sum of money, and a quantity of jewels, and eloped
with the Englishman. They were pursued, taken,
and committed to prison Thus detected, Nevison

would certainly have finished a short but villanous career in a foreign land, had he not fortunately effected his escape.

With so small difficulty he arrived in Flanders, and enlisted into a regiment of English volunteers under the command of the Duke of York. In that station he behaved with considerable reputation and even acquired some money; but his restless temper and disposition to acquire riches, by whatever means, did not permit him to remain in a situation of sobriety or industry. He deserted, went over to England, with his money, purchased a horse, together with other necessaries and commenced his depredations in a systematic form. His success was uncommon, and he every day found means to replenish his coffers, and to nourish his extravagance. Nor would he unite his fortune with any one, who, from selfish motives, might feel disposed to participate in his lucrative employment.

One day Nevison, who went otherwise by the name of Johnson, travelling on the road, and scouring about in search of a prize, met two countrymen, who, coming up towards him, informed him, that it was very dangerous travelling forward, for that the way was set, and that they had been robbed by three highwaymen, about half a mile off; and if he had any charge of money about him, it was his safest course to turn back. Nevison asking them what they had lost, they told him forty pounds: upon which he replied, turn back with me and shew me the way they took, and my life to a farthing, I'll make them return you your money again. They rode along with him till they came in sight of the highwaymen, when Nevison, ordering the country-

men to stay behind him at some distance, rode up,
and spoke to the foremost of them, saying, sir, by
your garb and the colour of your horse, you should
be one of those I look after; and if so, my business is to tell you, that you borrowed of two friends
of mine forty pounds, which they desire me to demand of you, and which, before we part, you must
restore. How! cried the highwaymen, forty pounds!
What! is the fellow mad? So mad, replied Nevison, that your life shall answer me, if you do not
give me better satisfaction. Upon which he drew
his pistol and suddenly clapped it to the other's
breast, who, finding that Nevison had also his rein,
and that he could not get his sword or pistols, yielded, telling him his life was at his mercy. No, said
Nevison, it is not that I seek, but the money you
robbed these two men of, who are riding up to me,
which you must refund.

The thief was forced to consent, and readily to
deliver such part as he had, saying, his companions
were in possession of the rest; so that Nevison,
having made him dismount, and taking away his
pistols, which he gave to the countrymen, ordered
them to secure him, and hold his own, while he took
the thief's horse, and pursued the other two, whom
he soon overtook: for they, thinking him their companion, stopped as soon as they saw him; so that
he came up to them in the midst of a common.
How now, Jack, said one of them, what made you
engage with yon fellow? No, gentlemen, replied
Nevison, you are mistaken in your man: Thomas
—— for by the token of your horse and arms, I
perceive you are Thomas —— he hath sent me to
you for the ransom of his life, amounting to no less

than the prize of the day, which if you presently
surrender, you may go about your business! if not,
I must have a little dispute with you at sword and
pistol! At which one of them fired at him, but
missing his aim, received Nevison's bullet in his
right shoulder; and being thereby disabled, Nevison was about to discharge at the other, when he
called for quarter, and came to a parley, which, in
short, was made up, with Nevison's promise to send
their friend, and their delivering all the ready money they had, amounting to a hundred and fifty
pounds. Having obtained this booty, he rode back
to the two countrymen, and released their prisoner,
giving them their whole forty pounds, with a caution for the future to look better after it, and not,
like cowards as they were, to surrender their money
on such easy terms again.

In all his exploits, Nevison was tender of the fair
sex, and bountiful to the poor. He was also a true
loyalist, and never levied any contributions upon the
royalists.

One day, fortunately encountering a rich usurer,
he stopped his coach, and demanded that he would
deliver the money which he had extorted from poor
widows and orphans. The pistol presented to his
breast, and the reproaches of the highwayman, filled
his guilty mind with inexpressible terror, and he
began to expostulate for his life. That shall be
granted, replied Nevison, upon condition of your
surrendering your gold. The other reluctantly drew
out sixty broad pieces of gold; but this sum being
inadequate to the necessities of Nevison, he constrained the usurer to mount upon the postilion's
horse, and allowed the coach with the three ladies

in it to proceed.   The poor Jew, now thinking that the hour was verily nigh at hand when he would be bereft of life and separated from his treasures, experienced all the violent emotions of terror, chagrin, and despair.   Nevison compelled him to draw a note upon sight for five hundred pounds upon a scrivener in London.   He then permitted him to ride after his friends to acquaint them with his misfortunes, while he himself rode all night, that he might have the money drawn before advice could be forwarded to stop the payment.

After several adventures of a similar nature, Nevison one day robbed a rich grazier of £450 and then proposed to himself to retire with the spoil.   Accordingly, he returned home, and was joyfully received by his father, who, not having heard of him of seven or eight years, supposed that he had been dead. He remained with his father until the day of the old man's death, living soberly and honestly as if no act of infamy had ever sullied his reputation.

Upon the death of his father, however, he returned to his former courses, and in a short time his name was a terror to every traveller on the road. To such an extent did he carry his plans that the carriers and drovers who frequented that road, willingly agreed to leave certain sums at such places as he appointed, to prevent their being stripped of their all.

Continuing his wicked course, he was at last apprehended, thrown into Leicester jail, put in irons, and strictly guarded ; but, in spite of all the precautions of the county, he effected his escape.

One day, two or three of his trusty friends visited him, one of whom, being a physician, gave out that he was infected with the plague, and that, unless he was removed to a larger room, where he might enjoy free air, he would not only himself perish, but communicate the infection to all the inmates of the jail. He was instantly removed; and the jailor's wife did not allow the jailor to go farther than the door of his apartment, for fear of the infection, which afforded Nevison and his friends time to perfect their scheme. The physician came twice or thrice every day to see him, and continued to declare his case hopeless. At last a painter was brought in who painted all his body with spots, similar to those that appear upon a person affected with the pestilence. In a few days after, he received a sleeping draught, and was declared to be dead. The inquest who sat upon the body were afraid to approach in order to make very minute inspection, and thus a verdict was returned that he had died of the plague. His friends now demanded his body, and he was carried out of prison in a coffin.

This insertion into a coffin only rendered him more callous and daring in vice. He, with redoubled vigour, renewed his depredations, and meeting the carriers and drovers, informed them that it was necessary to increase their rents, in order to refund his expenses while in jail and his loss of time.

It was at first supposed that it was his ghost, who carried on the same pranks that he had done in his lifetime. The truth of this, however, came to be suspected, and the jailor offered a reward of twenty pounds to any person that would apprehend and restore him to his former domicile.

Resolved to visit the capital, he upon his journey met a company of canting beggars, pilgrims, and

idle vagabonds. Continuing in their company for
some time, and observing the merry life that they
pursued, he took an opportunity to propose himself
a member of their honourable fraternity. Their
leader applauded his resolution, and addressed him
in the following words:—Do we not come into the
world arrant beggars, without a rag upon us? And
do not we all go out of the world like beggars, saving only a sheet over us? Shall we then be ashamed to walk up and down the world, like beggars,
with old blankets pinned before us? No! no! that
would be a shame to us, indeed. Have we not the
whole kingdom to walk in at our pleasure? Are
we afraid of the approach of quarter day? Do we
walk in fear of sheriffs, bailiffs, and catch-poles?
Who ever knew an arrant beggar arrested for debt?
Is not our meat dressed in every man's kitchen?
Does not every man's cellar afford us beer? And
the best men's purses keep a penny for us to spend.

Having by these words, as he thought, fully fixed
him in love with begging, he then acquainted the
company with Nevison's desire, in consequence of
which they were all very joyful. The first question
they asked him was, if he had any *loure* in his *bung?*
Nevison stared on them, not knowing what they
meant; till at last one of them informed him, it
was money in his purse. He told them he had but
eighteen pence, which he gave them freely. This,
by a general vote, was condemned to be spent in a
booze for his initiation. Then they commanded
him to kneel down, which being done, one of the
chief of them took a *gage* of *booze,* which is a quart
of drink, and poured the same on his head, saying, I do, by virtue of this sovereign liquor, install

thee in the Roage, and make thee a free denizen of our ragged regiment. So that henceforth it shall be lawful for thee to cant, only observing these rules :—First, that thou art not to wander up and down all countries, but to keep to that quarter that is allotted thee ; and, secondly, thou art to give way to any of us that have borne all the offices of the wallet before ; and, upon holding up a finger, to avoid any town or country village, where thou seest we are foraging for victuals for our army that march along with us. Observing these two rules, we take thee into our protection, and constitute thee a brother of our numerous society.

The leader having ended his oration, Nevison rose up, and was congratulated by all the company's hanging about him, like so many dogs about a bear, and making such a hideous noise, that the chief, commanding silence, addressed them as follows :— Now that thou art entered into our fraternity, thou must not scruple to act any villanies, whether it be to cut a purse, steal a cloak, bag, or portmanteau, convey all manner of things, whether a chicken, sucking pig, duck, goose, or hen, or to steal a shirt from the hedge ; for that he will be a *quier cove* (a professed rogue,) must observe these rules. And because thou art but a novice in begging, and understandest not the mysteries of the canting language, thou shalt have a wife to be thy companion, by whom thou mayest receive instructions. And thereupon he singled him out a girl of about seventeen years of age, which tickled his fancy very much ; but he must presently be married to her after the fashion of their patrico, who is, amongst beggars,

their priest. Whereupon the ceremony was per
formed after this manner :—

They took a hen, and having cut off the head,
laid the dead body on the ground, placed Nevison
on the one side, and his intended on the other ; this
being done, the priest, standing by, with a loud voice
bade them live together till death did them part ;
then shaking hands, and kissing each other, the ceremony of their wedding was over, and the whole
group appeared intoxicated with joy. Night ap
proaching, and all their money being spent, they be-
took themselves to a barn not far off, where they
broached a hogshead, and went to sleep.

Nevison, having met this odd piece of diversion
on his journey, slipped out of the barn when all were
asleep, took a horse, and posted directly away. But,
coming to London, he found there was too much
noise about him to permit him to tarry there ; he
therefore returned into the country, and fell to his
old pranks again. Several who formerly had been
robbed by him, happened to meet him, imagined
that his ghost walked abroad, having heard the re-
port of his pestilential death in Leicester jail. In
short, his crimes became so notorious, that a reward
was offered to any that would apprehend him, this
made many waylay him, especially two brothers,
named Fletcher, one of whom Nevison shot dead ;
but, going into a litle village about thirteen miles
from York, he was taken by captain Hardcastle, and
sent to York jail, where on the 15th of March, 1684,
he was tried, condemned, and executed, aged forty-
five.

WILLIAM DAVIS, COMMONLY CALLED
THE GOLDEN FARMER,

Was a native of North Wales, but he obtained the name of the Golden Farmer, from his custom of paying any considerable sum in gold. He was born in the year 1626. At an early period of life he removed to Sudbury, Gloucestershire, where he took a farm, married the daughter of a wealthy innkeeper, by whom he had eighteen children, and followed that employment merely to disguise the real character of a robber, which he sustained without suspicion for the space of forty-two years. He usually robbed alone. One day, meeting some stage coaches, he stopped one of them, full of ladies, all of whom complied with his demands, except a quaker, who vowed she had no money, nor any thing valuable about her; upon which, fearing he should lose the booty of the other coaches, he told her he would go and see what they could afford him, and return to her again. Having rifled the other three coaches, he was as good as his word; and the quaker persisting in her former statement, enraged the farmer to such a degree, that, seizing her by the shoulder, and employing language that it would be hardly proper to repeat, he so scared the poor quaker, as to cause her to produce a purse of guineas, a gold watch and a diamond ring. Whereupon, they parted as good friends as when they were first introduced to each other.

Upon another occasion, our desperado met the

B

duchess of Albermarle in her coach, as she was
riding over Salisbury Plain, but he encountered
greater difficulty in this case than he had contemp-
lated.   Before he could assault the lady he was compelled to engage a postilion, the coachman, and two
footmen ; but, having disabled them all by discharg-
ing several pistols, he approached his prey, whom
he found more refractory than the female quaker.
Perceiving another person of quality's coach approaching, with a retinue of servants, he was fain to
content himself by pulling three diamond rings from
her finger by force, snatching a gold watch from her
side, and venting a portion of abuse upon her obstinate ladyship.

It was not very long after this exploit, that our
adventurer met with Sir Thomas Day, a justice of
the peace, living at Bristol. They fell into discourse, and riding along, the Golden Farmer informed his new acquaintance, that a little while before,
he had narrowly escaped being robbed by a couple
of highwaymen, but, luckily, his horse had better
heels than theirs, and he got clear of them. Truly,
said Sir Thomas, that had been very hard ; but,
nevertheless, as you would have been robbed between sun and sun, the country, upon suing it,
would have been obliged to make good your loss.
Thus, chatting together, and coming to a convenient place, the Golden Farmer shot Sir Thomas's
man's horse under him, and compelling him to retire to a distance, presented a pistol to the knight's
heart, and demanded his money. I thought, sir,
said Sir Thomas, that you had been an honest man.
Your worship is mistaken, cried the farmer ; and if
you had any skill in physiognomy, you might have

perceived that my countenance is the very picture of necessity: so deliver me presently, for I'm in haste. Sir Thomas therefore, being constrained to give him the money he had about him, which was about sixty pounds in gold and silver; the other humbly thanked his worship, and told him, that what he had parted with was not lost, because he had been robbed between sun and sun, and could therefore come upon the county.

One Mr. Hart, a young gentleman of Enfield, who possessed a good estate, but was not overburdened with brains, riding one day over Finchley Common, where the Golden Farmer had been some hours hunting for prey, was met by him, and saluted with a smart slap of his drawn hanger upon his shoulders: a plague on you! said the farmer, how slow you are, to make a man wait all the morning; come, deliver what you have, and go to the devil for others! The young gentleman, rather surprised at this novel greeting, began to make several excuses, saying he had no money about him; but his incredulous antagonist took the liberty of searching him, and finding about him above a hundred guineas, he bestowed upon him two or three further slaps on the shoulders, telling him, at the same time, not to give his mind to lying in future, when an honest gentleman required a small gratuity from him.

Squire Broughton, a gentleman of the middle temple, was the next prey of Davis. They happened to meet at an inn on the road, and the Farmer pretended to be on his way to the capital, about an offence that a neighbouring farmer had committed against him, by allowing his cattle to break into his

fields. Meanwhile he requested that Squire Broughton would recommend him to an expert and faithful
agent to conduct his cause. Having spent this
night at the inn, they proceeded next morning on
their journey, when the Farmer addressed the counsellor, saying, pray, sir, what is meant by trover and
conversion, in the law of England? He replied,
that it signified, in our common law, an action
which one man has against another, who, having
found any of his goods, refuses to deliver them up
on demand, and perhaps converts them to his own
use.

Davis being now at a place convenient for his
purpose, very well, then, sir, said he, should 1 find
any money about you, and convert it to my use, it
is only actionable, I find. That is robbery, said the
barrister, which requires no less a satisfaction than
a man's life. A robbery, replied the Golden Farmer ;
why then I must commit one in my time : and presented his pistol. Surprised at his client's rough behaviour, the lawyer began to remonstate in forcible
terms upon the impropriety of his conduct, and con-
tended that it was contrary to both conscience and
law. He failed, however, to make an impression on
the Farmer, for he put his pistol to the breast of
the lawyer, and compelled him to deliver his money
amounting to about forty pounds.

The famous highwayman had only a few more
acts of violence to perform. His actions and character being now universally known, many a hue and
cry was sent after him, and conspired to his over-
throw. He was seized and imprisoned, tried and
condemned. He spent his time in prison in the

same way in which his former life had been passed,
and a violent death terminated his wicked course on
the 20th of December, 1698.

JONATHAN SIMPSON.

THIS individual was the son of a respectable gentleman in Launceston, in Cornwall, and put an apprentice to a linen draper. After serving his time
with great approbation, his father gave him £1500
to commence business for himself.

He had not been a year in business when he
married a merchant's daughter, and received with
her £2000 of portion. Such an accession to his
wealth enabled him to extend his business, and to
conduct it with ease. But money cannot procure
happiness. The affections of the young lady had
been gained by a man of less fortune, and, to please
her father, she had given her hand where she could
not bestow her heart; and, though married to
another, she continued in a degree of familiarity
with her former lover that excited her husband's
jealousy, the most violent of all the passions.

In a short time, after having lived in a very unhappy manner, Simpson took the opportunity to sell
all off, and, having shut up shop, went away with
what money he could raise, determined no longer to
remain in Bristol. He was now possessed of about
£5000, but his expenses were so extravagant, that
this large sum was soon exhausted. He then went
to the highway, committed a robbery, and would
certainly have been hanged, had not some of his

rich relations procured a reprieve. The difficulty of obtaining it may be guessed from the fact, that it arrived at Tyburn just when the rope was about his neck. Such was his obduracy, that when returning to Newgate behind one of the sheriff's men, the latter asked him what he thought of a reprieve when he was come to the gallows. No more than I thought of my dying day.

When he came to the prison door, the turnkey refused to receive him, saying, that he was sent to be executed, and that he was discharged of him, and would not permit him to enter without a new warrant. Upon which Simpson exclaimed, what an unhappy cast off dog am I, that both Tyburn and Newgate should in one day refuse to entertain me! Well, I'll mend my manners for the future, and try whether I can't merit a reception at them both, next time I am brought thither.

He immediately recommenced his operations and one day robbed a gentleman of his purse full of counters, which he supposed were gold. He kept them in his pockets, always anxiously looking out for his benefactor. After four months after, he met him upon Bagshot heath, riding in a coach: Sir, said he, I believe you made a mistake the last time I had the happiness of seeing you, in giving these pieces. I have been troubled ever since, lest you should have wanted them at cards, and am glad of this opportunity to return them ; only, for my care, I require you to come this moment out of your coach, and give me your breeches, that I may search them at leisure, and not trust any more to your generosity, lest you should mistake again. A pistol enforced his demand, and Simpson found a gold watch, a gold snuff box, and ninety-eight guineas, with five jacobuses.

At another time, he robbed Lord Delamere of three hundred and fifty guineas. He was almost unequalled in his depredations: in one day he robbed nineteen different people, and took above two hundred pounds; and, in the space of six weeks, committed forty robberies in the county of Middlesex. He even ventured to attack the duke of Berwick, and took from him articles to a very great value.

But wickedness has a boundary over which it cannot pass. Simpson attacked two captains of the guards: a strong struggle ensued: his horse was shot under him, and he was wounded in both arms, and one of his legs before he was taken. He was sent to Newgate, and now found that he was not refused entrance: and he soon also discovered, that Tyburn was equally ready to receive him. His execution took place on the 8th September, 1589.

WILLIAM CADY,

Was a native of Norfolk county, and the son of an eminent surgeon. After the preparatory steps of education, William went to the University of Cambridge, and was tutor to lord Townshend. He was during that time made bachelor of arts, and continued to pursue his studies until deprived of his father by death.

The loss of a prudent father to a young man, forms a remarkable era in his life. If he is left with an ample fortune, he has then the means of gratifying his wishes, whether in the fields of bene-volence or in that of dissipation ; and though left with no fortune, yet he is then at full liberty to fol-low his ruling inclination. Upon the intelligence of his father's death, William went to London and began to practise medicine. His first patient was his own uncle, who, being dangerously affected with an imposthume, was cured by him in the following manner:—

When he entered his uncle's bedchamber, his first care was to examine the state of the old gentleman's stomach ; for this purpose he ranged about the room, overturning every plate and dish, to discover what had been given him to eat. He at last disco-vered an old saddle, which he thought would answer for the intended experiment. Upon seeing this he cried out, uncle, your case is very desperate! Not so bad, I hope, said the uncle, as to make me past remedy. Heaven knows that, cried Cady, but a surfeit is a terrible thing, and I perceive that you have got a violent one. A surfeit! said the old gentleman; you mistake, nephew ; it is an impos-thume that I am troubled with. The deuce it is ! replied Cady : why, I could have sworn it had been a surfeit, for I perceive you have eaten a whole horse, and left us only the saddle ! At this he held up the saddle, and the old gentleman fell into such a fit of laughter as instantly broke his imposthume, so that he became quite well in less than a fortnight.

For this speedy and unexpected cure his uncle gave him fifty guineas, which supported his extrava-gance for one month. But his purse becoming empty, he took his leave of the healing art, in which he had been so successful, and commenced robber. His first adventure was with a captain of the guards and another gentleman, of whom he inquired the way to Staines, as he was a stranger. They inform- ed him that they were going to that place, and that they would be glad of his company. When he ar- rived at a convenient place, Cady shot the gentleman through the head, and, turning to the officer, told him that if he did not deliver, he should share the same fate. The other replied that he was a captain of the guards, Cady must fight if he expected to get any thing from him. If you are a soldier, cried Cady, you ought to obey the word of command, otherwise you know your sentence; I have nothing to do but tie you neck and heels. You are an uncon- scionable rogue, said the captain, to demand money of me, who never owed you any. Sir, replied Cady, there is not a man that travels the road, but owes me money, if he has any about him; therefore you are one of my debtors, if you do not pay me in- stantly, your blood shall satisfy my demand. The captain exchanged several shots with Cady; but his horse being killed under him he surrendered his watch, a diamond ring, and a purse of twenty guineas. William collected all he could, tied the captain neck and heels, nailed the skirts of his coat to a tree, and rode off in search of more booty.

His next encounter was with Viscount Dundee who commanded the forces of James VII of Scot- land, and the second of England, and fell in the bat- tle of Killiecrankie. Dundee was mounted upon horse back, attended by two servants. Cady rode up to them at full speed, and inquired if they did not see a man ride past with more than ordinary haste. Being quickly answered in the affirmative, he pantingly exclaimed that he had robbed him of twenty pounds which he was going to pay his landlord, and unless he recovered it, he was utterly ruined! The man who had ridden by was a confederate, and had done so by express concert. His lordship was moved with compassion, and ordered the two footmen to pursue the robber. When the servants seemed to have got to a sufficient distance, Cady turned upon his Lordship, and robbed him of a gold watch, a gold snuff box, and fifty guineas. He then shot the viscount's horse, and rode after the footmen, whom he found about a mile off with the supposed robber as their prisoner. These men were surprised when Cady desired them to let him go, and laughed at them for what they had done. They, however, refusing to part with their prey, a scuffle ensued, and one of the footmen being slain, the other fled, and found that his master had been dismounted and robbed.

Dundee complained of this injury at court, and a reward of two hundred pounds were offered to any person who should apprehend either Cady or his companion, who were both minutely described. To evade the diligent search which he was certain this proclamation would occasion, he went over to Flanders. As he had received a liberal education, he entered himself of the English seminary of Douay, and joining the fraternity of Benedictine friars, soon acquired an extraordinary character for learning and piety. The natural result was, that many penitents resorted to them for confession. The rigid sanctity and ecclesiastical duties of Cady were however, soon found rather troublesome companions, and he re-

solved to return to England, preferring his rambles
upon the highway to the devotions of the convent.
But as money was necessary for his voyage, his invention was again set in motion.

To effect his purpose, he feigned himself sick
and, being confined to his bed, he was visited by
many of those who formerly employed him as their
father confessor. He particularly fixed his attention upon two young women, who generally came
together, and were both very rich and very handsome. He had previously procured a brace of pistols. When the ladies next came to him and had
made their confession, he desired them presently to
attend him. He briefly informed them that he was
greatly in want of money, and that if they did not
instantly supply his wants, he would deprive them
of their lives, holding at the same time a pistol to
their breast. He then proceeded to rifle their pockets, where he found fifty pistoles. In addition to
this he compelled them to make an offering of two
diamond rings from their fingers; then, binding
them neck and heel, he informed the father of the
convent that he wished to walk a little in the fields,
and would soon return. It is needless to say that
he returned no more to his religious habitation, but
renewed his former mode of life.

Scarcely was he arrived in England when he met
a hop merchant, accompanied by his wife, upon
Black-heath, and commanded them to stand and deliver. The merchant made a stout resistance, firing two pistols, but without effect; so that he was
left at the mercy of the robber, who killed their
horse, and examining their pockets, found twenty

eight pounds upon the merchant, and half a crown upon his wife.

Cady then addressed her thus : Is this your way of travelling ? What! carry but half a crown in your pocket, when you are to meet a gentleman collector on the king's highway ? I'll assure you, madam, I shall be even with you, therefore off with that ring from your finger. She entreated him to spare her marriage ring as she would not lose it for double the value, for she had kept and worn it for these twenty years. The woman saw that all entreaties were vain, and hastily pulled off her ring, and thrust it into her mouth. Cady then stamped, raged, and swore that he would be even with her; and instantly shooting her through the head, went away perfectly unmoved, while the husband, being tied to a tree, was spectator of this horrid barbarity.

On his road to the capital, between Ferry-bridge and Doncaster, he met with Dr. Moreton, a prebendary of Durham, well mounted; but whether meditating on the amount of his tithes, or the next Sabbath's sermon, is uncertain. Cady instantly rode up to him and cried, 'Deliver, or you are a dead man !' The doctor, unaccustomed to such language, began to admonish him concerning the atrocity of his conduct, and the danger that he was in, both with respect to his body and his soul. Cady stared him in the face with all the ferocity he could muster, and informed him that his remonstrances were in vain, saying, that if he did not deliver him what he had, he would speedily send him out of the world. ' But then, (added Cady) that is nothing, because all the gentlemen of your cloth are prepared

for death. What, you unreasonable, you unmannerly dog! (continued he in a rage, unable to discover the doctor's cash,) what do you mean, to
meet a man in the midst of his journey, without
bringing him any money to pay his charges?' For
the doctor had taken care to hide his money in a
hedge; so that Cady, upon examining him, found
his pockets completely empty. The ruffian, convinced that a man of his appearance could not
travel without money, with dreadful imprecations
threatened that if he would not inform him what he
had done with it, he should never go home alive.
The doctor insisting that he had none, the wretch
instantly shot him through the heart.

He next undertook a journey to Norfolk to visit
his relations; but meeting a coach near that place,
in which were three gentlemen and a lady, he rode
up to it, and addressed them in his own language.
The gentlemen, however, were resolved to stand
upon the defensive, and one of them fired a blunderbuss at him, which only grazed his arm, without
doing any material injury. This put him into a
violent passion, and after taking a hundred and fifty
pounds from the company, he brutally added, that
the gentleman who fired at him should not pass un-
punished, and instantly shot him through the heart;
then, cutting the reins of the horse, he went off in
search of new plunder, and declined visiting his relations upon that occasion, lest he should have been
detected.

Directing his course to London, he came up with
a lady taking a ride for the benefit of the air, attended by a single footman, and fell upon her in a very

rude manner, pulling a diamond ring from her finger, a gold watch out of her pocket, and a purse with
eighty guineas; insulting her meanwhile with op-
probious language. Though the lady had commanded her footman not to interfere, yet the man
could not help complimenting Cady with some well-
merited appellations. The ferocious monster, without uttering a word, saluted him with a brace of bul-
lets in the head, and he fell upon the spot. Cady
was just about to prosecute his journey, when two
gentlemen, perceiving what he had done, rode up to
him with pistols in their hands. Cady, seeing his
his danger, fired at them, and shots were exchanged
with the greatest rapidity, until Cady's horse was
shot under him; and even then he struggled with
the greatest violence with the gentlemen, until his
strength was exhausted: he was then apprehended,
and carried to Newgate under a strong guard. There
he remained until the assizes, without shewing the
least signs of repentance, or tokens of regret. Upon
his trial he behaved with the most daring insolence,
calling the judges ' a huddle of alms-women,' treating
the jury in the same manner. The crime of which
he was accused was so clearly proved, that he was
sentenced to death, and committed to the condemned hole. But this place of darkness had no
effect upon his mind. He continued to roar, curse,
blaspheme, and get drunk, as he had always done.
It is probable that the hope of pardon, by the influence of some friends at court, tended to harden him
the more; but the number and enormity of his
crimes prevented James the Second from extending
his royal mercy to such a miscreant.

The day of execution being come, and the cart stopping as usual under St. Sepulchre's wall, while the bellman rang his bell, and repeated his exhortations, he began to swear and to rail, because they stopped to hear an old puppy chatter nonsense.

At Tyburn he acted in a similar manner, without either taking any notice of the ordinary, praying by himself, or addressing the people, he rushed into an eternal state to suffer the just punishment of his great and numerous offences. He died in the twenty-fifth year of his age, in the year 1687.

PATRICK O'BRIAN,

WAS a native of Ireland and his parents were very indigent. He came over to England, and enlisted in the Coldstream Guards. He was, however, not so dexterous in the use of arms as he was in the practice of all manner of vice. Patrick was resolved not to want money, if there was any in the country. He first ran into debt at all the public houses and shops that would trust him; then borrowed from every person, as long as he could find any that would believe him.

When fraud failed him he had recourse to force. Doctor Clewer, rector of Croydon, was the first whom he attacked. This man had been in his youth, tried at the Old Bailey, and burned in the hand for stealing a silver cup. Alluding to this, Patrick said, that he could not refuse lending a little assistance to one of his old profession. The Doctor assured him, that he had not made a word, if he had had any money about him; but he had not so much as a single farthing. Then, said Patrick, I must have your gown, sir. If you can win it, cried the doctor, you shall; but let me have the chance of a game at cards. To this O'Brian consented; and the Doctor, pulling out a pack of cards, they commenced. Patrick was victorious, and obtained the black gown.

One day, Patrick attacked a famous posture master, and commanded him to stand and deliver! The latter instantly jumped over his head, which led Patrick to suppose that it was the devil come to sport with him before his time. By this display of his agility, the harlequin escaped with his money, and had the good fortune never to afford an opportunity to O'Brian to be revenged of him for his fright.

Our adventurer at last commenced highwayman. For this purpose he purchased a horse and other necessaries, and began in due form. He one day met with the celebrated Nell Gwynne in her coach, and addressed her, saying:—Madam, I am a gentleman; I have done a great many signal services to the fair sex, and have, in return, been all my life maintained by them. Now, as I know that you are a charitable woman, I make bold to ask you for a little money, though I never had the honour of serving you in particular. However, if any opportunity shall ever fall in my way, you may depend upon it I will not be ungrateful. Nell made him a present of ten guineas, and he went off in quest of more plunder.

It was with O'Brian as with every other wicked man; he was solicitous to lead others to the same line of conduct. In particular, he seduced a young man, of the name of Wilt, who was apprehended and suffered for his first offence, O'Brian was also apprehended, and executed at Gloucester: and when he had hung the usual time, his body was cut down and given to his friends; but when carried home, he was observed to move, on which a surgeon was immediately sent for, who bled him; and othe means being used, he recovered life. The fact was kept a secret, and it was hoped that it would have had a salutary effect upon his future conduct. His friends were very willing to contribute towards his support, in order that he might live in the most retired manner, and O'Brian engaged to reform his life, and for some time kept his promise; but the impression of death and all its tremendous consequences, soon wearing off his mind, he returned to his vicious courses. Abandoning his friends, and purchasing a horse and all other necessaries, O'Brian again visited the road.

In about a year after his execution he met the very gentleman who was his former prosecutor, and attacked him in the same manner as before. The gentleman was surprised to see himself stopped by the very same person who had formerly robbed him, and who was executed for that crime. His consternation was so great that he could not avoid exhibiting it, and he addressed O'Brian, saying, how comes this to pass? I thought that you had been hanged a twelvemonth ago. So I was, and therefore you ought to imagine that what you now see is only my ghost. However, lest you should be so uncivil as to hang my ghost too, I think my best way to secure you. Upon this, he discharged a pistol through the gentleman's head, and alighting from his horse, cut his body in pieces with his hanger.

This barbarity was followed by a greater. O'Brian accompanied by four others, attacked the house of Launcelot Wilmot, Esq. of Wiltshire ; entered, and bound all the servants ; then went up to the gentleman's own room, and bound him and his wife. They next proceeded to the daughter's chamber, whom they stabbed to the heart, and having returned, in the same manner butchered the old people, and rifled the house to the amount of two thousand five hundred pounds.

This miscreant continued his depredations two years longer, until one of his accomplices confessed his crime, and informed upon all who were concerned. Our adventurer was seized at his lodgings at Little Suffolk-street, and conveyed to Salisbury, where he acknowledged the crime. He was a second time executed, and, to prevent another resuscitation, was hung in chains, near the place where the crime was perpetrated, on the 30th of April 1689.

JOHN SHEPPARD.

JOHN SHEPPARD was born in the parish of Stepney, near London, in the year 1702. His father was a carpenter, and he died when he was so young, that he could not recollect ever seeing him. Thus the burthen of his maintenance, together with his brother and sister, lay upon his mother, who soon procured him admission into the workhouse in Bishopgate street, where he continued a year and a half, and in that time received an education sufficient to qualify him for the trade his mother designed him, viz. a carpenter: accordingly he was recommended to Mr. Wood, in Wych street, Drury lane, and bound to him for seven years; the lad proved an early proficient.

Being an ingenious hand, he soon became master of his business, and gave such satisfaction to his master's customers, that he had the character of a very sober, orderly boy; but alas, unhappy youth! before he had completed six years of his apprenticeship, he commenced a fatal acquaintance with one Elizabeth Lyon, otherwise called Edgeworth Bess, from a town of that name in Middlesex, where she was born, the reputed wife of a soldier, and who lived a debauched life.

Our young hero became soon enamoured with her, and they cohabited together as man and wife. This was the foundation of his ruin.

Sheppard grew weary of the yoke of servitude, and began to dispute with his master, telling him that his way of jobbing from house to house was not sufficient to furnish him with a due experience in his trade, and if he would not seek to undertake some building, he would step into the world for better information.

Mr. Wood, a mild honest man, gave him every indulgence, and Mrs Wood exhorted him against the company of this prostitute; but he, prompted and hardened by this harlot, d——d her blood, threw a stick at her, and beat her to the ground.

Being at work at Mr. Britt's the Sun alehouse,
near Islington, he, on a trivial occasion, fell upon
his master, and beat and bruised him in a most
shameful manner. Such a sudden and deplorable
change was there in the behaviour of this promising
man ! Next ensued a neglect of duty both to God
and his master : laying out at nights, perpetual jar-
ring animosities. These acts were the consequences of his intimacy with this harlot, who, by the sequel, will appear to have been a main loadstone in
bringing him to the fatal tree.

Mr. Wood having reason to suspect that Sheppard had robbed a neighbour, began to be in great
fear and terror for himself : and when his man came
not home in due season at night, barred him out ;
but he made a mere jest of locks and bolts, and entered in at pleasure ; and when Mr. Wood and his
wife have had all the reason in the world to believe
he was locked out, they found him in his bed the
next morning; such was the power of his early
magic.

Edgeworth Bess having stolen a gold ring from a
gentleman, whom she had picked up in the street,
was sent to St. Giles's round house. Sheppard went
immediately to his consort ; and after a short discourse with Mr. Brown, the beadle, and his wife,
who had the care of the place, he fell upon the poor
old couple, took the keys from them, and let his lady
out, in spite of all the outcries and opposition they
were capable of making.

About July, 1720, he was sent by his master, to
perform a repair at the house of Mr. Braines, a
piece broker in White horse yard ; and from thence

he stole a roll of fustian, containing 24 yards, which was afterwards found in his possession.

This is supposed to be the first robbery he ever committed, and it was not long before he repeated another upon the same Mr. Braines, by breaking into his house in the night-time, and taking out of the till £7 in money, and goods to the amount of £14 more; how he entered the house was a secret, till his being at last committed to Newgate, when he confessed that he took up the iron bars at the cellar window; and after he had done his business, he nailed them down again, so that Mr. Braines never believed that his house had been broke, and a woman, a lodger in the house, lay all the while under the weight of suspicion of committing the robbery.

Sheppard and his master parted ten months before the expiration of his apprenticeship; a woeful parting to the former, he was gone from a good and careful patronage, and lay exposed to, and complied with, the temptations of the most wicked wretches the town could afford, such as Joseph Blake, alias Blueskin; Dowling, James Sykes, alias Hell and Fury, and which last was the first that betrayed and put him into the hands of justice, as will presently appear.

Having deserted his master's service, he took shelter in the house of Mr. Charles, in May-fair; and his landlord having occasion for some repairs in the house, engaged a Mr. Panton, a carpenter, to undertake it, and Sheppard to assist him as a journeyman; but before the work was completed, Sheppard took an opportunity to rob the people of the following effects, viz. £7 10s. in specie, five large silver spoons, six plain forks ditto, four tea-spoons, six plain gold rings, and a cypher ring, four suits of wearing apparel, besides linen to a considerable value. This fact he confessed to the Rev. Mr. Wagstaff, before his escape from the condemned cell at Newgate.

Sheppard being on his wicked range in London, committing robberies wherever he could, one day met with an old acquaintance, James Sykes, alias Hell and Fury, sometimes a chairman, and sometimes a running footman. He was invited by him to go to one Sedgate's, a victualling-house, near the Seven Dials, to play at skittles.

Sheppard complied, and Sykes secretly sent for Mr. Price, a constable of St. Giles's parish, and charged him with his friend, for robbing Mrs. Cook, &c. Sheppard was carried before Justice Parry, who ordered him to St. Giles's roundhouse, till the next morning, for further examination. He was confined in the upper part of the place, being two stories from the ground; but before two hours, by only the help of a razor, and a stretcher of a chair, he broke open the top of the roundhouse, and tying together a sheet and a blanket, by them descended into the church-yard, and escaped, leaving the parish to repair the damage.

On the following evening, Sheppard, with another robber, named Benson, was passing through Leicester fields, where a gentleman stood accusing a woman with an attempt to steal his watch. A mob was gathered about the disputants. Sheppard's companion got in among them, and picked the gentleman's pocket in earnest of his watch, and then ensued an outcry of stop thief! Sheppard and

Bensons took to their heels : but Sheppard was seized, and was conveyed to St. Ann's round-house in Soho, and was kept secure till the next morning, when Edgeworth Bess came to visit him, who was seized also. They were carried before Justice Waller, when the people of Drury-lane and Clare-market appeared, and charged them with the robberies before mentioned ; but Sheppard pretending to impeach certain accomplices, the justice committed them to the New Prison, with an intent to have them removed to Newgate, unless there came from them some useful discoveries.

He and his mate were now in a strong and well-guarded prison, himself loaded with a pair of double links, and bazils of about 14lb. weight, and confined together in the safest apartment, called Newgate ward.

Sheppard, conscious of his crimes, and knowing the information he had made to be but a blind scheme that would avail nothing, began to meditate an escape. They had been thus detained four days, and their friends having the liberty of seeing them, furnished them with implements proper for his design ; accordingly he went to work, and on the 25th of May, being Whit Sunday, at about two o'clock in the morning, completed a practical breach, and sawed off his fetters ; having, with unheard of diligence and dexterity, cut off an iron bar from the window, and took out a mutin, or bar of the most solid oak, about six inches in thickness, by boring it through in many places with great skill and labour. They had twenty-five feet to descend. Sheppard fastened a sheet and a blanket to the bars, caused madam to take off her gown and petticoat, and sent her out first.   She being more corpulent than himself, it was with great difficulty he got her through the interval; but on observing his directions, she was instantly down, more frightened than hurt. Our hero followed and lighted with ease and pleasure.   But where had they escaped to? why out of one prison into another.

The reader is to understand that the New Prison and Clerkenwell Bridewell lay contiguous to each other, and they had got into the yard of the latter, and had a wall of twenty-two feet high to scale before their liberty was perfected.   Sheppard far from being unprepared to surmount this difficulty, had his gimlets and piercers ready, and made a scaling ladder.   While the keepers and prisoners of both places were asleep in their beds, he mounts with his lady, and in less than ten minutes carries both her and himself over the wall, and completes an entire escape.

Although his escape from the condemned hole in Newgate made a far greater noise in the world than from the New Prison, it has been allowed by all the gaol keepers in London, that one so extraordinary was never performed in England before.   The broken chairs and bars are kept in the New Prison, to testify and preserve the memory of this villain.

Sheppard not warned by this admonition, returns back like a dog to his vomit, and again comes to his master's neighbourhood in Wych street, and concerts measures with Anthony Lamb, an apprentice to Mr. Carter, a mathematical instrument maker, for robbing Mr. Burton, a master tailor, who lodged in Mr. Carter's house. Charles Grace, a cooper, being let into the secret, consented and resolved to act his part, and the 16th of June was appointed.

Lamb let Grace and Sheppard into the house at midnight, and they all went to Mr. Burton's apartment armed with pistols, and entered undisturbed. Grace was posted at Burton's bedside with a loaded pistol, with positive orders to shoot him through the head in case he awoke, Sheppard being engaged in opening the trunks and boxes in the mean time.

It luckily happened for Mr. Burton, that he slept more sound than usual that night, having come from a merry making with some friends. They carried off in notes, bonds, guineas and clothes, made and unmade, to the value of between two and three hundred pounds, besides a panuasay suit of clothes worth about twenty pounds more, which having been made for a corpulent gentleman, Sheppard had them reduced and fitted to his own size and wear. Grace and Sheppard having disposed of the goods at an ale-house in Newtoner's Lane, (a rendezvous for robbers and ruffians) took their flight, and Grace was not heard of after. Lamb was apprehended, and carried before Justice Newton, and made an ample confession, and there being nothing but that against him at his trial, he came off with sentence of transportation ; he, as well as Sheppard, confirmed all the above particulars, and with this addition, viz, that it was agreed among them to have murdered all the people in the house, save one person.

About the latter end of the same month, June, Mr. Kneebone, a woollen draper, near the New Church in the Strand, received a caution from the father of Anthony Lamb, who intimated to Mr.

Kneebone that his house was intended to be broke open and robbed that very night.

Mr. Kneebone prepared for the event, ordered his servants to sit up, and gave directions to the watchman in the street to observe his house. About two o'clock in the morning, Sheppard and his gang being about the door, a maid servant went to listen, and heard one of the wretches say, d—— him, if they could not enter that night, they would another, and would have three hundred pounds of his money. They then went off, and nothing was heard of them till Sunday, the 12th day of July following; when Joseph Blake, alias Blueskin, John Sheppard, and William Field, (as himself swore) came about twelve o'clock at night, and cut two large oaken bars over the window, at the back part of the house in Little Drury Lane, and so entered. Mr. Kneebone and his family being at rest, they proceeded to open a door at the foot of the cellar stairs, with three bolts, and with a large padlock upon it: and then came up into the shop, and wrenched off a hasp and padlock that went over the press, and arrived at their desired booty; they continued in the house three hours, and carried off with them 108 yards of broad cloth, five yards of blue baize, a light tie wig, a beaver hat, two silver spoons, a handkerchief, and penknife; in all to the amount of about fifty pounds.

The Sunday following, Sheppard and Blueskin robbed Mr. Pargiter, a chandler of Hampstead, near the Half-way-house. Sheppard, after his being taken at Finchley, was particularly examined about this robbery. The Rev. Mr. Wagstaff received a letter from an unknown hand, with some questions to be proposed to Sheppard, viz: Whether he did not rob one Mr. Pargiter, and how much money he took from him? Whether he was drunk or not: and if he had any rings or watch about him when robbed? He said Pargiter was very much in liquor, having a great coat, neither rings on his fingers, or watch, and only three shillings in his pocket, which they took from him, and that Blueskin knocked him down twice with the end of his pistol to make sure work, (though excess of drinking had done that before): but Sheppard did in kindness raise him up as often.

The next time they stopped a stage coach, and took from one of the passengers in it twenty shillings, and were so expeditious in the matter, that scarcely a word was spoke. Now Mr. Sheppard's long and wicked course was seemingly drawing to a period. Mr. Kneebone having applied to Jonathan Wild, and set advertisements in the papers, complaining of his robbery; the following night, Edgeworth Bess was taken in a brandy shop, near Temple Bar, by Jonathan Wild; she being much terrified, discovered where Sheppard was. A warrant was accordingly issued by Justice Blackerby, and the next day he was apprehended at the house of Blueskin's mother, in Rosemary-lane, by one Quilt, a domestic of Mr. Wild's, though not without great opposition, for he presented a loaded pistol to Quilt's breast, and attempted to shoot him, but the pistol missed fire. He was brought back to New prison, confined in the dungeon, and the next day taken before Justice Blackerby. Upon this examination, he confessed the three robberies on the highway before mentioned, as also his robbing Mr. Brains, Mr. Burton, and Mr. Kneebone. He was committed to

Newgate, and the ensuing sessions at the Old Bailey, he was tried upon the three following indictments :

John Sheppard, of the parish of St. Martin in the Fields, was indicted for breaking the house of William Phillips, and stealing divers goods; but there not being sufficient evidence against the prisoner, he was acquitted. He was indicted a second time, for breaking open the house of Mary Cook, and stealing divers goods; but the evidence against the prisoner being deficient, as to this indictment, he was again acquitted. He was indicted a third time, for breaking the house of William Kneebone, and stealing 108 yards of woollen cloth, the 12th of July.

Jonathan Wild deposed, that Mr. Kneebone came to him, and desired that he would enquire after his goods; that the prisoner had been concerned in the robbery, he having before committed some robberies in the neighbourhood. That he enquired after him, having heard of him before, and he was informed that he was an acquaintance of Jonathan Blake, alias Blueskin, and William Field; whereupon he sent for William Field, who came to him; and he told him if he would make an ingenuous confession, he believed he could prevail upon the court to make him an evidence. Then he did make a discovery of the prisoner, upon which he was apprehended, and also of others, and gave an account of some pieces of the cloth, which were found accordingly.

W. Field deposed, that the prisoner told him and Joseph Blake, that he knew a KEN where they might get something of worth; that they went to take a view of the prosecutor's house, but disapproved of the attempt, as not thinking it easy to be performed; but the prisoner said it might easily be done. he knowing the house, and having lived with the prosecutor; they thereupon he cut the cellar bar, went into the the cellar, got into the shop, and brought out three parcels of cloth, which they carried away. The prisoner had also confessed the fact when he was apprehended, and likewise before the justice. The fact being clearly proved, the jury found him guilty of the indictment.

Sentence of death was pronounced on him accordingly. Several other prosecutions might have been brought against him: but this was thought sufficient to rid the world of so notorious an offender. He begged earnestly for transportation to the remotest part of his majesty's dominions, and pleaded youth and ignorance, as the causes which had precipitated him into guilt: but the court, deaf to his importunities, knowing his repeated crimes to be equally flagrant, gave him no satisfactory answer. He returned to his dismal abode, the condemned hole, where were nine more unhappy wretches in as dreadful circumstances as himself. The king being at Windsor, the malefactors had a longer respite than usual. During that recess, James, Haram, Lumdy, Davies, and Sheppard, agreed upon an escape, concerted measures, and provided instruments, to make it effectual; it was on this day Davis gave Sheppard the watch-springs, files, saws, &c. to effect his own release; and knowing that a warrant was hourly expected for his execution with two others, on the Friday following, he thought it time to look about him, for he waited for his trial, saw his conviction, and heard his sentence with some patience; but finding himself irrespitably decreed for death, he could sit passive no longer, and the very day of the execution of the former, while they were having their fetters taken off, in order for going to the tree, that day he began to saw; Saturday made a progress, but Sunday omitted by reason of the concourse in the lodge. On Monday the death-warrant came from Windsor, appointing that he, with Joseph Ward and Anthony Upton, should be executed on the Friday following, being the 4th of September. The keepers acquainted him therewith, and desired him to make good use of the short time allotted him; he thanked them, and said, he would follow their advice, and prepare. Edgeworth Bess, and another woman, had been with him at the door of the condemned cell the greater part of the afternoon; between five and six o'clock he desired the other prisoner, except Stephen Fowles, to remain above, while he offered something in private to his friends at the door. They complied, and in this interval he got the spike asunder, which made way for him to pass with his heels foremost, by the assistance of Fowles, whom he most ungenerously betrayed to the keepers after his being taken, and the fellow was severely punished for it.

Having now got clear of his prison, he took coach, disguised in a night gown, at the corner of Old Bailey, along with a man who waited for him in the street, and was supposed to be one Page, a butcher; and ordered the coachman to drive to Blackfriar's stairs, where his prostitute gave him the meeting; and the three took boat, and went on shore at the Horse Ferry, at Westminster; and, at the White Hart, they went in and drank, and staid some time; from thence they adjourned to a place in Holborn, where, by the help of a saw, he quitted the chains he had brought with him from Newgate, and then, like a free man, took a ramble through the city, and came to Spitalfields, and there lay with Edgworth Bess.

It may be easy to imagine what an alarm his escape gave the keepers of Newgate, three of their people being at the farther end of the lodge, engaged in discourse concerning his wonderful escape from the New Prison, and what caution ought to be used, lest he should give them the slip, at the very instant he effected it.

Edgworth Bess had been apprehended by Jonathan Wild, and committed to the Poultry-compter by Sir Francis Forbes, one of the aldermen of London, for aiding and assisting Sheppard in his escape; the keepers and others terrified her as much as possible, to discover where he was; but had it been her inclination, it was not in her power to tell, as it appeared soon after.

The people about the Strand, Wych-street, and Drury-lane, whom he had robbed, and who had prosecuted him, were under great apprehensions and terror; and in particular Mr. Kneebone, on whom he vowed revenge, because he lately refused to sign a petition in his behalf to the Recorder of London. This gentleman was forced to keep armed people up in his house every night, till he was retaken, and had the same fortified in the strongest manner. Several other shopkeepers in that neighbourhood were also put to great expence and trouble, to guard against the villain.

The keepers of Newgate, (whom the rash world loaded with infamy, stigmatized and branded with

the title of persons guilty of bribery, for conniving
at his escape) contributed their utmost to unde-
ceive a wrong notioned people. Their diligence
was indefatigable, sparing neither money nor time,
night nor day, to bring him back to his deserved
justice. After much intelligence, which they bought
or received, they had one which proved very successful; having learnt for certainty that his haunts
were about Finchly Common; and being well assured of the house where he lay, on Tuesday, the
10th of September, a number of men, both of spirit
and conduct, furnished with arms proper for their
design, went for Finchley, some in a coach and four
and others on horseback; they dispersed themselves
about the Common aforesaid, in order to take their
view; they had not long been there before they
came in sight of Sheppard, in company with William
Page, habited like two butchers, in blue frocks, with
aprons tucked round their waists.

Upon Sheppard's seeing Mr. Langley, one of the
head turnkeys of Newgate, he said to his companion,
Page, I spy a stag: upon which their courage dropt,
knowing that now their wicked way of business was
drawing to an end; however, to make their flight as
secure as they could, they thought it adviseable to
take to a foot path, to cut off the pursuit of the
Newgate cavalry; but this did not prove successful,
Mr. Langley came up with Page, who was hinder-
most, and dismounting with pistol in hand, commanded Page to throw up his hands, which he
tremblingly did, begging for life, desiring him to
FISK him, viz. search him, which he accordingly
did, and found a broad knife, and a file; having thus
disarmed him, he takes the CHUB along with him in

quest of the slippery eel, Sheppard, who had taken shelter in an old stable belonging to a farm-house; the pursuit was close, the house invested, and a girl seeing his feet, she discovered him. Mr. Austin, a turnkey, first attacked his person; Mr. Langley seconded him, and Ireton, the officer, helped to inclose. He being shocked with fear, told them he submitted, and desired they would let him live as long as he could, which they did, and used him mildly; upon searching him they found a broad knife; and now having gained their point, and made themselves masters of what they had often endeavoured for, they came with their lost sheep to a house on the common, that sold liquors, with this inscription on the sign, I have brought my hogs to a fine market; which our two unfortunate prisoners under their then unhappy circumstances, had too sad reason to apply to themselves. Sheppard had by this time recovered his surprise, grew calm and easy, and desired them to give him some brandy, which they did, and were all friends and good company.

They adjourned with their prisoners to another place, where there was a coach and four waiting to convey them back to town with speed and safety, where John Sheppard arrived at his old mansion about two in the afternoon. The joy of the people of Newgate on this occasion was inexpressible, and nothing but smiles and bumpers were seen in the lodge for many days together; but Jonathan Wild, who happened to be gone on a wrong scent after him to Stourbridge, lost a share of the glory.

The Rev. Mr. Wagstaff, who officiated in the absence of the ordinary, renewed his former acquain-

D

tance with John Sheppard, and examined him in a particular manner concerning his escape from the condemned cell; but he entirely disowned that all or any belonging to the prison were privy thereto. He declared that Edgworth Bess, who had hitherto passed for his wife, was not really so.

He was continually meditating a second escape, as appeared by his own hardiness, and the instruments found upon him on Saturday the 12th, and Wednesday the 16th of September: the first time a small file was found in his bible; and the second time two files, a chisel, and a hammer were hid in the rushes of his chair; and whenever a question was put to him, by what means these implements came into his hands, he would fly out, and say, how can you always ask me these and such like questions? And in a particular manner, when he was asked, whether his companion Page, was an accomplice with him, in the affair of the watches, or any other? He replied, that if he knew, he would give no direct answer.

It was thought necessary by the keepers to remove him from the condemned hole, to a place called the castle, in the body of the jail, and to chain him down to two large staples in the floor. The concourse of people of the first fashion to see him was exceedingly great, and he was always cheerful and pleasant to a degree, and turned almost every thing that was said into a jest and banter.

Being one Sunday at chapel, a gentleman belonging to the lord mayor asked a turnkey which was Sheppard? The man pointed to him. Says Sheppard, yes, sir, I am the Sheppard, and all the gaolers in the town are my flock, and I cannot stir into

the country, but they are all at my heels bawling
after me, &c. He told Mr. Robins the city smith,
that he had procured him a small job, and that whoever
he was that put the spikes in the condemned hole
was an honest man, for a better piece of metal I
never wrought in all my life. He was loath to believe his frequent robberies were an injury to the
public, for he used to say, that if they were ill in
one respect, they were as good in another, and
though he cared not for working much himself, he
was desirous that others should not be idle, and
more especially those of his own trade, who were
always repairing breaches.

When serious, and that was but seldom, he would
reflect on his past wicked life; he declared, that for
several years of his apprenticeship he had an utter
aversion to the women of the town, and used to pelt
them with dirt when they fell in his way, till a button maker, his next door neighbour, had set up a
victualling house in Newtoner's lane, where himself and other apprentices resorted on Sundays, and
at all other opportunities.—At this house began his
acquaintance with Edgworth Bess, his sentiments
being strangely altered, and from an aversion to
these prostitutes, he had a more favourable opinion,
and often conversed with them, till he contracted
an ill distemper, which, as he said, he cured by a
medicine of his own preparing.

He inveighed bitterly against his brother Thomas, for putting him into the information of Mrs.
Cook's robbery, and pretended that all the mischiefs
that attended him were owing to that circumstance;
he acknowledged that he was concerned in that business, and his said brother broke into his lodgings,

and stole from him more than his share of the acquired booty.

He oftentimes averred, that William Field was not concerned in Kneebone's robbery, but that being a brother of the quill, Blueskin and himself told him the particulars, and the manner of the facts, and that all he swore against him was false; and that he had no other authority for it than what came out of their (Sheppard and Blueskin's) mouths, who had actually committed the fact.

On Wednesday, October the 14th, the sessions began at the Old Bailey, and Jack knew that the keepers would then have so much business attending the court, as would leave them but little leisure to visit him; and therefore thought this would be the only time for him to make a push for his liberty.

The next day, about two o'clock in the afternoon, one of the keepers carried Jack his dinner, and as usual, examined his irons, found all fast, and so left him. He had hardly been gone an hour before Jack went to work. The first thing he did, he got off his handcuffs, and then with a crooked nail, which he found upon the floor, opened the great padlock that fastened his chain to the staple. Next he twisted asunder a small link of the chain between his legs, and drawing up his feet locks as high as he could, he made them fast with his garters.

He attempted to get up the chimney, but had not advanced far, before his progress was stopped by an iron bar that went across within side: and therefore, being descended, he went to work on the outside, and with a piece of broken chain, picked out the mortar, and removed a small stone or two,

about six feet from the floor; he got out the iron
bar, which was an inch square, and near a yard
long, and this proved of great service to him. He
presently made so large a breach, that he got into
the Red Room over the castle; here he found a
large nail, which was another very useful imple-
ment. The door of this room had not been opened
for seven years past; but in less than seven minutes he wrenched off the lock, and got into the
entry leading to the chapel. Here he found a door
bolted on the other side, upon which he broke a
hole through the wall, and pushed the bolt back.
Coming now to the chapel door, he broke off one
of the iron spikes, which he kept for farther use,
and so he got into the entry between the chapel and
the lower leads. The door of this entry was very
strong ,and fastened with a strong lock, and what
was worse, the night had overtaken him, and he
was forced to work in the dark. However, in half
an hour, by the help of the great nail, the chapel
spike, and the iron bar, he forced off the box of the
lock, and opened the door, which led him to another yet more difficult; for it was not only locked,
but barred and bolted; when he had tried in vain
to make this lock give way, he wrenched the fillet
from the main post of the door, and the box and
staples came off with it; and now St. Sepulchre's
chimes went eight. There was yet another door
between him and the lower leads, but it being only
bolted withinside, he opened it easily, and mounting the top of it, he got over the wall, and then to
the upper leads.

The next consideration was, how to get down;
for which purpose, looking round him, and finding

the top of the turner's house, adjoining to Newgate,
was the most convenient place to alight upon, he
resolved to descend thither; but as it would have
been a dangerous leap, he went back to the castle
the same way as he came, and fetched a blanket
which he used to lie upon. This he made fast to
the wall of Newgate with the spike he stole out of
the chapel, and sliding down, dropping upon the
turner's leads, and then the clock struck nine.

Luckily for him the turner's garret door on the
leads happened to be open. He went in, and crept
softly down one pair of stairs, when he heard company in a room below. His irons gave a clink,
when a woman started and said, Lord, what noise
is that? Somebody answered, the dog or cat.
Thereupon Sheppard returned to the garret, and
having continued there about two hours, he ventured down a second time, when he heard a gentleman take leave of the company, and saw the maid
light him down stairs. As soon as the maid came
back, and had shut the chamber door, he made the
best of his way to the street door, unlocked it, and
made his escape, at twelve o'clock at night.

It is uncertain where he took up his lodging for
the remaining part of that night, or rather morning;
or when, or how, he got the irons off his legs; but,
on the first of November, not only his feetlocks,
but his handcuffs too, were found in a room belonging to Kate Cook and Kate Keys, in Cranbourn-
alley.

He had not been many days at liberty, before he
wrote the two following letters; and, dressing himself at night, like a porter, went to Mr. Applebee's
house, in Blackfriars, who at that time printed what

is termed the dying speeches of the persons executed, and left them with his servant maid.

Mr. Applebee,

This with my kind love to you, and pray give my kind love to Mr. Wagstaff, hoping these few lines will find you in good health, as I am at present; but I must own you are the loser for want of my dying speech, but to make up your loss, if you think this sheet worth your while, pray make the best of it. Though they do say I am taken among the smugglers, and put into Dover Castle, yet I hope I am among smugglers still. So no more, but your humble servant,

JOHN SHEPPARD.

P. S.—I desire you will be the postman with this letter to Mr. Austin, the jail keeper; so farewell; now I quit the English shore.—NEWGATE FAREWELL.

Mr. Austin,

You was pleased to pass your jokes upon me, and did say, you should not have been angry with me, had I took my leave of you; but now pray keep your jokes to yourself: let them laugh that win; but now it is an equal chance, you to take me, or I to go away; but I own myself guilty of that ill manners; but excuse me, for my departure being private and necessary, spoiled the ceremony of bidding adieu. But I wish you all as well as I am at present. But pray be not angry for the loss of your irons: had you not given them I had not taken them away ; but really I had left them behind me had convenience served. So do not be angry.

And what is amiss done, you write, for my scholarship is but small. This from your fortunate prisoner,

JOHN SHEPPARD.

In a few days after his leaving these letters, he broke a shop in Monmouth-street, and stole some wearing apparel. On the 29th of October he broke open the house of Robert Rawlins, a pawn broker in Drury-lane, from whence he took a sword, a suit of wearing apparel, a snuff box, rings, watches, and goods, to a considerable value.

And now Jack resolved to appear like a gentleman among his old friends in Drury-lane, and Clare-market. He strutted about in a fine suit of black, a light tie wig, and a ruffled shirt, with a silver hilted sword by his side, a diamond ring on his finger, and a gold watch in his pocket, notwithstanding he knew there was a diligent search made for him.

On the 31st of October he dined with his two women, Cook and Keys, at a public house in Newgate street, where they were very merry together. About four in the afternoon, they took coach, and drawing up the windows passed through Newgate, which was then similar to Temple-bar, and so to the Sheers alehouse, in Maypole alley, by Clare-market; where, in the evening, he sent for his mother, and treated her with some brandy. As she knew the danger he was in, she advised him to take care of himself, and keep out of the way; but Jack had been drinking very hard, and was grown too wise to take counsel, and too valiant to fear any thing; and, therefore, leaving his mother, he strolled about in the neighbourhood from alehouse to gin shop, till near twelve o'clock, when he was apprehended by means of an alehouse boy, who had accidentally seen him. Poor Jack was then drunk, and could make no resistance, and was once more conveyed to Newgate.

Infinite numbers of citizens came to Newgate to behold Sheppard's workmanship; and Mr. Pitt and his officers very readily conducted them up stairs, that the world might be convinced there was not the least room to suspect either negligence or connivance in the servants. Every one expressed the greatest surprise imaginable: and declared themselves satisfied with the measures they had taken for the security of their prisoner. One of the sheriffs came in person, and went up the castle to be satisfied with the situation of the place, &c. attended by several of the city officers.

The court being set at the sessions house, the keepers were sent for and examined; the magistrates expressed great surprise that so horrid a wretch had escaped justice, having intended that he should be brought down to the court the last day of the sessions, and ordered for execution in two or three days after, if it appeared he was the person condemned for breaking open Mr. Kneebone's house and had been ordered for execution.

He undoubtedly performed the chief part of his last escape in the darkest part of the night, and without the least glimpse of a candle. In a word, he actually did with his own hands, in a few hours, what several of the most skilful artists allow could not have been accomplished by a number of persons, furnished with proper implements, and every other advantage, in a whole day.

Never was there any thing better timed. The keeper and all their assistants, being obliged to give a close attendance on the sessions at the Old Bailey, which held for about a week, and Blueskin having confined Jonathan Wild to his chamber by stabbing him very severely in the throat, at the time of his trial at the season's house, a more favourable op·portunity could not have presented itself for Sheppard's purposes. The gailors suffered, much by the opinion the ignorant part of the people entertained of the matter; and nothing would satisfy some, but that they not only connived, but even as·sisted him in breaking their own walls and fences, and that for this reason too, viz: that he should be at liberty to instruct and train up others in the method of house breaking, and fill the town with a new set of rogues, to supply the places of those transported. It is now necessary that we return to the behaviour of Sheppard a few days before his last flight.

Mr. Figg, the famous prize·fighter, coming to see him in Newgate, there passed some pleasant raillery between them. After Mr. Figg was gone he declared he had a mind to send him a formal challenge to fight him at all weapons in the strong room; and that, let the consequence be what it would, he would call at Mr. Figg's house, in his way to execution, and drink a merry glass with him, by way of reconciliation.

He complained of his nights, saying, it was dark with him from five in the evening till seven in the morning: and not being permitted to have either bed or candle, his situation was dismal; that he never slept, but had some confused doses: yet, he said, he considered all this with the temper of a philosopher.

Neither his sad circumstances, nor the solemn exhortations of the several divines who visited him, were able to divert him from his ludicrous way of expression. He said, they were all gingerbread fellows, who came rather out of curiosity than charity; or to form papers and ballads out of his behaviour.

When he was visited in the castle by the Rev. Mr. Wagstaff, he put on the appearance only of a preparation for his end, as appeared by his frequent attempts made upon an escape; and when he has been desired to discover those who put him upon the means of escaping, and furnishing him with implements, he would passionately, and with a motion of striking, say, Ask no questions; one file is worth all the bibles in the world. When asked, if he had not put off all thoughts of an escape, and entertained none but those of death? he indirectly would answer, by way of question, whether they thought it possible, or probable, for him to effect his release, when manacled in the manner he was? When moved to improve the few moments that seemed to remain of his life, he did, indeed listen to, but not regard the design and purport of the admonition, interrupting it with something new of his own, either with respect to his accomplices or actions, and all too with pleasantry and gaiety of expression. Indeed, when he was at chapel he always appeared very serious and attentive; though both before and immediately after, he made himself as merry as possible, and endeavoured all he could to prevent any religious discourse.

The 10th of November he was carried to the King's Bench bar, at Westminster, there the record of his conviction being read, and an affidavit made, that he was the same John Sheppard mentioned in that record, Mr. Justice Power awarded sentence of death against him, and a rule of court was made for his execution on Monday following.

The day came, but Jack had some hopes of eluding justice. Somebody had furnished him with a penknife; this he put naked into his pocket with the point upwards; and as he told one whom he thought he could trust, his design was to lean forward in the cart, and cut asunder the cord that tied his hands together, and when he came near Little Tunstile, to throw himself over among the crowd, and run through the narrow passage, where the officers could not follow him on horseback, but must be forced to dismount; and, in the mean time, doubted not, but by the mob's assistance, he should make his escape.

It is not unlikely that he pleased himself with these thoughts, when he said, I have now as great satisfaction at heart, as if I was going to enjoy an estate of two hundred pounds a year; though the chaplain understood it in a different sense. But this hopeful scheme was discovered, in the press yard in Newgate, just as he was going into the cart; though it was not prevented without the loss of some blood. One Watson, an officer, too incautiously examining Jack's pockets, unluckly cut his own fingers —Sheppard had still another project in his head.

He earnestly desired some of his acquaintance, that after his body was cut down, they would, as soon as possible, put it into a warm bed, and try to let him blood; for he said, he believed, if such care was taken, they might bring him to life again.

At the place of execution he behaved himself very gravely; confessed in particular, that he robbed Dr. Phillips and Mrs. Cook, though, for want of proper evidence, the jury had acquitted him of both; and he declared, that when he and Blueskin robbed Mr. Kneebone, William Field was not with them.

He was executed at Tyburn, on Monday, November 16th, 1725, in the 23rd year of his age. He died with great difficulty, and much pitied by the mob. When he had hung about a quarter of an hour, he was cut down by a soldier, and delivered to his friends, who carried him to the Barley Mow, in Long-acre, and he was buried the same evening, in St. Martin's church-yard.

In a paper written by Sheppard during his confinement in the middle stone room, and left with the Ordinary, he returns his hearty thanks to the Rev. Dr. Bennet, the Rev. Dr. Burney, the Rev. Mr. Wagstaff, the Rev. Mr. Hawkins, the Rev. Mr. Flood, and the Rev. Mr. Edwards, for their charitable visits and assistance to him; as also his thanks to those worthy gentlemen who so generously contributed to his support in prison.

I hope, says he, none will be so cruel as to reflect on my poor distressed mother, the unhappy parent of two miserable wretches, myself and brother; the last gone to America for his crimes, and myself going to the grave for mine.—I beseech the

Supreme Being to pardon my numberless and enormous crimes, and to have mercy on my poor departing soul.

In a postscript to the paper alluded to, he says—After I had escaped from the castle, concluding that Blueskin would have been decreed for death, I did fully purpose to have gone and cut down the gallows the night before his execution.

No felon ever made more noise in the world. He was for a considerable time the common subject of conversation, and his picture was engraved by several artists, representing the manner of his escape out of the condemned hole, and the castle in Newgate, besides other prints of his effigies.

The principal of which was a Mezzotinto, done from the original picture, painted by Sir James Thornhill.

RICHARD TURPIN.

THE transactions of this most notorious offender made a greater noise in the world, than those of almost any other malefactor previous to his time.

Richard Turpin was born at Hampstead, in Essex, where his father followed the occupation of a butcher, with a fair reputation; and after being the usual time at school, he was bound apprentice to a butcher in Whitechapel, but did not serve out his time; for his master discharged him from his house for brutal and egregious conduct, which was not in the least diminished by his parents' improper indulgence in supplying him with money, which enabled

him to cut a swell round the town among the blades
of the road and turf, whose company he affected to
keep. His friends thinking that marriage, and a
settlement in life, would bring him over from his
irregular courses, persuaded him to marry, which he
did, with one Hester Palmer, a young woman of decent family at East Ham, in Essex; but he had not
been married long before he fell into his old course
again, and soon became acquainted with a gang of
thieves, whose depredations terrified the whole county of Essex, and the neighbourhood of London.—
His share of the spoils was not sufficient, it appears,
to support him in his extravagance; for he joined
sheep stealing to foot pad robbery: and was at last
obliged to fly from his place of residence for stealing a young heifer, which he killed and cut up for
sale. Soon after this, he stole two oxen from one
Farmer Giles, of Plaistow, and drove them to a butcher's slaughtering house near Waltham Abbey.
Giles's servants came to this place in pursuit of the
cattle, where finding two carcases cut up, that answered the description of their master's property in
size, and shrewdly suspecting Turpin, who did not
deny being the owner of the goods, they made a
strict search after the skins, and having found them,
they had not the smallest doubt of his having stolen
the identical beasts they were in search of. No
doubt remaining who was the robber, a warrant was
procured for his apprehension; but he soon got
scent that the runners were in pursuit of him. He
made his escape out of the window of the house
where he was, just at the moment they were entering the door. Finding his situation at Waltham
Abbey rather perilous, he retreated into the hun-

dreds of Essex, where he found greater security ;
but as he could not live long without a fresh supply
of money, he hit upon a new scheme to support
himself; and that was to rob the smugglers he happened to meet with on the road; but he took care
not to attack the gang, only such solitary travellers
as fell in his way, and then did it with a colour of
justice ; for he constantly pretended to have a de-
putation from the Customs, and so took their property in the king's name.

He got tired of this kind of business after a
while ; and the retirement to which he was condemned, and this pursuit, not suiting the volatility
of his disposition, he went in search of the gang
with whom he had before connected himself, the
principal part of whose depredations were committed upon Epping Forest and the adjacent parts ; but
this business not succeeding to their expectations,
they determined to commence house-breaking, and
in this they were encouraged by joining with Gregory's gang, as it was then called ; a company of
desperadoes that made the Essex and adjacent roads
very dangerous to travel.   They formed themselves
into a body by Turpin's directions, and went round
the country at night, and whatever house they knew
had any value in it they marked.   Their method
was, one to knock at the door, when, as soon as it
was opened, the rest rushed in and plundered; and
such were their impudence and rapacity, that they
were not satisfied with the money they found,
plate, watches, or rings, but even took away the
household goods, if any suited them.

Somehow or other Turpin became acquainted
with the circumstances of an old woman who lived

at Loughton, who always kept a quantity of ready cash by her; whereupon he and his gang agreed to rob her; and when they came to the door, Wheeler knocked at it, and Turpin and the rest forcing their way into the house, blindfolded the old woman and her maid, tied the legs of her son, a well-grown lad, to the bedstead, and proceeded to rob the house; but not at first finding the wished for booty, they all set about a consultation what to do to get at it; for they were certain she must have a considerable sum concealed in the house. Turpin began to examine her, where her money and effects were hid; telling her, at the same time, that he knew she had money, and it was in vain to deny it, for have it he would. The old gentlewoman being very loth to part with her money, persisted in it that she had none, and would not declare any thing more of the matter; upon which some of the gang were inclined to believe her, and were sorry for their disappointment; but Turpin as strenuously insisting she had money, as she that she had none, he at last, with horrid oaths and imprecations, swore he would put her on the fire. She continued obstinate for all that, imagining he meant only to threaten her; and so very fond was she of her darling gold, that she even suffered herself to be served as he had declared, and endured it for some time; till the anguish at last forced her to make a discovery, which when she had done, they took her off the grate and robbed her of all they could find.

The next person they robbed was a farmer's at Ripple side, near Barking; where the people not coming to the door as soon as they wanted them, they broke it open. They first of all, according to their old scheme, gagged, tied and blindfolded all they found in the place capable of opposing them ; and then robbed the house of £700, which delight- ed Turpin so much, that he exclaimed, " Aye, this is the thing ! that's your sort for the rag, (a cant term for money) if it would last !"   And they safely retired with their prize, which amounted to £80 a man.   This robbery was committed in the begin- ning of the year, 1730.   This success so much flushed Turpin and his associates, that several others joined them, insomuch that they became a formidable crew, and many times, when together, defied the legal authority of the magistrates ; and their adroitness was such, that they escaped detec- tion for many months.

Some little time after, they determined to attack the house of Mr. Mason, the keeper of Epping Forest, who was pitched upon to feel the effects of their resentment for his former vigilance in disturb- ing their poaching excursions into his district. But Turpin was not concerned in this affair ; for he happened at that time to be in London, when drink- ing too freely he forgot his appointment ; but the job was done by Rust, Rose, and Fielder, who pre- viously bound themselves together by an oath not to leave a whole thing in the house.   Fielder got over a wall and broke in backwards, when letting in his companions, they proceeded to their busi- ness.   Mr. Mason was at home, sitting up by the fire in his bed room, with his father, an aged gen- tleman.   After their usual means of tying their hands and feet, they asked the old man if he knew them ; but answering he did not, they carried him down into the kitchen, and put him under the dresser. Mr. Mason had a sack put over his head, and tied round his waist; and in the flurry his little girl got out of the bed, and without clothes on, hid herself in the hog-stye. Turpin's absence from this expedition was an unfortunate circumstance to the forest keeper's family, for they proceeded to greater lengths in their mischief than he would have permitted them, had he been present: as he was always satisfied with plunder, without adding cruelty to oppression. They now went up stairs, and broke every article of furniture in the house. The china and glass made a dreadful ringing: the chairs were piled upon the fire: looking glasses, drawers, and tables, were beat to pieces with bed-posts; while the bed and carpets were cut without remorse. This wanton havoc produced them but little, besides the brutal satisfaction of revenge; and they would have retired without a single guinea, had it not been, that in the general wreck of every thing, a china punch-bowl was broke, that stood a little out of the way, upon an upper shelf, and out of it dropped 122 guineas and moidores, which they picked up, and retired with, after they had done all the mischief they possibly could, and got safe off, no doubt very much satisfied with the severe retaliation they had made. They then took the road to London; and going through Whitechapel, they met Turpin, with whom they went to the Bunhouse, in Rope fields, where they shared the bounty, which proves the old adage, "there is honour among thieves," though he had not taken any active part in the execution of the robbery.

The next robbery of note they committed was about seven or eight o'clock in the evening. Rust,

Turpin, Field, Walker, and three others, came to
the house of Mr. Saunders, a wealthy farmer, at
Charlton, in Kent, and knocking at the door, inquired if Mr. Saunders was at home.   Being answered he was, and the door opened, they all rushed
in, went directly to the parlour, where Mr. Saunders, his wife, and some friends, were at cards;
but desired them not to be frightened, for that they
would not hurt their persons if they sat still and
made no disturbance.   The first thing they laid
hands on, was a silver snuff-box, which lay upon the
table before them, and open his closets, boxes, es-
critoire, from whence they took upwards of one hundred pounds in money, and all the plate in the
house, a velvet hood, mantle, and other things.
Whilst this was doing, the servant maid got loose
and ran up stairs, barred herself in one of the
rooms, and called out for assistance, in hopes of
alarming the neighbourhood; but one of the rogues
ran up stairs after her, and with a poker broke open
the door, brought her down again and bound her,
and all the rest of the family; then they rifled the
house of divers other things of value; and finding,
in their search, some bottles of wine, ate mince pie,
and obliged the company to drink a glass of water,
and putting some drops in it, gave it to her, and
were very careful to recover her.   They staid a considerable time in the house, after feasting and pack-
ing up their booty; and when they departed, they
declared, that if any of the family gave out the least
alarm within two hours, or even advertised the
marks of the plate they had taken, they would remember them for it, for they would return and murder them at a future time.   This robbery was con-

certed at the George at Woolwich, from whence
they proceeded to put their design in execution;
and when they had effected it they crossed the water, and brought their goods to an empty house in
Ratcliffe Highway, provided for them by one of
Dick Swift's acquaintance, where they deposited
their plunder, and divided their produce.

They next proceeded into Surrey, where Turpin,
Rust, Swift, Fielder, and Walker, robbed Mr. Sheldon's house, a lone building, near Croydon church,
where they arrived about seven o'clock in the evening. They began their operations here by securing
the coachman in the stable attending the horses,
whom they bound hand and foot, and afterwards
locked him in safe. His master being in an out-
house, and hearing some strange voices in the yard,
was proceeding that way to know the cause, when
he was met by Turpin and Walker, who seizing
hold of him, compelled him to shew them the way
into the house, which when they had got into they
secured the door, and confined the rest of the family
in one room, over which, within and without, they
set a guard. Mr. Sheldon's servant man unluckily
coming to the door from abroad, was first knocked
down, and then dragged into the passage and tied,
while they ransacked the house. But they were
much disappointed; for they found but little plate
and no cash. From Mr. Sheldon's person they took
eleven guineas; two of which Turpin returned him,
begging pardon for what they had done, and wished
him a good night.

These robberies had hitherto been carried on entirely on foot, with only the occasional assistance
of a hackney coach; but now they aspired to appear

on horseback, for which purpose they hired horses at the Old Leaping Bar, in High Holborn, from whence they set out about two o'clock in the afternoon, and arrived at the Queen's Head, near Stanmore, at five, where they staid to regale themselves. It was by these means that Wood, the master of the house, had so good an opportunity of observing the horses, as to remember the same again when he saw them afterwards in King-street, Bloomsbury, where they were taken. About five o'clock they went from Mr. Wood's, at the Queen's Head, to Stanmore, and staid there from six until about seven o'clock, and then all went away together for Mr. Laurence's, which was about a mile from thence, where they arrived about half-past seven. Mr. Laurence had just been paying off some workmen, who were discharged, and gone from the house. On their arrival at Mr. Laurence's they alighted from their horses at the outer gate; and Fielder getting over the hatch into the sheep yard, met with Mr. Laurence's boy, just putting up some sheep. They seized and presented a pistol to him, Fielder saying he would shoot him if he offered to cry out; and then took off the boy's garters, and tied his hands; inquiring what servants Mr. Laurence kept, and who was in the house, which they obliged him to tell them. They told him they would not hurt him, but that he must go to the door with them; and when they knocked at it, if any body within should ask who it was, that the boy was to answer, and bid them to open the door to let him in, and they would give him some money. Accordingly they led the boy to the door, and calling out to Mr. Laurence, the man servant, supposing it to be some

of the neighbours only, opened the door, upon which
they all rushed in with pistols in their hand, crying
out with horrid imprecations, how long have you
lived here ? and seizing Mr. Laurence and his man,
threw a cloth over their faces, and then took the boy,
and led him into the next room, with his hands tied,
demanding of him what fire-arms Mr. Laurence had
in the house ; and being told there was none but
an old gun, they went and fetched that, and broke
it to pieces ; then took Mr. Laurence's man, and
binding his hands, led him to the room where the
boy was, and made him sit down there ; and also
bound Mr. Laurence. Turpin cut down his breeches,
and they fell to rifling his pockets, out of which
they took one guinea, one Portugal piece of thirty-
six shillings, about fifteen shillings in silver, and
his keys. They said the money was not enough,
that they must have more, and drove Mr. Laurence
up stairs ; where coming to a closet, although they
had taken the key from Mr. Laurence before, and
had it in their custody, yet they broke open the door,
and took out from thence two guineas, ten shillings
in silver, a silver cup, thirteen silver spoons, two
gold rings, and what they could find ; and in their
search meeting with a bottle of elder wine, they
obliged the servants to drink twice of it. They
brought Mr. Laurence down stairs again and threatened to cut his throat ; and Rose put a knife to it,
as if he intended to do it, to make him confess what
money was in the house. One of them took a
chopping bill, and threatened to cut off his leg.
They then broke his head with their pistols, and
dragged him about by the hair of the head. Another
of them took a kettle of water off the fire, and flung

it upon him; but did no other harm than wetting him, by reason the maid had just before taken out the greatest part of the boiling water, and filled it again with cold. After this they dragged him about again, swearing they would ' do for him,' if he did not immediately inform them where the rest of his money was nid. They then proceeded to make further search; and found £20 in a chest, which with plate, linen, &c, they packed up, then locked all the people in the parlour, and swore they would shoot every one they found loose, when they returned, which would be in half an hour.

Such frequent robberies, and the particulars of this atrocious one, being represented to the King, a proclamation was issued for the apprehenson of the offenders, and a pardon and fifty pounds were offered to any of the party who would impeach his accomplices. This, however, had no effect; for they continued their depredations with more systematic ingenuity, and at such distances, that none could be aware of their approach. The success they met with elated their spirits, and encouraged them to bid defiance to the executive laws of the country.

In the mouth of danger, and in the midst of alarm which their audacities had occasioned, Turpin, and his gang, were as careless as they were heedless.

The White Hart, at the upper end of Drury lane, was their place of rendezvous. Here they planned their nightly visits, and there divided their nightly spoil, and spent the property they unlawfully acquired. The gang all this time consisted of a great number, from the bold adventurer on horseback, to the pitiful stripper of children's clothes. From hence there issued a select band to rob a Mr. Francis, a farmer near Marylebone, where they arrived about dusk: and while they were making their observations on the premises, one of them perceiving somebody in the cow house, they went in, and finding a man there, they seized and bound him, swearing they would shoot him if he made any attempt to loosen himself, or cry out. They then proceeded to the stable, where was another of the farmer's servants, whom they served in the same manner. Scarce had they performed this, before Mr. Francis, who had been abroad, coming home, was met at the gate, as he was going up to his door. Three of the gang laying their hands upon his shoulder, prevented him from going any further; and the farmer not at first apprehending them to be thieves, but frolicsome fellows, only said to them, Methinks you are mighty funny, gemmen. On which, shewing their pistols, they told him no harm should come to him, if he would give an order to his daughter for one hundred pounds in cash: which Mr. Francis refused to do, alleging his incapacity, not having half so much money by him: they forced him by the arm into the stable to his man, where they bound him also, and left him under the care of Rust and Bush, who stood over them with loaded pistols, whilst the rest went to the house. Upon knocking at the door, Miss Francis opened it, supposing it to be some of the men, when Wheeler and four others rushing in, they secured her also. Turpin coming in with the last, prevented them from being too violent with the young lady; only threatening, if she made any resistance, she would be worse used. The maid servant hearing this, cried out, Lord, Mrs.

Sarah, what have you done? On which one of
them struck the maid, and another Miss Francis,
and swore they would murder them if they did not
hold their peace. Mrs. Francis hearing the disturbance, and being apprehensive of some danger, cried
out, Lord, what's the matter? On which Fielder
stepped up to her, and cried, D——n you for an old
b——h, I'll stop your mouth presently; and immediately broke her head with the handle of his whip;
and then tied her down in a chair, bleeding as she
was.

The maid and daughter were bound in the kitchen, and Gregory was set to watch them, who
stood over them with a pistol in his hand, to prevent
their crying out for assistance, or endeavouring to
get their liberty, whilst the other four were rifling
the house. In it they found thirty-seven guineas,
and ten pounds in silver, which they took away
with them; as also, several articles of jewellery,
plate, linen, &c.

When they came to divide the plunder, Turpin
prevented them from cheating one another, which
some seemed inclined to do; and he gave to each
of them £10 2s. 6d. The guineas were secreted
by him that had laid hands on them, from the rest
of his companions, which, when Turpin afterwards
found out, he made him pay severely for: for he informed against him to the officers of justice, which
occasioned his being taken up, and he was shortly
afterwards executed at Tyburn.

They formed a design to rob Justice Ashe, near
Leigh, in Essex, but were interrupted by some
neighbouring farmers; their attempt became known,
and their daring conduct alarmed the whole coun-

try, nobody thinking themselves safe; upon which
Mr. Thompson, one of the king's forest-keepers,
went to the Duke of Newcastle's office, and obtained his majesty's promise of a reward of one hundred pounds for whoever should apprehend any of
them. This made them rather more shy than they
were before; but, however, they could not conceal
themselves entirely; they still frequented their old
haunts; which some of the justice's men, hearing
that a number of them usually met at an ale-house
in an alley in Westminster, they went thither, where
finding Turpin, Fielden, Rose, and Wheeler, after a
short conflict, with cutlasses, the three last were
secured; but not till one Bob Berry, a cork cutter,
had his arm dangerously cut across a little below
the elbow. During the scuffle, Turpin made his
escape out of a window, and getting a horse, rode
away immediately. Wheeler turned evidence, and
the two others were hanged in chains. This affair
broke up the gang.

Turpin being now left to himself, had more prudence than to follow the house-robbing immediately
after, particularly as he was so well known; and
having some money in his pockets, he took a resolution to be concerned with no other gang, but to
act entirely on his own account. With this view
he set off to Cambridge, which he judged would be
the best place, as he was not known in that part
of the country. Near Alton, he met with an
odd encounter, which got him the best companion
he ever had, as he often declared. King, the highwayman, as he was returning from this place for
London, being well dressed and mounted, Turpin,
seeing him have the appearance of a substanstial

gentleman, rode up to him, and thinking him a fair mark, bid him stand and deliver, and therewith producing his pistols, King fell a laughing at him, and said, what, dog rob dog! come, come, brother Turpin, if you don't know me, I know you, and should be glad of your company. After a mutual communication of circumstances to each other, they agreed to keep company, and divide good or ill fortune as the trumps might turn up.

They met with various fortune : but being both too well known to remain long in a place, and as no house that knew them would receive them in it, they formed the resolution of making themselves a cave, covered with bavins and earth. And for that purpose fixed upon a convenient place, enclosed with a thicket, situated on the Waltham side of Epping, near the sign of the King's Oak. Here they excavated, and covered with thicket, wood, and quickset, a place large enough to receive them and their horses; and while they lay quite concealed themselves, could, through several holes, discover the passengers as they went along the road ; and as thought proper, would issue out, and rob them in such bold and daring style, that they were more admired than blamed.

The very higglers on the road did not always esscape their requisitions, but they were mostly repaid again ; whilst those that went armed, lost their piecesi were wounded, and robbed of all they carried about them.

Turpin's wife was their messenger, went to market for victuals for them, supplied them with linen, and frequently remained there a whole week at a time. In this place, Turpin lived, eat, drank and

lay, for the space of six years, during the first three
of which he was enlivened by the drollery of his
companion, Tom King, who was a fellow of infinite
wit in telling stories and of unshaken resolution in
attack or defence.

These forest partners used frequently to issue
from their cell, like the thieves from the cave of Gil
Blas, and take a ride out in quest of plunder. Riding towards Bungay, in Suffolk, they met two young
women who had just received a considerable sum
for corn. King proposed to rob them, Turpin endeavoured to dissuade him from it, alleging that
they were two pretty inoffensive girls, and he would
not be concerned in it. King swore he would rob
them, and accordingly did, against Turpin's consent,
which occasioned a dispute between them.

Turpin having lost his horse, he stole one out of
a close. This was a black one; and some people
being at work in a field within sight, he threw a
handful of silver among them, and made off: but
the same evening he changed his black one for a
chesnut mare, which he found in a field, and upon
her he made the best of his way to the forest.

He next stopped a country gentleman, who clap-
ping spurs to his horse, Turpin followed him, and
firing a pistol after him which lodging two balls in
his horse's buttocks, the gentleman was obliged to
surrender. He robbed him of fifty shillings, asking
him if that was all, and the gentleman saying he
had no more, Turpin searched him, and found two
guineas more in his pocket book, out of which he
returned him 5s. but at the same time told the gentleman it was more than he deserved, because of his
intention to have cheated him.

Turpin had gone on for a long time in a most notorious and defying way, stopping the mail and other
coaches and robbing them of their contents, and the
reward for apprehending him had induced many to
attempt it.   Amongst the rest was the ranger,
Thompson's man.   This fellow must needs go in
company with a higgler.   Turpin was unarmed,
standing alone ; and not knowing the man, took him
for one poaching for hares, and told him he would
get no hares near that thicket.   No, says the fellow,
but I have got a Turpin, and presenting his piece at
him, commanded him to surrender.   Turpin stood
talking with him, and receding back to his cave, laid
hold of his carbine, and shot him dead, at which the
higgler made off.   This man's death obliged Turpin
to make off precipitately ; so he went further into
the country in search of King ; and sent his wife a
letter to meet him at a public house in Hertford,
who accordingly went, with two of Squire H———'s
servants.   She waited for him about half an hour,
and when he came to the house, he asked for her by
a fictitious name, left on purpose.   He soon found
she was there : and in going to her through the kitchen he saw a butcher to whom he owed £5.   The
butcher taking him aside, come Dick, says he, it
would be of great service.   Turpin replied his wife
was in the next room, she had money, and he would
get some of her, and pay him presently.   The butcher apprised two or three that were present who it
was, and that he would get his five pounds, and then
take him, but Turpin, instead of going to his wife,
jumped out of the next window, took horse, and went
away immediately, without seeing her ; while the
butcher waited some time in expectation of receiv-

ing his five pounds. Affairs wore a serious aspect for a while, and Turpin was obliged to be very cautious in his approaches to the metropolis.

Turpin and King being driven about, they joined with one Potter, a daring roadsman, who had a good horse. In his company they stopped several gentlemen on horseback, and in post chaises, from whom they levied considerable sums. Turpin, the better to disguise himself, now wore sometimes a miller's frock, quite white: at other times he had a black one on, like a waggoner. In this disguise, but upon a good horse, he ventured over the forest, towards London, when within three hundred yards of the Green Man, he overtook one Mr. Major, the owner of White stockings, the race-horse; and, although they were so near the houses, Turpin ventured to rob him. He took from him his whip, and finding he had a better horse than his, made him dismount, change, and stay till he had changed saddles likewise, and then rode towards London. Mr. Major got to the Green Man, and acquainted Mr. Bayes of it, who immediately said, I dare swear it is Turpin has done it, or one of that crew, and I'll endeavour to get intelligence of your horse. This that they have left you is stole, and I would have you advertise it. This was accordingly done, and the horse proved to have been stolen from Arrowsmith. This robbery was committed on Saturday night: and on Monday following, Mr. Bayes received intelligence that such a horse as Mr. Major had lost, was left at the Red Lion Inn, in Whitechapel. He accordingly went thither, and found it to be the same; and then resolved to wait till somebody came to fetch it.   Nobody came at time it was left for: but about eleven o'clock at night King's brother (as it was afterwards proved) came for the horse; upon which they seized him immediately and taking him into the house, said he bought it, and could produce proof of it.   But Mr. Bayes looking on the whip in his hand, found the button half broke off, and the name Major upon it, which proved a confirmation of the thing.   They charged a constable with him; but he seemed frightened, and they declared that they did not believe but the horse was for somebody else, and if he would tell them where they waited, he should be released, he told them that there was a person in a white duffled coat, waiting for it in Red Lion street.   They then immediately went out; and finding him as directed, perceived it was King, and coming round him attacked him.   King immediately drew a pistol, which he clapped to Mr. Bayes breast; but it luckily flashed in the pan; upon which King struggled to get out his other, that he twisted round his pocket, but could not.   Turpin, who was but a small distance on horseback, came up, when King cried out, d—ye, shoot him, Dick, or we shall be taken; at which instant Turpin let fly one of his pistols, and the other directly afterwards.   Both shots missed Bayes but severely wounded King in two places, who cried out, why Dick, you have killed me, or nearly so. Turpin hearing this, and finding his case desperate indeed, rode away as fast as possible.   Some accounts say that King died a week after; but with more certainty it may be asserted, that he was the masked highwayman that was shot near Enfield, by the King's German messenger, in attempting to rob him in a post-chaise. This happened but a short time afterwards. Turpin and King never met after this; but King called him a coward, and one wanting resolution.

Bayes soon after this got intelligence that Turpin might be found at a noted house by Hackney Marsh, and that when he rode out, he always had three brace of pistols about him, and a carbine slung. Upon enquiry this was found to be true, which made Mr. Bayes desist in the pursuit. Turpin for a while shewed great signs of uneasiness, often using something like the following expressions to the landlord: why, Sam, what shall I do? D— that fellow, Dick Bayes, I'll be the death of him, I will. Where shall I go? For I have lost the best companion I ever had in my life; I have shot poor King in endeavouring to rescue him from the shark's paws. He retained this resolution to the last; but he never had an opportunity to put his revenge in practice.

The public heard very little of Turpin for near two years after this. The first notice of him was from the minister of Long Sutton, in Lincolnshire, who was magistrate of the place. There he was taken into custody; but he escaped from the constable as he was conducting him back from examination, and hastened to Welton in Yorkshire, where he assumed his wife's maiden name, (Palmer) and took upon himself to appear as a gentleman.

He took a large house at Brough, near South Cave, in Yorkshire, from whence to Welton, he carried on an extensive trade in horses, selling and exchanging; and at the time of the races he is said to have realized about one thousand pounds, which

F

enabled him now (Mr. John Palmer) to keep the first company stirring in those parts.

On one of these occasional visits to Brough he fell in with the celebrated Dickey Dickenson, the humourous governor of Scarborough Spa, to whom he sold a horse, which four year afterwards was claimed by Squire More as his property, he having lost it from the Marshes in Lincolnshire. He went first to Long Sutton, in Lincolnshire, where the people, he thought, would not know him ; and as he abounded in money, he proposed to himself to commence a dealer in horses.

It is very remarkable that, for such a course of time as from the date of the King's reward of £200 for his apprehension, he should still go on with his depredations with the most audacious impunity, insomuch that it affected the national character in the eyes of foreigners, who could not help remarking, that the native bravery of the English was supine in bringing such a daring offender to justice. In fact, his feats of equestrian agility were so surprising, and his identity so uncertain, that to these circumstances alone may be ascribed his long evasion from the iron hand of the law. He had been at Luton, and drank very freely at the Cock there. Early in the morning he set off, and robbed a gentleman of fifty guineas and a valuable watch, in the environs of London. Apprehensive of being known and pursued, he spurred his horse on, and took the northern road, and, astonishing to relate, reached York the same evening, and was noticed playing at bowls in the bowling-green with several gentlemen there, which circumstance saved him from the hands of justice for that time. The gentleman he robbed knew him to be Turpin, and caused him to be pursued and taken at York. He afterwards swore to him and the horse he rode on, which was the identical one he arrived upon in that city; but on being in the stable, and his rider at play, all in twenty-four hours, his alibi was admitted; for the magistrates of York could not believe it possible for one horse to cover the ground, being upwards of one hundred and ninety miles, in so short a space. He is reported, upon this occasion, to have used his horse to raw beef upon the bit in his mouth. Some go so far as to say he always rode with fowls' guts tied round. Be this so or not, it was a race that equalled, if not surpassed, the first achievements of turf velocity.

Another time he robbed a poor woman returning from Ferrybridge, where she had been to sell some commodities; and soon after hearing she was distressed by her landlord for rent, he contrived to relieve her in the following singular manner. He found out her abode, and threw into the window, through the glass, a leather bag, containing gold and silver to the amount of six pounds; perhaps the produce of a recent robbery.

For the last two years of his life he seemed to have confined his residence mostly to the county of York, where he was but little known, and kept company with the best yeomen of the county. He often went with the neighbouring gentlemen in their parties of hunting and shooting; and one evening, on a return from an expedition of the latter kind, he saw one of his landlord's cocks in the street, at which he shot, and killed. One Hall, his neighbour, seeing him shoot the cock, said to him, Mr.

Palmer, you have done wrong to shoot your landlord's cock; whereupon Palmer said, if you will
stop till I have charged my piece, I will shoot you
too.   Mr. Hall hearing this, went and told the landlord what Palmer had done and said, and had him
immediately apprehended, and on refusing to find
sureties, was committed to prison.   Informations
poured in from various parts, implicating his conduct, and in less than two months, persons from
Lincolnshire claimed a mare and foal, and likewise
a horse, which he had stolen in that county.   Captain Dawson, of Ferraby, was one among the
claimants.   His horse was that which Turpin, alias
Palmer, rode when he came to Beverley, and which
he had stolen from off Hickington Fen, in Lincolnshire.   After five months' imprisonment, he wrote
to his brother as follows :—

Dear Brother,
     I am sorry to acquaint you, that I am now un-
der confinement in York Castle for horse stealing,
if I could procure an evidence from London to give
me a character, that would go a great way towards
my good, and might prove in the end to my enlarge-
ment and acquittal.   It is true I have been here a
long while, but never wrote before.   Few people
knew me.   For Heaven's sake, dear brother, do not
neglect me; you will know what I mean when I
say I am your's,
                              JOHN PALMER.

His brother refused to take the letter; and it was
returned unopened to the post-office in Essex, because the brother would not pay for it.   This letter

being accidentally seen by a Mr. Smith, a school-master of the town, he recognized the hand-writing to be Turpin's, for he had taught him to write at his father's. This coming to the knowledge of the magistrates, they subpœned Mr. Smith, by whom it was discovered that this said John Palmer was the real Richard Turpin.

On a rumour that the noted Turpin was a prisoner in York Castle, persons flocked from all parts of the country to take a view of him, and debates ran very high whether it was the real person or not. Among others who visited him, was a young fellow who pretended to well acquainted with the famous Turpin, having regarded him for a considerable time with looks of great attention, he told the keeper he would bet him half a guinea he was not Turpin the horse-stealer; on which the prisoner whispering to the turnkey, said, lay him, Jack, and I'll go you halves.

During his abode in the Castle, the turnkeys are said to have made more than £100 by shewing him, and selling him and his acquaintances and visitors liquors.

The trial of Turpin took place at York Castle on the 22nd of March, 1739, before the Hon. Sir William Chapple, for stealing a black gelding, the property of Thomas Creasy. Upon his trial, Smith the schoolmaster, proved his identity. During his trial, his conduct seemed to affect the hearers. He had two trials, in both of which he was convicted on the fullest evidence. When asked by the judge why sentence of death should not be pronounced against him, he said, he thought it very hard, as he was not prepared for his defence, having been in-

formed that his trial would be removed to Essex.
His lordship observed, that whoever told him so
was highly to blame, but it was his duty, the jury
having found him guilty of a crime worthy of death,
to pronounce sentence against him.

He wrote to his father, upon being convicted, to
use his interest to get him off for transportation;
but his fate was at hand; his notoriety caused all
application to be ineffectual. To this letter the father returned the following answer :—

Dear Child,

I received your letter this instant, with a great
deal of grief. According to your request, I have
wrote to your brother John and Madam Park, to
make what intercession can be made to Colonel
Watson, in order to obtain transportation for your
misfortunes; which had I £100. I would freely
part with to do you good. In the mean time
my prayers are for you: and for God's sake give
your whole mind to beg of God to pardon your
many transgressions, which the thief received pardon for upon the cross at the last hour, though a
very great offender. The Lord be your comfort,
and receive you into his everlasting kingdom. I am
your distressed and loving father,

JOHN TURPIN.

The morning before Turpin's execution, he paid
£3 19s amongst five men, who were to follow the
cart as mourners, with hatbands and gloves, and
gave gloves and hatbands to several persons more.
He also left a gold ring, and two pair of shoes and
clogs, to a married woman at Brough, that he

was acquainted with ; though he at the same time acknowledged he had a wife and child of his own.

He was carried in a cart to the place of execution, on Saturday, April 7th, 1739, with John Stead, condemned also for horse-stealing. He behaved himself with amazing assurance, and bowed to the spectators as he passed. It was remarkable that as he mounted the ladder, his right leg trembled, on which he stamped it down with an air, and with undaunted courage looked about him; and after speaking near half an hour to the topsman, threw himself off the ladder, and expired in about five minutes.

He was buried next morning in St. George's Church-yard, without Fisher-gate Postern, with this inscription, *R T.* 29. [He confessed to the hangman that he was 33 years of age.] The grave was dug very deep ; and the persons whom he appointed as mourners, as abovementioned, took all possible care to secure the body ; notwithstanding which, early on Tuesday morning, some persons had taken it up. The mob having got scent where it was carried to, and suspecting it was to be anatomized, went to a garden, in which it was deposited. and brought away the body through the streets of the city in a sort of triumph, almost naked, being only laid on a board, covered with straw, and carried on four men's shoulders and buried it in the same grave, having first filled the coffin with slacked lime.

CLAUDE DU VALL

THIS noted person was born at Domfront in Normandy. His father was a miller. He was brought up in the Catholic faith, and received but an indifferent education. But although his father was careful to train up his son in the religion of his ancestors, he was himself utterly without religion.

Du Vall's parents were exempted from the trouble and expense of rearing their son at the age of thirteen. We first find him at Rouen, the principal city of Normandy, in the character of a stable boy. Here he fortunately found return horses going to Paris: upon one of these he was permitted to ride, on condition of assisting to dress them at night. His expenses were likewise defrayed by some English travellers he met upon the road.

Arrived at Paris he continued at the same inn where the Englishmen put up, and by running messages, or performing the meanest offices, subsisted for a while. He continued in this humble station until the restoration of Charles II., when multitudes from the continent resorted to England. In the character of a footman to a person of quality, Du Vall also repaired to England. The universal joy which seized the nation on that event contaminated the morals of all : riot, dissipation, and every species of profligacy abounded. The young French footman entered keenly into these amusements. His funds, however, being soon exhausted, he deemed it no great crime for a Frenchman to exact con-

tributions from the English ; in other words to rob
on the highway.   In a short time, he became so
great an adept in his new employment, that he had
the honour of being first named in an advertisement
issued for the apprehending of some notorious robbers.

One day, Du Vall and some others met a knight
and his lady travelling alone in their carriage.   Seeing themselves in danger of being attacked, the lady resorted to a flageolet, and commenced playing,
which she did very dexterously.   Du Vall taking
the hint, pulled one out of his pocket, and began to
play, and in this posture approached the coach.
Sir, said he to the knight, 'your lady performs excellently, and I make no doubt she dances well;
will you step out of the coach, and let us have the
honour to dance a courant with her upon the heath?'
'I dare not deny any thing, sir,' replied the knight
readily, 'to a gentleman of your quality and good
behaviour; you seem a man of generosity, and you
are perfectly reasonable.'   Immediately the footman
opened the door and the knight came out.   Du Vall
leaped lightly off his horse, and handed the lady
down.   It was surprising to see how graceful he
danced upon the grass : scarcely a dancing master
in London, but would have been proud to have
shown such agility in a pair of pumps, as Du Vall
evinced in a pair of French boots.   As soon as the
dance was over, he handed the lady to the coach,
but just as the knight was stepping in, sir,' said he,
'you forget to pay the music.'   His worship replied, that he never forgot such things, and instantly
put his hand under the seat of the coach, pulled out
one hundred pounds in a bag, which he delivered

to Du Vall, who received it with a very good grace, and courteously answered, 'sir, you are liberal, and shall have no cause to regret your generosity; this hundred pounds, given so handsomely, is better than ten times the sum taken by force. Your noble behaviour has excused you the other three hundred pounds, which you have in the coach with you.' After this, he gave him his word that he might pass undisturbed, if he met any other of his crew, and then wished him a good journey.

At another time, Du Vall and some of his associates, met a coach on Blackheath, full of ladies, and a child with them. One of the gang rode up to the coach, and in a rude manner robbed the ladies of their watches and rings, and even seized a silver sucking bottle of the child's. The infant cried bitterly for its bottle, and the ladies earnestly entreated that he would only return the article to the child, which he barbarously refused. Du Vall went forward to discover what detained his accomplice, and the ladies renewing their entreaties to him, he instantly threatened to shoot his companion, unless he returned that article, saying, 'Sirrah, can't you behave like a gentleman, and raise a contribution without stripping people? but, perhaps, you had some occasion for the sucking-bottle, for, by your actions, one would imagine you were hardly weaned.' This smart reproof had the desired effect, and Du Vall, in a most courteous manner, took his leave of the ladies.

One day, Du Vall met Roper, master of the hounds to Charles II., who was hunting in Windsor forest; and, taking the advantage of a thicket, demanded his money, or he would instantly take his life. Roper, without hesitation gave him his purse, containing at least, fifty guineas : in return, for which, Du Vall bound him neck and heels, tied his horse to a tree beside him, and rode across the country.

It was a considerable time before the huntsmen discovered their master. The Squire being at length released, made all possible haste to Windsor, unwilling to venture himself into any more thickets that day, whatever might be the fortune of the hunt. Entering the town, he was accosted by Sir Stephen Fox, who inquired if he had any sport. 'Sport!' replied Roper, in a great passion, 'yes, sir, I have have had sport enough, from a villain who made me pay full dear for it; he bound me neck and heels, contrary to my desire, and then took fifty guineas from me to pay him for his labour which I had much rather he omitted.'

England now became too contracted a sphere for the talents of our adventurer; and, in consequence of a proclamation issued for his detection, and his notoriety in the kingdom, Du Vall retired to his native country. At Paris, he lived in a very extravagant style, and carried on war with rich travellers and fair ladies, and proudly boasted that he was equally successful with both; but his warfare with the latter was infinitely more agreeable, though much less profitable, than with the former.

There is one adventure of Du Vall at Paris which we shall lay before our readers. There was in that city a learned Jesuit, confessor to the king, who had rendered himself eminent, both by his politics and avarice. His thirst for money was insatiable, and increased with his riches. Du Vall devised the fol-

lowing plan, to obtain a portion of the immense
wealth of this avaricious father.

To facilitate his admittance into the Jesuit's company, he dressed himself as a scholar, and waiting
a favourable opportunity, went up to him very confidently, and addressed him as follows :—'May it
please your reverence, I am a poor scholar, who
have been several years travelling over strange
countries, to learn experience in the sciences, prin-
cipally to serve my own country, for whose advantage I am determined to apply my knowledge, if I
may be favoured with the patronage of a man so
eminent as yourself.' 'And what may this knowledge of yours be? replied the father, very much
pleased. If you will communicate anything to me
that may be beneficial to France, I assure you, no
proper encouragement will be wanting on my side.'
Du Vall, upon this, growing bolder, proceeded :—
'Sir, I have spent most of my time in the study of
almychy, or the transmutations of metals, and have
profited so much at Rome and Venice, from great
men learned in that science, that I change several
metals into gold, by the help of a philosophical
powder which I can prepare very speedily.

The father confessor was more elevated with this
communication, than all the discoveries he had obtained in the way of his profession, and his knowledge even of the royal penitent's most private secrets
gave him less delight than the prospect of immense
riches which now burst upon his mind. Friend,
said he, such a thing as this will be serviceable to
the whole state, and particularly grateful to the king,
who, as his affairs go at present, stands in great
need of such a curious invention. But you must

let me see some proof of your skill, before I credit what you say, so far as to communicate it to his majesty, who will sufficiently reward you, if what your promise be demonstrated. Upon this, the confessor conducted Du Vall to his house, and furnished him with money to erect a laboratory, and to purchase such other materials as were requisite, in order to proceed in this invaluable operation, charging him to keep the secret from every living soul. Utensils being fixed, and every thing in readiness, the Jesuit came to witness the wonderful operation. Du Vall took several metals and minerals of the basest sort, and then put them in a crucible, his reverence viewing every one as he put them in. Our alchymist had prepared a hollow tube, into which he conveyed several sprigs of real gold; with this seeming stick he stirred the operation, which with its heat, melted the gold, and the tube at the same time, so that it sank imperceptibly into the vessel. When the excessive fire had consumed all the different materials which he had put in, the gold remained pure, to the quantity of an ounce and a half. This the Jesuit ordered to be examined, and, ascertaining that it was actually pure gold, he became devoted to Du Vall, and blinded with the prospect of future advantage, credited every thing the imposter said, furnishing him with whatever he demanded, in hopes of being made master of this important secret. The confessor was as candid as Du Vall could wish; he shewed him all his treasures, and several rich jewels which he had received from the king; hoping by these obligations, to incline him to discover his wonderful secrets with more alacrity. In short, he became so importunate, that Du Vall was apprehensive of too minute an inquiry, if he denied the request any longer : he therefore appointed a day when the whole was to be disclosed. In the mean time, he took an opportunity of stealing into the chamber where the riches were deposited, and where his reverence generally slept after dinner; finding him in deep repose, he gently bound him, then took his keys, and unhoarded as much of his wealth as he could carry off unsuspected, after which, he quickly took leave of him and France.

It is uncertain how long Du Vall continued his depredations after his return to England ; but we are informed, that in a fit of intoxication he was detected at the Hole in-the-Wall, in Chandos street, committed to Newgate, convicted, condemned, and executed at Tyburn, in the twenty seventh year of his age, on the 1st of January, 1669.

SAWNEY BEANE.

THE following narrative presents such a picture of human barbarity, that were it not attested by the most unquestionable historical evidence, it would be rejected as fabulous and incredible.

Sawney Beane was born in the county of East Lothian, about eight miles east of Edinburgh, in the reign of James I. of Scotland. His father was a hedger and ditcher, and brought up his son to the same laborious employment. Naturally idle and vicious, he abandoned that place in company with a young woman equally idle and profligate, and retired to the deserts of Galloway, where they took up their habitation by the sea side.

The place which Sawney and his wife selected for their dwelling was a cave of about a mile in length, and of considerable breadth, so near the sea, that the tide often penetrated into the cave above two hundred yards. The entry had many intricate windings and turnings, leading to the extremity of the subterraneous dwelling, which was literally ' the habitation of cruelty.' In this cave, they commenced their depredations. To prevent the possibility of detection, they murdered every person they robbed. Destitute also of the means of obtaining any other food, they resolved to live upon human flesh. Accordingly, when they had murdered any man, woman, or child, they carried them to their den, quartered them, salted the limbs, and dried them for food. In this manner they lived, carrying on their depredations and murder, until they had eight sons and six daughters, eighteen grandsons and fourteen granddaughters, all the offspring of incest.

But though they soon became numerous, yet such was the multitude which fell into their hands, that they had often a superabundance of provisions, and would, at a distance from their own habitation, throw legs and arms of dried human bodies into the sea by night. These were often cast out by the tide, and taken up by the country people to the great consternation and dismay of the surrounding inhabitants. Nor could any one eiscover what had befallen many friends, relations, and neighbours, who had fallen into the hands of these merciless cannibals.

In proportion as Sawney's family increased, eve-

ry one that was able acted his part in these horrid
assassinations. They would sometimes attack four
or six men on foot, but never more than two upon
horseback. To prevent the possibility of escape,
they would lie in ambush in every direction, that if
they escaped those who first attacked, they might
be assailed with renewed fury by another party, and
inevitably murdered. By this means they always
secured their prey, and prevented detection.

At last, however, the vast number who were slain,
roused the inhabitants of the country, and all the
woods and lurking places were carefully searched ;
yet, though they often passed by the mouth of the
horrible den, it was never once suspected that any
human being resided there. In this state of uncer-
tainty and suspense concerning the authors of such
frequent massacres, several innocent travellers and
innkeepers were taken up on suspicion, because the
persons who were missing had been last in their
company, or had resided at their houses. The effect of this well meant and severe justice, constrained the greater part of the innkeepers in those parts
to abandon such employments, to the great incon-
venience of these who travelled through that district.

Meanwhile, the country became depopulated, and
the whole nation was at a loss to account for the
numerous and hitherto unheard of villanies and
cruelties that were perpetrated, without the slight-
est clue to the discovery of the abominable actors.

At last, however, they were discovered under the
following circumstances. One evening, a man and
his wife were riding home upon the same horse
from a fair which had been held in the neighbourhood,

and, being attacked, the husband made a most vigorous resistance. His wife, however, was dragged from behind him, carried to a little distance, and her entrails instantly taken out. Struck with grief and horror, the husband continued to redouble his efforts to escape, and even trod some of the assassins down under his horse's feet. Fortunately for him, and for the inhabitants of that part of the country, in the mean time, twenty or thirty in a company came riding home from the fair. Upon their approach, Sawney and his blood-thirsty crew fled into a thick wood, and hastened into their infernal den.

This man, who was the first that ever escaped out of their hands, related to his neighbours what had happened, and showed them the mangled body of his wife lying at a distance, the blood thirsty wretches not having had time to carry it along with them. They were all struck with astonishment and horror, took him with them to Glasgow, and reported the whole adventure to the chief magistrate of the city, who, upon this information, instantly wrote to the king, informing him of the matters.

So much importance had the affair assumed, that in a few days, his majesty in person, accompanied by four hundred men, went in quest of the perpetrators of these horrid cruelties. The man whose wife had been murdered before his eyes, went as their guide, with a great number of blood hounds, that no possible means might be left unattempted to discover the haunt of such execrable villains.

They searched the woods, and traversed and examined the sea shore; but though they passed by the entrance into the cave, they had no suspicion that any creature resided in that dark and dismal

G

abode. Fortunately, however, some of the blood
hounds entered the cave, raising an uncommon
barking and noise, an indication that they were about
to seize their prey. The king and his men returned, but could scarcely conceive how any human being could reside in a place of utter darkness, and
where the entrance was difficult and narrow; but as
the blood hounds increased in their vociferation,
and refused to return, it occurred to all that the cave
ought to be explored to the extremity. Accordingly,
a sufficient number of torches were provided; the
hounds were permitted to pursue their course; a
great number of men penetrated through the intricacies of the path, and at length arrived at the private
residence of the horrible cannibals.

They were followed by all the band, who were
shocked by a sight unequalled in Scotland, if not in
any part of the universe. Legs, arms. thighs, hands,
and feet, of men, women, and children, were suspended in rows like dried beef. Some limbs and
other members were soaked in pickle; with a great
mass of money, both of gold and silver, watches,
rings, pistols, clothes, both of linen and woollen,
with an immense quantity of other articles, were
either thrown together in heaps or suspended upon
the sides of the cave.

The whole cruel, brutal family, to the number
formerly mentioned, were seized; the human flesh
buried in the sand of the sea shore; the immense
booty carried away, and the king marched to Edinburgh with the prisoners. This new and wretched
spectacle attracted the attention of the inhabitants,
who flocked from all quarters to see, as they passed
along, so bloody and unnatural a samily, which had

increased, in the space of twenty five years, to the number of twenty seven men and twenty-one women. Arrived at the capital, they were all confined in the tolbooth under a strong guard, and were next day conducted to the place of execution in Leith walk, and executed without any formal trial, it being considered unnecessary to try those who were avowed enemies to all mankind, and of all social order.

The enormity of their crimes dictated the severity of their death. The wretched mother of the whole crew, the daughters and grand children, after being spectators of the death of the men, were cast into three separate fires and consumed to ashes. Nor did they, in general, display any signs of repentance or regret, but continued, with their last breath, to pour forth the most dreadful curses and imprecations upon all around, and upon those who were instrumental in consigning them to the hands of a tardy but a certain and inevitable justice.

THOMAS WITHERINGTON.

THIS individual was the son of a gentleman of Carlisle, in the county of Cumberland, who possessed a considerable estate, and brought up his children suitable to his condition. Thomas, the subject of this memoir, received a liberal education, as his father intended that he should be free from toil and hazard of business. The father dying, Thomas came into possession of the estate, which soon procured him a rich wife, who afterward proved the chief cause of his ruin. She was loose in her conduct, and violated her matrimonial obligations, which drove him from his house to seek happiness in the tavern, or in the company of abandoned women. These by degrees perverted all the good qualities he possessed ; nor was his estate less subject to ruin and decay; for the mortgages he made on it, in order to support his luxury and profusion, soon reduced his circumstances to the lowest ebb. Undisciplined in poverty, how could a man of his late affluent fortune, and unacquainted with business, procure a maintenance? He was possessed of too independent a spirit to stoop either to relations or friends for a precarious subsistence, and to solicit the benevolence of his fellow men was what his soul abhorred. Starve he could not, and only one way of living presented itself to his choice—levying contributions on the road. This he followed for six or seven years with tolerable success ; and we shall now relate a few of his most remarkable adventures.

Upon his first outset he repaired to a friend, and with a grave face lamented his late irregularities, and declared his determination to live by some honest means; but for this purpose he required a little money to assist him in establishing himself, and hoped his friend would find it convenient to accommodate him. His friend was overjoyed at the prospect of his amendment, and willingly lent him fifty pounds, with many blessings and exhortations.

Witherington, however, frustrated the expectations of his friend, and with the money bought himself a horse and other necessaries fit for his future enterprises.

He stopped one night at Keswick in Cumberland,

where he met with the dean of Carlisle. Being equally learned, they found each other's company very agreeable, and Witherington passed himself off for a gentleman who had just returned from the East Indies with a handsome competency, and was returning to his friends at Carlisle, among whom he had a rich uncle, who had lately died and left him sole heir to his estate. True, said the dean, I have often heard of a relation of Mr. Witherington's being in the East Indies; but his family, I can assure you, have received repeated information of his death, and what prejudice this may have done to your affairs at Carlisle, to-morrow will be the best witness. The dean then told him his own history, and concluded in the following words :—And I am now informed that, to support his extravagance, Mr. Witherington frequents the road, and takes a purse wherever he can extort it. Our adventurer seemed greatly hurt at this account of his cousin's conduct, and thanked the doctor for his information. Being both very fond of their bottle, they spent the evening very agreeably, promising to travel together on the following day to Carlisle.

On coming to a wood on the road, Witherington rode close up to the dean, and whispered into his ear, sir, though the place at which we now are is private enough, yet willing that what I do should be still more private, I take the liberty to acquaint you, that you have something about you that will do me an infinite piece of service. What's that? answered the doctor; you shall have it with all my heart. I thank you for your civility, said Witherington. Well then, to be plain, the money in your breeches pocket will be very serviceable to me at

the present moment.   Money! rejoined the doctor;
sir, you cannot want money; your garb and person
both tell me you are in no want.   Ay, but I am;
for the ship in which I came over happened to be
wrecked, so that I have lost all that I brought from
India; and I would not enter Carlisle for the world
without money in my pocket.   Friend, I may urge
the same plea, and say I would not go into that
city without money for the world; but what then?
If you are Mr. Witherington's nephew as you pretend to be, you would not thus peremptorily demand
money from me, for at Carlisle your friends will
supply you; and if you have none now I will bear
your expenses to that place.   Sir, said Witherington, the question is not whether I have money or
not, but concerning that which is in your pocket;
for, as you say, my cousin is obliged to take purses
on the road, and so am I; so that if I take your's,
you may ride to Carlisle, and say that Mr. Witherington met you and demanded your charity.   After
much expostulation, the dean alarmed at the sight
of a pistol, reluctantly surrendered his purse, containing about fifty guineas, and the scoundrel set off
in quest of more prey.

Witherington subsequently went to Newcastle,
and put up at an inn where some commissioners
had that day to make choice of a schoolmaster for a
neighbouring parish.

The salary was handsome, and consequently the
competitors were numerous; and, thinking himself
possessed of sufficient qualifications, Witherington
bethought him of standing a candidate, for which
purpose he borrowed coarse plain clothes from the
landlord, that he might correspond in appearance

with the conduct he meant to pursue. Repairing to the kitchen, and sitting down by the fire, he called for a mug of ale, and put on a dejected countenance. A freeholder, who came to vote, observing him as he stood warming himself by the fire, took particular notice of his countenance, and entered into conversation with him. He very modestly informed the freeholder that he had come with the intention of standing a candidate, but when he saw so many gay young men as competitors, and fearing that every thing would be carried by interest, he resolved to return home. Nay, replied the honest freeholder, as long as I have a vote, justice shall be done; and never fear, for egad, I say, merit shall have the place and if thou be found the best scholar thou shalt certainly have it; and to show you I am sincere, I now, though you are a stranger to me, promise you my vote, and my interest likewise. Witherington thanked him for his civility, and consented to wait for the trial. A keen contest took place between two of the most successful candidates when our adventurer was introduced as a man who had so much modesty as to make him fearful of appearing before so great an assembly, but who nevertheless wished to be examined.

He confronted the two opponents, and exposed their ignorance to the trustees, who were all astonished at the stranger. He showed it was not a number of Greek and Latin sentences that constituted a good scholar, but a thorough knowledge of the nature of the book which he read, and the ability to discover the design of the author. Suffice it to say, that Witherington was installed into the office with all the usual formalities.

Conducting himself with much moderation and humility, the churchwardens of the parish took a great fancy to him, and made him overseer and tax-gatherer to the parish; and the rector likewise committed to his care the collection of his rents and tithes. This friendly disposition towards Witherington extended itself over the parish, and never was a man believed to be more honest or industrious. Of the latter qualification, we must say, in this instance he showed himself possessed; but of the former he had never any notion. His opinion had great weight with the heads of the parish, and he proposed the erection of a new school-house, and for this purpose offered, himself, to sink a year's salary towards a subscription. It was willingly agreed to, and contributions came in from all quarters, and a sum exceeding £700 was speedily raised. The mind of Witherington was now big with hope, but, being discovered by two gentlemen who had come from Carlisle, he made off with all the subscriptions and funds in his possession, leaving the parish to reflect upon the honesty of their schoolmaster and their own credulity.

He next went to Buckinghamshire, and staid at an inn in the county town, where he fell into the company of some farmers, who, he quickly discovered, had come to meet their landlord with their rents. They were all tenants of the same proprietor, and poured out many complaints against him for his injustice and harshness, in not allowing some deduction from their rents, or time after the quarter day, when they met with the severe losses from bad weather or other causes. He learned that this landlord was very rich, and so miserly that he denied himself even the necessaries of life; Witherington, therefore, determined, if possible, to rifle him before he departed.

The landlord shortly arrived, and the company were shown into a private room; Witherington upon pretence of being a friend of one of the farmers and a lawyer, accompanied them. He requested a sight of the last receipts, and examined them carefully, and then addressing the landlord, sir, said he, these honest men, my friends, have been your tenants for a long time, and have paid their rents very regularly: but why they should be so fond of your farms at so high a rent I am unable to comprehend, when they may get other lands much cheaper; and that you should be so unreasonable as not to allow a reduction in their rents in a season like this, when they must lose instead of gain by their farms. It is your duty, sir, to encourage them, and not to grind them so unmercifully, else they will soon be obliged to leave your farms altogether. The landlord endeavoured to argue the case; and the farmers, seeing the drift of Witherington refrained from interfering. It is unnecessary, resumed Witherington, to have more parley about it; I insist, on behalf of my friends here, that you remit them at least £150, of the 300 you expect them to pay you, for I am told that you have more than enough to support yourself and family. Not a sous, replied the landlord. We'll try that presently. But pray, sir, take your pen, ink, and paper, and in the mean time, write out their receipts, and the money shall be forthcoming immediately. Not a letter till the money is in my hands. It must be so, then, answered Witherington; you will force a good natured man to use extremities with you : and so saying, he laid a brace of loaded pistols on the table. In a moment the landlord was on his knees, crying, Oh! dear sir, sweet sir, kind sir, merciful sir, for God of Heaven's sake, sir, don't take away the life of an innocent man, sir, who never intended harm to any one sir. Why, what harm do I intend you, friend? Cannot I lay the pistols I travel with on the table, but you must throw yourself into this unnecessary fear? Pray, proceed to the receipts, and write them in full of all demands to this time, or else,—Oh, good sir! Oh, dear sir! you have an intention—pray, dear sir, have no intention against my life. To the receipts then, or by Jupiter Ammon! I'll——O yes, I will, sir. With these the old landlord wrote the full receipts, and delivered them to the respective farmers.

Come, said Witherington, this is honest, and to shew you that you have to do with honest people, here is the £150 ; and I promise you, in the name of these honest men, that if they succeed well, you shall have the other half next quarter day. The farmers paid the money, and departed astonished, and not a little afraid, at the consequences of this proceeding. Witherington ordered his horse, and inquired of the oastler the road the old gentleman had to travel, and presently took his departure.

He chose the road which the old gentleman had to travel, and soon observed him jogging away in sullen silence, with a servant behind him. When he observed our hero, he would have fled, but Witherington seized the bridle of his horse, forced him to proceed, bantering upon the folly of hoarding up riches, without enjoying it himself, merely for some spendthrift son to squander after his death. For, he continued, money is a blessing sent us from heaven, in order that, by its circulation, it may afford nourishment to the body politic; and if such wretches as you, by laying up thousands in your coffers to no advantage, cause a stagnation, there are thousands in the world that must feel the consequences, and I am to acquaint you of them; so that a better deed cannot be done, than to bestow what you have about you upon me; for to be plain with you, I am not to be refused; and hereupon he presented his pistol. The old gentleman, in trepidation for his life, resigned his purse, containing more than three hundred and fifty guineas: and Witherington, unbuckling the portmanteau from behind the servant, placed it on his own horse, and left the landlord with an admonition, to be in future affable and generous to his tenants for they were the persons who supported him, adding, that if he ever again heard complaints from them, he would visit his home, and partake liberally of what he most coveted.

The country, after this adventure, was up in pursuit of Witherington, and he retired to Cheshire with great expedition, where he committed numerous depredations; at length he repaired to the London road, where he perpetrated a robbery between Acton and Uxbridge; after which he was detected and committed to Newgate, where he led a most profligate life till the day of his execution.

He was executed with Jonathan Woodward, and James Philpot, two most notorious house breakers, who had once before received mercy from king James I. upon his accession to the throne.

JAMES BATSON.

WE give the history of this robber in his own words :

I suppose, he says, that, according to custom, the reader will expect some relation of my genealogy, and as I am a great admirer of fashion I shall gratify his curiosity. My father had the good fortune to marry a woman well skilled in rope dancing and vaulting, and who could act her part uncommonly well. Though above fifty years of age, and affected with phthisic, she died in the air. To avoid seeing other women fly as she had done, her husband would not marry again, but diverted himself with keeping a puppet show in Moorfields, considered the most remarkable that had been seen in that place. My grandfather was also so little, that the only difference between him and his puppets was, that they spoke through a trunk, and he without one. He was however, so eloquent, and made such lively speeches, that his audience was never rendered drowsy. All the apple women, hawkers, and fish-women, were so charmed by his wit, that they would run to hear him, and leave their goods without any guard but their own straw hats.

My father had two trades, or two strings to his bow : he was a painter and a gamester, and master much alike at both ; for his painting could scarcely rise so high as a sign post, and his hand at play was of such an ancient date, that it could scarcely pass. He had one misfortune, which, like original sin, he entailed upon his children ; and that was, his being born a gentleman, which is as bad as being a poet, few of whom escape eternal poverty.

My mother had the misfortune to die longing for mushrooms. Besides myself, she left two daughters, both very handsome and very young; and though I was then young myself, yet I was much better skilled in sharping than my age seemed to promise. When the funeral sermon was preached, the funeral rites performed, and our tears dried up, my father returned to his daubing, my sisters to their stitching, and I was despatched to school. I had such an excellent memory, that, though my dispositions were then what they have continued to be, yet I soon learned as much as might have been applied to better purposes than I have done. My tricks upon my master and my companions were so numerous, that I obtained the honourable appellation of the little Judas. My avaricious disposition soon appeared, and if my covetous eyes once beheld any thing, my invention soon put it in my possession. These, however, I could not obtain gratis, for they cost me many a boxing bout every day. The reports of my conduct were conveyed home, and my eldest sister would frequently spend her white hands upon the side of my pate; and sometimes carried her admonitions so far as politely to inform me, that I should prove a disgrace to the family.

It was my good fortune, however, not to be greatly agitated by her remonstrances, which went in at one ear and out at the other. It happened, however, that my adventures were so numerous, and daily increasing in their magnitude, that I was dismissed the school with as much solemnity, as if it had been been by beat of drum. After giving me a complete drubbing, my father carried me to a barber, in order to be bound as his apprentice. I was first sent to the kitchen, where my mistress soon provided me with employment, by shewing me a parcel of dirty clothes, informed me, that it made part of the apprentices' work to clean them. 'Jemmy,' said she, 'mind your heels, there's good boy!' I hung down my head, tumbled all the clouts into a trough, and washed them as well as I could. I so managed the matter, that I was soon discarded from my office, which was very fortunate for me, for it would have put an end to Jemmy in less than a fortnight.

The third day of my apprenticeship my master having given me a note to receive money, there came into the shop a ruffian with a pair of whiskers, and told my master he would have them turned up. The journeyman not being at hand, my master began to turn them up himself, and desired me to heat the irons. I complied, and just as he had turned up one whisker, there happened a quarrel in the street, and he ran out to learn the cause. The scuffle lasting long, and my master desirous to see the end as well as the beginning of the bustle, the spark was all the time detained in the shop, with the one whisker ornamented, and the other hanging down like an aspen leaf. In a harsh tone, he asked me if I understood my trade: and I, thinking it derogatory to my understanding to be ignorant, boldly replied that I did; 'Why, then,' said he, ' turn up this whisker for me. or I shall go into the street as I am, and kick your master.' I was unwilling to be detected in a lie, and deeming it no difficult matter to turn up a whisker, never showed the least concern, but took up one of the irons, that had been in the fire ever since the commencement of the street bustle, and having to try it on, and willing to appear expeditious, I took a comb, stuck it into his bristly bush, and clapped the iron to it: no sooner did they meet than there arose a smoke, as if it had been out of a chimney, with a whizzing noise, and in a moment all the hair vanished. He exclaimed furiously, thou son of a thousand dogs! dost thou take me for St. Lawrence, that thou burnest me alive! With that he let fly such a bang at me, that the comb dropped out of my hand, and I could not avoid in my fright, laying the hot iron close along his cheek: this made him give such a shriek as raised the whole, and he, at the same time, drew his sword, to send me to the other world. I, however, recollected this proverb, ' that one pair of heels is worth two pair of hands,' ran so nimbly into the street, and fled so quickly from that part of the town, that though I was a good runner, I was amazed when I found myself about a mile from home, with the iron in my hand, and the remainder of the whisker sticking to it. As fortune would have it, I was near the dwelling of the person who was to pay the note my master gave me: I went and received the money, but deemed it proper to detain it in lieu of my three days' wages.

This money was all exhausted in one month, when I was under the necessity of returning to my father's house. Before arriving there, I was informed, that he was gone into the country to receive a large sum of money which was due to him, and therefore went boldly in, as if the house had been

my own. My grave sisters received me very coldly,
and severely blamed me for the money which my father paid for my pranks. Maintaining, however,
the honour of my birthright, I kept them at considerable distance. The domestic war being thus
prolonged, I one day lost temper, and was resolved
to make them feel the consequences of giving him
sour beer; and, though the dinner was upon the
table, I threw the dish at my eldest sister, and the
beer at the younger, overthrew the table, and marched out of doors on a ramble. Fortunately, however, I was interrupted in my flight by one who informed me that my father was dead, and in his testament had very wisely left me sole heir and execu-
tor. Upon this I returned, and soon found the tones
and tempers of my sisters changed, in consequence
of the recent news. I sold the goods, collected the
debts, and feasted all the rakes in the town, until
not one farthing remained.

One evening, a party of my companions carried
me along with them, and opening the door of a certain house, conveyed from thence some trunks,
which a faithful dog perceiving, he gave the alarm.
The people of the house thus alarmed, attacked the
robbers, who threw down their burdens to defend
themselves; meanwhile, I skulked into a corner,
trembling. The watch made their appearance, and
seeing three trunks in the street, two men dangerously wounded, and myself standing at a small distance, they seized me as one concerned in the robbery. Next day I was tried, and my defence being
frivolous and unsatisfactory, I was about to be hoist-
ed up by the neck, and sent out of the world in a

disgraceful manner, when a reprieve came, and in two months, a full pardon.

After this horrid fright, (I was not disposed to visit the dwelling of my grandfather,) I commenced travelling merchant, and according to my finances, purchased a quantity of wash-balls, tooth picks, and tooth powders. Pretending they came from Japan, Peru, or Tartary, and extolling them to the skies, I had a good sale particularly among the gentry at the playhouse. Upon a certain day, one of the actresses, a beautiful woman of eighteen, and married to one of the actors, addressed me, saying, 'she had taken a liking to me, because I was a confident, forward, sharp youth; and therefore, if I would serve her, she would entertain me with all her heart; and that when the company were strolling, I might beat the drum, and stick up the bills.' Deeming it an easier mode of moving through the world, I readily consented, only requiring two days to dispose of my stock, and to settle all my other accounts.

In my new profession my employments were various; some of which, though not very pleasant, I endeavoured to reconcile myself to, inasmuch as they were comparatively better than my former. In a little time I became more acquainted with the temper of my master and mistress, and became so great a favourite, that fees and bribes replenished my coffers from all expectants and authors who courted their favour. Unfortunately, one day, in their absence I was kindly invited by some of the party to take a short walk, and going into a tavern, commenced playing at cards till my last farthing was lost. Determined, if possible, to be revenged of

H

my antagonist, I requested him to run home for more money, it was regularly granted. I ran and seized an article belonging to my mistress, pawned it for a small sum, which soon followed my other stores. Evils seldom come alone: I was in this situation not only deprived of my money, but also obliged to decamp.

The next adventure of Baston was to enlist as a soldier. It happened, however, that his captain cheating him out of his pay, caused a grievous quarrel. Baston soon found it was dangerous to reside in Rome and strive with the pope. His captain, upon some pretence of bad conduct, had him apprehended, tried, and condemned to be hanged. The cause of this harsh treatment was a very simple one: 'For, says Baston, I was one day drinking with a soldier, and happened to fall out about a lie given. My sword unluckily running into his throat, he kicked up his heels, all through his own fault, for he ran upon my point, so that he may thank his own hastiness.' Upon this our hero says, as if it had been a thing of nothing, or as a matter of pastime, they gave sentence that I should be led in state through the streets, then mounted upon a ladder, kick up my heels before all the people, and take a swing in the open air, as if I had another life in my knapsack. A notary informed me of this sentence, who was so generous that he requested no fee, nor any expenses for his trouble during the trial. The unfeeling jailor desired me to make my peace with the Maker, without giving me one drop to cheer my desponding heart. Informed of my melancholy condition, a compassionate friar came to prepare me for another world, since the inhabitants of this were so ready to bid me farewell. When he arrived, he enquired for the condemned person, I answered, 'Father I am the man though you do not know me.' He said, 'dear child, it is now time for you to think of another world, since sentence is passed, and therefore you must employ the short time allowed you in confessing your sins, and asking forgiveness of your offences.' I answered, 'reverend father, in obedience to the commands of the church, I confess but once in the year, and that is the Lent; but if according to human laws, I must atone with my life for the crime I have committed, your reverence being so learned, must be truly sensible that there is no divine precept which says, 'thou shalt not eat nor drink;' and therefore, since it is not contrary to the law of God, I desire that I may have meat and drink, and then we will discourse of what is best for us both: for I am in a Christian country, and plead the privileges of the sanctuary.'

'The good friar was much moved at finding me so jocular, when I ought to have been serious, and began to preach to me a loud and long sermon upon the parable of the lost sheep, and the repentance of the thief. But the charity bells, that ring when criminals are executed, knolling in mine ears, made a deeper impression than the loud and impressive voice of the friar. I therefore kneeled down before my ghostly father, and confessed my sins; he then gave me his blessing, and poor Batson expected soon to take his flight from the present world.

'But, having previously presented a petition to the Marquis D'Este then commanding officer, he at that critical moment called me before him. He, being a merciful man, respited my sentence, and sent me to the galley for ten years. Some friends farther interfered, and informed the marquis, that the accusation and sentence against me, were effected by the malice of the captain, who was offended because I had insisted for the whole of my listing money. The result was, that he ordered me to be set at liberty, to the disappointment of my captain, together with that of the multitude and executioner.

'The deadly fright being over, and my mind restored to tranquillity, I went forth to walk, and to meditate upon what method I was to pursue in the rugged journey of life. Every man has his own fortune, and as good luck would have it, I again met with a recruiting officer, who enlisted me, and from partiality took me home to his own quarters. The cook, taking leave of the family, I was interrogated if I understood any thing in that line. To this I replied, as usual, in the affirmative, and was accordingly installed into the important office of a cook.

In the course of a military life, my master took up his winter residence at Bavaria, in the house of one of the richest men in those parts. To save his property, however, the Bavarian pretended to be very poor, drove away all his cattle, and removed all his stores to another quarter. Informed of this, I waited upon him, and acquainted him that, as he had a person of quality in the house, it would be necessary to provide liberally for him and his servants. He replied, that I had only to inform him what provisions I wanted, and he would order them immediately. I then informed him, that my mas-

ter always kept three tables, one for the gentlemen
and pages, a second for the butler and under officers, a third for the footmen, grooms, and other li-
veries; for these tables he must supply one ox, two
calves, four sheep, twelve pullets, six capons, two
dozen of pigeons, six pounds of bacon, four pounds
of sugar, two of all sorts of spice, a hundred eggs,
half a dozen dishes of fish, a pot of wine to every
plate, and six hogsheads to stand by. He blessed
himself, and exclaimed, if all you speak of only be
for the servants' tables, the village will not be able
to furnish the master's. To this I replied, that my
master was such a good-natured man, that, if he
saw his servants and attendants well provided, he
was indifferent to his own table; a dish of imperial
stuffed meat, with an egg in it, would be sufficient
for him. He asked me of what that same imperial
siuffed meat was composed? I desired him to send
for a grave-digger and a cobbler, and while they
were at work, I would inform him what there was
wanting. They were instantly called. I then took
an egg, and putting it into the body of a pigeon,
which I had already gutted with my knife, said to
him, now, sir, take notice; this egg is in the pigeon,
the pigeon is to be put into a partridge, the partridge into a pheasant, the pheasant into a pullet, the
pullet into a turkey, the turkey into a kid, the kid
into a sheep, the sheep into a calf, the calf into a
cow; all these creatures are to be pulled, flead, and
larded, except the cow, which is to have her hide
on; and as they are through one into another, like
a nest of boxes, the cobler is to sew every one of
them with an end, that they may not slip out; and
the grave-digger is to throw up a deep trench, into

which one load of coals is to be cast, and the cow
to be laid on the top of it, and another load above
her; the fuel set on fire, to burn about four hours,
more or less, when the meat being taken out, is in-
corporated, and becomes such a delicious dish, that
formerly the emperors used to dine upon it on their
coronation day; for which reason, and because an
egg is the foundation of all that curious mass, it is
named the imperial egg-stuffed meat. The landlord was not a little astonished, but after some conversation we understood each other, and my master
left the matter to my care.

In the course of my negotiations with the landlord, I incurred the displeasure of my master, who
discovering my policy, came into the kitchen, seized
the first convenient instrument, and belaboured me
unmercifully. He was, however, punished for his
rashness, by the want of a cook for two weeks.

The scoundrels of the French were audacious
enough to pay us a visit while we remained here.
I was ordered out with the rest, but I kept at the
greatest distance, lest any bullet should have mistaken me for any other person. No sooner did I
receive the intelligence that the French were conquered, than I ran to the field of battle, brandishing
my sword, and slashing and cutting among the
dead men. It unfortunately happened, however,
that as I struck one of them with my sword, he uttered a mournful groan, and, apprehensive that he
was about to revenge the injury done to him, I ran
off with full speed, leaving my sword in his body.
In passing along, I met with another sword, which
saved my honour, as I vaunted that I had seized it
from one on the field of battle.

While thus rambling through the field of blood and danger, my master was carried home mortally wounded, who called me a scoundrel, and cried, why did not you obey? Lest, sir, replied I, I should have been as now you are. The good man soon breathed his last, leaving me a horse and fifty ducats.

Being again emancipated from the bond of servitude, I began to enjoy life, and continued to treat all my acquaintances as long as my money would permit. The return of poverty, however, made me again enlist under the banners of servitude.

About this time a singular occurrence happened to me. I chanced to go out into the street, when my eye-sight was so affected, that I could not discern the candles suspended in a candle-maker's shop, and taking them for raddishes, I thought there was no great harm though I should taste one of them. Accordingly, laying hold of one, down fell the whole row, and being dashed to pieces upon the floor, a scuffle ensued; I was taken into custody, and made to pay the damage, which operated to restore my sight to its natural state.

Not long after this adventure, I was assailed with love for the fair sex, and, after some sighs and presents, I was bound to a woman for better or for worse, and continued with her until the charms of the marriage state and pleasure of domestic life began to pall upon me, and an ardent desire to return to my old course of adventure took possession of my mind. Towards the attainment of this desirable end. I one day kicked my wife out of doors, dressed myself, and prepared to sally forth. I had no sooner effected this liberation, than a tavern was my first resting-place to recruit my spirits and to redeem lost time.

I at last formed the resolution of returning to my native home, and there spending the evening of my bustling life in calm repose. After travelling many a tedious mile, I got to London, arrived in the capital, I went directly to my father's house, but found it in the possession of another, and my sisters departed this life. As both of them had been married, and had left children, there was no hope of any legacy by their death: I was therefore under the necessity of doing something for a living. Finding the gout increasing upon me, I, by the advice of an acquaintance, took a public house; and, as I understood several languages, thought I might have many customers from among foreigners.

Batson then gravely concludes his own narrative in these words :—

I intend to leave off my foolish pranks, and as I have spent my juvenile years and money in keeping company, hope to find some fools as bad as myself, who delight in throwing away their estates and impairing their health.

He accordingly took a house in Smithfield, and acquired a considerable sum. But, being desirous to make a fortune with one dash, he hastened his end. Among others that put up at his house was a gentleman who had purchased a large estate in the country, and was going to deliver the cash. The ostler observed to his master, that the bags belonging to the gentleman were uncommonly heavy when he carried them into the house. They mutually agreed to rob, and afterwards to murder him; and the ostler accomplished the horrid deed. But, differing about the division of the spoil, the ostler got drunk, and disclosed the whole matter. The house was searched, and the body of the gentleman found, and both murderers were seized, tried, and condemned. The ostler died before the fatal day, but Batson was executed, and according to the Catholic faith, died a penitent, a year before the restoration of king Charles II.

THOMAS RUMBOLD.

RUMBOLD was the son of honest and industrious parents who lived at Ipswich, in Suffolk. In his youth he was apprenticed to a bricklayer; but evil inclinations gaining an ascendancy over his mind, he quitted his employment before a third part of his time was expired. In order to support himself after having absconded, and conceiving a great desire to see London, he repaired thither, and soon confederated himself with a gang of robbers. In conjunction with these he shared in many daring exploits, but wishing to try his skill and fortune alone, he left them, and repaired to the road.

He travelled from London with the intention of way-laying the archbishop of Canterbury. Having got sight of the party between Rochester and Sittingbourne in Kent, he got into a field, and placing a tablecloth on the grass, on which he placed several handfuls of gold and silver, took a box and dice out of his pocket, and commenced a game at hazard by himself. His grace observing him in this situation, sent a servant to inquire the meaning; who upon coming near Rumbold, heard him swearing and rioting about his losses, but never paid the least attention to his questions. The servant returned and informed the prelate, who alighted, and seeing none but Rumbold, asked him whom he was playing with. Pray, sir, said Rumbold, be silent—five hundred pounds lost in a jiffey! His grace was about to speak again—Ay, continued Rumbold, continuing to play on, there goes a hundred more! Pr'ythee, said the archbishop, do tell me whom you play with. Rumbold replied, with ———, naming some one who perhaps never had existence. And how will you send the money to him? By his ambassadors, quoth Rumbold; and, considering your grace as one of them extraordinary, I shall beg the favour of you to carry it to him. He accordingly rose and rode up to the carriage, and placing on the seat £600 rode off. He proceeded on the road he knew the archbishop had to travel, and both, having refreshed at Sittingbourne, again took the road, Rumbold preceding the bishop by a little distance. He waited at a convenient place, and again seated himself on the grass in the same manner as before, only having very little money on the cloth. The bishop again observed him, and now believing him really to be a mad gamester, walked up to him, and just as his grace was going to accost him, Rumbold cried out with great seeming joy, six hundred pounds! What! said the archbishop, losing again? No by G—! replied Rumbold, won six hundred pounds! I'll play this hand out, and then leave off while I'm well. And of whom have you won them? said his grace. Of the same person that I left the six hundred pounds for with you before dinner. And how

will you get your winnings? Of his ambassador,
to be sure, said Rumbold : so, presenting his pistol
and drawn sword, he rode up to the carriage, and
took from the seat his own money, and fourteen
hundred pounds besides, with which he got clear off.

With part of this money Rumbold bought himself
an eligible situation ; but still he could not give up
his propensity of appropriating to himself the purses
of others. For many miles round London he had
the waiters and chambermaids of the inns enlisted
into his service : and though, to appearance, in an
honest way of gaining a livelihood, he continued
his nefarious courses to a great extent. He was
not, indeed, always successful ; for having once been
apprised of two rich travellers being at an inn where
one of his assistants was, he left London immediately, and waited on the road which he had been informed the travellers were to take ; long, however,
he might have waited, for the travellers were too
cunning, and pretended to be travelling to the place
which they had last left. Determined, however,
not to return without doing some business, he
waited on the road ; the earl of Oxford, attended by
a single footman, soon appeared, and being known
to his lordship, he disguised himself by throwing
his long hair over his face, and holding it with his
teeth. In this clumsy mask he rode up, and threatened to shoot both the servant and him if they made
the least resistance. Expostulations were vain, and
he proceeded to rifle the earl, in whose coat and
waistcoat he found nothing but dice and cards, and
was much enraged, till, feeling the other pockets,
he discovered a nest of goldfinches, (guineas) with
which he was mightily pleased, and said he would

take them home and cage them : recommending his lordship to return to his regiment and attend to his duty, giving him a shilling as an encouragement.

As Rumbold was riding along the road, he met a country girl with a milkpail on her head, with whose beauty and symmetry of shape he was greatly taken. Having entered into conversation, Rumbold alighted, and, excusing himself for the freedom, sat beside her while she milked her cows. Pleased with each other's company, they made an assignation the same evening; our adventurer was to come to her father's house at a late hour, and pretending to have lost his road, solicit a night's lodging. The plan was accordingly followed out; but they were disappointed in each other's society that evening, for some one of the family kept astir all night. Determined, however, not to leave his fair convert, he pretended in the morning to be taken dangerously ill, and the good farmer rode off immediately for medical assistance. All the power of surgery however, could not discover his ailment. The farmer kindly insisted upon his remaining where he was until he should recover, to which he, with great professions of gratitude, assented. Completely overpowered by such generosity, Rumbold wished to make some apparent return; and borrowing a name, he was a bachelor of property in a certain county; that he had hitherto remained secure against the attacks of beauty, but that he now was vanquished by the attractions of his daughter, and hoped if the girl had no objections, that a proposal of marriage would not be unacceptable to the family. The farmer, in his turn, overcome by such a mark of condescension, expressed himself highly gratified by the proposal; and, after communicating it to the family, all were agreeable, and none more so than the girl. The idea of adding gentility to the fortune which the farmer intended for his daughter, quite elated him, and made him extremely anxious to gain the favour of the suitor. Rumbold followed out the design, and his endearments with the daughter were thus more frequent than he expected. His principal design was to sift the girl as to the quantity of money her father had in the house, and where it lay; but he was chagrined when informed that there were only a few pounds, for that a few days before they met, her father had made a great purchase which took all his ready money. Seeing, now, that there was no chance of gleaning the father's harvest, he resolved to leave the family, and, accordingly, one evening took his march secretly, leaving the girl a present of twenty pieces of gold inclosed in a copy of verses.

He proceeded on the road, and met with no person worthy his notice until the following day, when a singular occurrence happened to him. Passing by a small coppice between two sand hills, a gentleman, as he supposed, darted out upon him, and commanded him to stand and deliver. Rumbold requested him to have patience, and he would surrender all his property; when putting his hand in his pocket, he drew a pistol, and fired at his opponent without the shot taking effect. If you are for sportt cried the other, you shall have it! and instantly shot him slightly in the thigh; and at the same time drawing his sword, he cut Rumbold's reins at one blow; thus rendering him unable to manage his horse. Rumbold fired his remaining pistol, and again missed his adversary, but shot his horse dead.   Thbs dismounted, the gentleman made a thrust at him with his sword, which, missing Rumbold, penetrated his horse, and brought them once more upon an equal footing.   After hard fighting on both sides, our adventurer threw his adversary, bound him hand and foot, and proceeded to his more immediate object of rifling.   Upon opening his coat, he was amazed to discover he had been fighting with a woman.   Raising her in his arms, he exclaimed, pardon me, most courageous Amazon, for thus rudely dealing with you; it was nothing but ignorance that caused this error; for, could my dim sighted soul have distinguished what you were, the great love and respect I bear your sex would have deterred me from contending with you; but I esteem this ignorance of mine as the greatest happiness, since knowledge, in this case, might have deprived me of the opportunity of knowing there could be so much valour in a woman.   For your sake, I shall for ever retain a very high esteem for the worst of females.   The Amazon replied, that this was neither a place nor opportunity for eloquent speeches, but that, if he felt no reluctance, she would conduct him to a more appropriate place ; to which he readily consented.   They entered a dark wood, and following the windings of several obscure passages, arrived at a house upon which, apparently the sun had not been accustomed to shine.

A number of servants appeared, and bustled about their lady, whose disguise was familiar to them ; but they were astonished to see her return on foot, attended by a stranger.

Being conducted into an elegant apartment, and

having been refreshed by whatever the house afforded, they became very familiar, and Rumbolt pressed
his companion to relate her history, which, with
great frankness, she did in the following words:—

I cannot, sir, deny your request, since we seem
to have formed a friendship which, I hope, will turn
out to our mutual advantage. I am the daughter
of a sword cutler; in my youth my mother would
have taught me to handle a needle, but my martial
spirit gainsaid all persuasions to that end.

I never could bear to be among the utensils of
the kitchen, but was constantly in my father's shop,
and took wonderful delight in handling the warlike
instruments he made; to take a sharp and well
mounted sword in my hand, and brandish it, was
my chief recreation. Being about twelve years of
age, I studied by every means possible how I might
form an acquaintance with a fencing master. Time
brought my desire to an accomplishment; for such
a person came into my father's shop to have a blade
furnished, and it so happened that there was none
to answer him but myself. Having given him the
satisfaction he desired, though he did not expect it
from me, among other questions I asked him if he
was not a professor of the noble science of self-de-
fence, which I was pretty sure of from his postures,
looks, and expressions. He answered in the affirmative, and I informed him I was glad of the opportunity, and begged him to conceal my intention,
while I requested he would instruct me in the art
of fencing. At first he seemed amazed at my proposal; but, perceiving I was resolved in good earnest, he granted my request, and appointed a time
which he could conveniently allot to that purpose.

In a short time I became so expert at the back-sword and single rapier, that I no longer required his assistance, and my parents never once discover-ed this transaction.

I shall waive the exploits I did by the help of my disguise, and only tell you that, when I reached the age of fifteen, an innkeeper married me, and carried me into the country. For two years we lived peaceably and comfortably together; but at length the violent and impetuous temper of my husband called my natural humour into action. Once a week we seldom missed a combat, which generally proved very sharp, especially on the head of the poor innkeeper; the gaping wounds of our discontent were not easily salved, and they in a manner became incurable. I was not much inclin-ed to love him, because he was a man of a mean and dastardly spirit. Being likewise stinted in cash my life grew altogether comfortless, and I looked on my condition as altogether insupportable, and, as a means of mitigating my troubles, I was com-pelled to adopt the resolution of borrowing a purse occasionally. I judged this resolution safe enough, if I were not detected in the very act; for who could suspect me of being a robber, wearing abroad man's apparel, but at home a dress suitable to my sex? Besides, no one could procure better information, or had more frequent opportunities than myself; for, keeping an inn, who could ascertain what booty their guests carried with them better than their landlady?

As you can vouch, sir, I knew myself not to be destitute of courage : what, then, could hinder me from entering on such enterprises? Having thus resolved, I soon provided myself with the necessary habiliments for my scheme, carried it into immediate execution, and continued with great success, never having failed till now. Instead of riding to market, or travelling some five or six miles about some piece of business, (the usual pretences with which I blinded my husband,) I would when out of sight, take the road to the house in which we now are, where I metamorphosed myself, and proceeded to the road in search of prey.

Not long since, my husband had one hundred pounds due to him about twenty miles from home, and appointed a certain day for receiving it. Glad was I to hear of this, and instantly resolved to be revenged on him for all the injuries and churlish outrages he had committed against me; I knew very well the way he went, and also the time he intended to return. I waylaid him, and had not to wait above three hours, when my lord and master made his appearance, whistling with joy at his heavy purse. I soon made him change the tune to a more doleful ditty in lamentation of his bad fortune. I permitted him to pass, but soon overtook him, and keeping close by him for a mile or two, at length found the coast clear, and, riding up and seizing his bridle, presented a pistol to his breast, and in a hoarse voice demanded his purse, else he was a dead man. This imperious don, seeing death before his face, had nearly saved me the trouble by dying without compulsion; and so terrified did he appear, that he looked more like an apparition than any thing human. Sirrah! said I, be expeditious; but a dead palsy had so seized every part of him, that his eyes were incapable of directing his hands

I

to his pockets. I soon recalled his spirits by two or three sharp blows with the flat of my sword, which speedily awakened him, and, with great trembling and submission, he resigned his money. After I had unhorsed him, I cut the reins and saddle girths, beat him most soundly, and dismissed him, saying, now, you rogue, I am even with you; have a care, the next time you strike a woman, (your wife, I mean,) for none but such as dare not fight a man, will lift up his hand against the weaker vessel. Now you see what it is to provoke them, for, if once irritated, they are restless till they accomplish their revenge to their satisfaction; I have a good mind to end your wicked courses with your life, inhuman varlet, but I am loth to be hanged for nothing, I mean for such a worthless fellow as you are.

Farewell! this money shall serve me to purchase wine to drink a toast to the confusion of all unmanly husband.

This extraordinary character was about to proceed with the narration of her exploits, when the servants announced the arrival of two gentlemen. Our heroine left the room, and returning with her friends apologised to our adventurer for the interruption, but hoped he would not find the company of her companions disagreeable, whom he soon discovered to be likewise females in disguise. The conversation now became general, and upon condition of Rumbold stopping all night with them, the Amazon promised to finish her adventures next day. This accorded with the wishes of Rumbold; and when they retired to rest, he found the same room was destined for them all.

His curiosity was, however, overcome by his covetousness ; for, rising early next morning, and finding all his companions asleep, he rifled their pockets of a considerable quantity of gold, and decamped with great expedition, thus disappointing the reader in the continuation of a narrative hardly to be credited from its singularity.

Our adventurer frequently observed a goldsmith in Lombard street counting large bags of gold, and he became very desirous to have a share of that glittering hoard. He made several unsuccessful attempts ; but having in his possession many rings, which he had procured in the way of his profession, he dressed himself in the habit of a countryman, attended by a servant, and going to the goldsmith, perceiving it to be a diamond of considerable value, and from the appearance of Rumbold supposing him to be ignorant of its real worth, after examining it, with some hesitation estimated its value at ten pounds.

To convince the countryman that this was its full value, he showed him a diamond ring much superior in quality, which he would sell him for twenty pounds. Rumbold took the goldsmith's ring to compare with his own, and, fully acquainted with its value, informed him that he had come to sell, but that it was a matter of small importance to him whether he purchased or sold. He accordingly pulled out a purse of gold, and laid down the twenty pounds for the ring. The goldsmith stormed and raged, crying that he had cheated him, and insisted on having back his ring. Rumbold, however, kept hold of his bargain, and replied, that the other had offered him the ring for twenty pounds; that he had a witness of his bargain ; there was his money, and he hoped that he would give him a proper exchange for his gold.

The goldsmith's indignation increasing at the prospect of parting with his ring, he carried the matter before a justice. Being plaintiff, he began his tale by informing the magistrate, that the countryman had taken a diamond ring from him worth a hundred pounds, and would give him but twenty pounds for it. Have a care, replied Rumbold, for if you charge me with taking a ring from you, which is, in other words, stealing, I shall vex you more than I have yet done. He then told the magistrate the whole story, and produced his servant as a witness to the bargain. The goldsmith now became infuriated, exclaiming that he believed the country gentleman and his servant were impostors and cheats! Rumbold said he would do well to take care not to make his cause worse; that he was a gentleman of three hundred pounds per annum ; and that being desirous to sell a ring at its just price to the goldsmith, the latter endeavoured to cheat him, by estimating it far below its value. The magistrate, therefore decided in favour of Rumbold, appointing him to pay only the twenty pounds in gold, without any change.

The riches of Lombard-street still continuing to attract the attention of Rumbold, he one day traversed that street, attended by a boy whom he had trained in his service. The boy ran into a shop where they were counting a bag of gold, seized a handful, and then let it fall on the counter, and ran off. The servants pursued the boy, and charged the boy with having some money, Rumbold approached to the assistance of the boy, and insisted that the boy had not stolen a farthing of their money, and that the goldsmith should suffer for his audacity. The goldsmith and Rumbold came to high words, and mutual volleys of imprecations were exchanged. The latter then enquired what sum he charged the boy with having stolen. The goldsmith replied, that he did not know, but that the bag originally contained a hundred pounds.

Upon this, Rumbold insisted that he would wait until he saw the money counted. He tarried about half an hour, and the money was found complete. The goldsmith made an apology to Rumbold for the mistake; but the latter replied, that, as a gentleman, no one should put upon him such an affront with impunity. After some strong expressions on both sides, Rumbold took his leave, assuring his antagonist that he should hear from him. The goldsmith was arrested the day following, in an action of defamation. The man who arrested him, being bribed by our adventurer, advised him to compromise the matter; urging, that the gentleman he had injured was a person of quality, and if he persisted in the action, it would expose him to severe damages. With some difficulty the matter was settled, by the goldsmith giving Rumbold twenty pounds in damages.

A jeweller in Foster-lane next supplied the extravagances of Rumbold. He had often disposed of articles for that jeweller, who had full confidence in Rumbold's fidelity. One day having observed in his shop a very rich jewel, he acquainted the jeweller that he could sell it for him. Happy at such information, he delivered it to Rumbold, who carried it to another jeweller to have a false one, exactly similar, prepared. He then embraced an opportunity to leave the counterfeit jewel with the jeweller's wife, in his absence. Shortly afterwards, he met the jeweller in the street, who said he never expected to have been so used by him; and threatened to bring the matter under the cognizance of a judge; but Rumbold retreated to a remote part of the city.

Rumbold was one day sauntering in the vicinity of Hackney, when his intention was directed towards a house, which he earnestly desired to possess. He approached the house, knocked at the door, and inquired if the landlord was at home. He soon appeared; when Rumbold politely informed him, that, having been highly pleased with the appearance of his house, he was resolved to have one built after the same model, and requested the favour of being permitted to send a tradesman to take its exact dimensions. This favour was readily granted; when our adventurer went to a carpenter, and informed him that he wished him to go along with him to Hackney to measure a house, in order that he might have one built on a similar construction. They accordingly went, and found the gentleman at home, who kindly entertained Rumbold, while the carpenter took the dimensions of every part of the house.

The carpenter, being amply rewarded, was dismissed, and, by the aid of the draught of the house taken by him, Rumbold drew up a lease, with a very great penalty in case of failure to fulfil the agreement. Being provided with witnesses to the deed, he went and demanded possession. The gentleman was surprised, and only smiled at the absurdity of the demand. Rumbold commenced a lawsuit for the possession of the house, and his witnesses swore to the validity of the deed. The carpenter's evidence was also produced, many other circumstances were mentioned to corroborate the fact, and a verdict was obtained in favour of Rumbold's claim. But the gentleman deemed it proper to pay the penalty rather than to lose his house.

Rumbold, disguised in the apparel of a person of quality, one day waited on a scrivener, and acquainted him that he had immediate occasion for a hundred pounds, which he hoped he would be able to raise for him upon good security. The scrivener inquired who were the securities, and Rumbold named two respectable citizens, whom he knew to be at that time in the country; which satisfying the money-lender, he desired our adventurer to call next day. In the mean time, the lender made inquiry after the stability of the securities, and found he had not been imposed upon as to their respectability. Our adventurer again waited upon the scrivener, who having agreed to advance the sum, Rumbold sent for two of his accomplices, who personated his securities, and, after a little preliminary caution, signed the bond for him under their assumed names; and, upon Rumbold's receiving the money, they immediately took their leave. The name which Rumbold assumed on this occasion was of further service to him; for it happened to be that of a gentleman in Surrey, whom he met with, after this adventure, at an inn. Having learned what time the gentleman intended to remain in town, and the name and situation of his estates, he determined to render his chance meeting of service to him. He accordingly again waited on the same scrivener, and informed him that he had occasion for another hundred, but did not wish to trouble any of his friends to become security for such a trifle; for that, as he possessed a good estate, it might be advanced upon his own bond; and that if the scrivener could spare a servant to ride the length of Surrey, he would then learn the extent of his estate, and be enabled to remove any scruple whatever. A servant was accordingly sent, and directed to go and make enquiry after the property of the stranger whom Rumbold had met at the inn. Returning in a few days, Rumbold found the scrivener very condescending, and prodigal of congratulations upon the possession of so pleasant and valuable a property, and said he would not have scrupled if the loan had been for a thousand. Rumbold, finding him thus inclined, doubled the sum, and, after giving his own bond for two hundred pounds, left the scrivener to seek redress as he best could.

Rumbold thus supported himself by exercising his ingenuity at the expense of others, and by this means amassed a considerable sum of money. He was not so addicted to these bad habits but that he felt an inclination to retire from scenes so fraught with danger and infamy. For this purpose he placed money in the hands of a private banker, with a design of living frugally and comfortably upon the interest. This banker unfortunately failed, and made off with all Rumbold's property; so that he was once more reduced to the necessity of having recourse to his old employment.

The first exploit recorded of Rumbold after his re-appearance in public, is the following:—He stopped at a tavern, where he called for a flaggon of beer, which was handed him in a silver cup, as was customary at that time. Being in a private room and alone, he called to the landlord to partake of his noggin, and they continued together for some time, until the landlord had occasion to leave him. Soon after, he went to the bar, and paid for his beer, while the waiter at the same time went for the cup: missing which, he called Rumbold back and asked him for the cup, 'Cup' said Rumbold, 'I left it in the room.' A careful search was made, but to no effect; the cup could not be found, and the landlord openly accused Rumbold of the theft. He willingly permitted his person to be searched, which proved equally unsuccessful; but the landlord still persisted in maintaining that Rumbold must have it, or at all events, that he was chargeable with the loss, and would have the matter investigated by a justice, before whom they immediately went. The landlord stated the case, while Rumbold complained loudly of the injury done him by the suspicion; and from his never endeavouring to run off when he was called back, and submitting so readily to be searched, the justice dismissed him and fined the landlord for his rashness.

During their visit to the justice, some of Rumbold's associates entered the same inn, where, according to arrangement, they found the cup fixed under the table with soft wax, and made off with it without the least suspicion.

The last recorded adventure of Rumbold was one which is now very common in the metropolis. Having observed a countryman pretty flush of money, he and his accomplices followed him; but from Hodge's attention to his pocket, they failed in several attempts to pick it. Our practitioners, however, taking a convenient opportunity and place, one of them went before and dropped a letter, while another kept close to the countryman, and upon seeing it, cried out, 'See, what is here?' But, although the countryman stooped to take it up, our adventurer was too nimble for him, and having it in his hand, observed, 'here is somewhat besides a letter.' 'I cry halves,' said the countryman. 'Well,' said Rumbold, 'you stooped, indeed, as well as I; but I have it. However I will be fair with you; let us see what it is, and whether it is worth dividing; and thereupon broke open the letter, in which was enclosed a chain or necklace of gold. 'Good fortune,' said Rumbold, 'if this be real gold.' 'How shall we know that?' replied the countryman; 'let us see what the letter says;' which was as follows :—

'Brother John,
'I have here sent you back the necklace of gold you have sent me, not from any dislike I have to it, but my wife is covetous, and will have a bigger. This comes not to above seven pounds, and she would have one of ten pounds; therefore, pray get it changed for one of that price, which please to send by the bearer, to your loving brother,

J. THORNTON.'

Nay, then, we have good luck, observed the cheat. 'But I hope,' said he, to the countryman, you will not expect a full share, for, you know, I found it; and, besides, if one should divide it, I know not how to break it in pieces without injuring it; therefore, I had rather have my share in money. 'Well, said the countryman, I will give you your share in money, provided we divide equally.' 'That you shall,' said Rumbold, 'and therefore I must have three pounds ten shillings, the price in all being, as you see, seven pounds.' 'Ay,' said the countryman, thinking to be cunning with our adventurer, 'it may be worth seven pounds in money, fashion and all; we must, however, not value that, but the gold; therefore, I think three pounds in money, is better than half the chain, and so much I'll give, if you'll let me have it.' 'Well, I'm contented,' said Rumbold: 'but then you shall give a pint of wine, over and above.' To this the other agreed, and to a tavern they went, where the bargain was ratified. There Rumbold and the countryman quickly disposed of two bottles of wine. In the mean time, one of Rumbold's companions entered the inn, inquiring for a person who was not there. Rumbold informed the stranger (as he pretended to be) that he would be there presently, as he had seen him in the street, and requested him to come in and wait for him. Upon this the stranger sat down to wait the arrival of his friend. In a little time, Rumbold proposed to remove into a larger apartment, where they commenced playing at cards, to amuse themselves until the gentleman expected, should arrive.

Rumbold and his associate then began their amusement, the countryman being a stranger to the game. After he had continued a spectator of the good fortune of the adventurer, who in general van-

quished the stranger, the countryman was at length
prevailed upon to run halves with the unfortunate
gamester.   For awhile the same good fortune smiled upon them, and the stranger in a rage, at his
great losses, refused to proceed.   But after a few
bottles more were emptied, the long expected gentleman never appearing, they renewed their amusement ; and fortune deserting Rumbold and the countryman who seconded him, in a short time the latter
found himself without a shilling.

The landlord was then called to assist in drinking
the money gained, and, being informed how they
had cheated the countryman, was resolved to exert
his ingenuity at their expense.   Meanwhile several
associates of Rumbold, who had been respectively
employed in similar adventures, entered the room,
joined in their conversation, and participated in their
wine.   The landlord was at last requested to bring
in supper, which was done with great alacrity.   The
bottle continuing to move with great rapidity, the
company were in general all intoxicated before they
sat down to supper.   When it was brought in, however, they commenced with great avidity, and soon
dispatched a shoulder of mutton, and two capons ;
and under the influence of wine, all fell asleep with
the dishes before them.

In the morning, the countryman, in order to get
money to carry him home, resolved to sell the chain
in his possession : he accordingly went to a goldsmith, but to his additional mortification, was informed that, instead of gold, it was nothing but
brass gilded over.   He acquainted the goldsmith
with the entire matter, who went along with him to
a justice to obtain a warrant, for the apprehension

of Rumbold and his associates; but before their arrival, they had fled with their spoil.

After this adventure, Rumbold had several narrow escapes; but, continuing his nefarious practices, he was at length detected, tried, and was condemned and executed at Tyburn in the year 1689.

JOHN COTTINGTON, *alias* MULLED SACK.

THE father of this individual was a haberdasher in Cheapside, but living above his income, he died so poor that he was interred by the parish. He had eighteen children, fifteen daughters and three sons. Our hero was the youngest of the family, and at the age of eight he was bound apprentice to a chimney sweeper. In his fifth year, deeming himself as expert at his profession as his master, he left him, and acting for himself, soon acquired a great run of business.

Money now coming in upon him, he frequented the tavern, and, disdaining to taste any thing but mulled sack, he acquired that appellation. One evening he there met with a young woman, with whom he was so enamoured, that he took her 'for better for worse.' But, not enjoying that degree of comfort in this union which his imagination had painted to him, he frequented the company of other women, until it became necessary to make contributions to supply their pressing necessities. His first trials were in pockets of watches, and any small sum he could find. Among others, he robbed a

lady famous among the usurers, of a gold watch set
with diamonds, and another lady of a like piece of
luxury, as she was entering a church to hear a celebrated preacher.   By the aid of his accomplices,
the pin was taken out of the axle of her coach,
which fell down at the church door, and in the
crowd, Mulled Sack, being dressed as a gentleman,
gave her his hand, while he seized her watch.   The
lady did not discover her loss, until she had been
some time in church.

It is stated that upon a certain occasion he had
the boldness to attack the pocket of Oliver Cromwell, and that the danger to which he was then exposed, determined him to leave that sneaking trade,
and enter upon the profession of public collector
upon the highway.

He entered into partnership with a Tom Cheney.
Their first adventure was attacking Colonel Hew-
son, who had raised himself from a cobler to a colonel.   He was riding at some distance from his
regiment upon Hounslow Heath, and even in the
sight of some of his men, these two thieves robbed
him.   The pursuit was keen : Tom's horse falling,
he was apprehended, but Mulled Sack escaped.
The prisoner, being severely wounded, entreated
that his trial might be postponed on that account.
But, on the contrary, lest he should die of his
wounds, he was condemned at two o'clock, and executed that evening.

One Horne was the next accomplice of Mulled
Sack.   His companions were, however, generally
unfortunate.   Upon their first attempt, Horne was
pursued, taken, and executed.

Thus twice bereft of his associates, he acted

alone, but generally committed his depredations on the republican party, who then had the wealth of the nation in their possession. Informed that the sum of four thousand pounds was on its way to London, to pay the regiments of Oxford and Gloucester, he concealed himself behind a hedge where the waggon was to pass, presented his pistols, and the guard supposing that many more must have been concealed, fled, and left him the immense prize.

When not employed as a chimney sweep, which profession he still occasionally pursued, he dressed in high style, and is said to have received more money by robbery than any man of that age. One day being informed that the receiver general was to send up to London six thousand pounds, he entered his house the night before, and rendered that trouble unnecessary. Upon the noise which this notorious robbery occasioned, Mulled Sack was apprehended; but through cunning, baffling the evidence, or corrupting the jury, he was acquitted.

Some time after, he robbed and murdered a gentleman, and for fear of detection, went to the continent, and was introduced into the court of King Charles the Second. Upon pretence of communicating information, he came home and applied to Cromwell, confessed his crime, but proposed to purchase his life by important information. But whether he failed in his promise, or that Cromwell considered that such a notorious offender was unworthy to live, cannot be ascertained; this however is certain, that he was tried and executed in the forty-fifth year of his age, in the month of April, 1659.

CAPTAIN JAMES HIND.

THE father of this individual was an industrious saddler. He was a native of Chipping Norton, Oxfordshire, where James was born. As he was his only son, he received a good education, and remained at school till he was fifteen years of age. He was then sent as an apprentice to a butcher in that place, and continued in that employment two years. Upon leaving his master's service, he applied to his mother for money to bear his expenses to London, complaining bitterly of the quarrelsome temper of his master. The mother yielded, and gave him three pounds, and with a sorrowful heart took farewell of her beloved son.

Arrived in the capital, he soon contracted a relish for the pleasures of the town. His bottle and a female companion became his principal delight, and occupied much of his time. He was unfortunately detected one evening with a woman of the town who had just robbed a gentleman, and was confined till next day. He was acquitted because no evidence appeared against him, but the woman was sent to prison.

Captain Hind, soon after this accident, became acquainted with one Allan, a famous highwayman. While partaking of the bottle, their conversation became mutually so agreeable, that they consented to unite their fortunes.

When they had concerted their measures, they set out in quest of prey. They fortunately met a gentleman and his servant travelling along the road. Hind being raw and inexperienced, Allan was desirous to have a proof of his courage and address; he therefore remained at a distance while Hind boldly rode up to them and took from them fifteen pounds, at the same time returned one to bear their expenses home. This he did with so much grace and pleasantry, that the gentleman vowed he would not injure a hair of his head though it were in his power.

About this period, the unfortunate Charles I. suffered death for his political principles. Captain Hind conceived an inveterate enmity to all those who had stained their hands in their sovereign's blood, and gladly embraced every opportunity to wreak his vengeance upon them. In a short time, Allan and Hind met the usurper, Oliver Cromwell, riding from Huntingdon to London. They attacked the coach, but Oliver being attended by seven servants, Allan was apprehended, and it was with no small difficulty that Hind made his escape. The unfortunate Allan was soon after tried, and suffered death for his audacity. The only effect which this produced upon Hind was to render him more cautious in his future depredations. He could not, however, think of abandoning a course on which he had just entered, and which promised so many advantages.

The captain had ridden so hard to escape from Cromwell and his train that he killed his horse, and having no money to purchase a substitute, he was under the necessity of trying his fortune upon foot, until he should find means to get another. It was not long before he espied a horse tied to a hedge

K.

with a saddle on and a brace of pistols attached to it. He looked round and observed a gentleman on the other side of the hedge. This is my horse, exclaimed the captain, and immediately vaulted into the saddle. The gentleman called out to him that the horse was his. Sir, said Hind, you may think yourself well off that I have left you all the money in your pocket to buy another, which you had best lay out before I meet you again, for fear you should be worse used. So saying, he rode off in search of new booty.

There is another story of Hind's ingenious method of supplying himself with a horse upon one occasion. It appears that, being upon a second extremity reduced to the humble station of a footpad, he hired a sorry nag, and proceeded on his journey. He was overtaken by a gentleman mounted on a fine hunter, with a portmanteau behind him. They entered into such topics as are common to travellers, and Hind was very eloquent in the praise of the gentleman's horse, which inclined the other to descant upon the qualifications of the animal. There was upon one side of the road a wall, which the gentleman said his horse would leap over. Hind offered to risk a bottle on it, to which the gentleman agreed, and quickly made his horse leap over. The captain acknowledged that he had lost his wager, but requested the gentleman to let him try if he could do the same ; to which he consented, and the captain, being seated in the saddle of his companion, rode off at full speed, and left him to return the other miserable animal to its owner.

At another time the captain met the regicide Hugh Peters in Enfield chase, and there command-

ed him to deliver his money. Hugh, who was not
deficient in confidence, began to combat Hind with
texts of scripture, and to cudgel our bold robber
with the eighth commandment: it is written in the
law, said he, that 'Thou shalt not steal;' and fur-
thermore, Solomon, who was surely a very wise
man, spoke in this manner, 'Rob not the poor, because he is poor.' Hind was desirous to answer
him in his own strain, and for that purpose began
to rub up his memory for some of the texts he had
learnt when at school. Verily, said Hind, if thou
hadst regarded the divine precepts as thou oughtest
to have done, thou wouldst not have wrested them
to such an abominable and wicked sense as thou
didst the words of the prophet, when he said, 'Bind
their kings with chains, and their nobles with fetters of iron.' Didst thou not then, detestable hypocrite, endeavour, from these words, to aggravate thy
royal master, whom thy cursed republican party unjustly murdered before the gate of his own palace ?
Here Hugh Peters began to extenuate that proceeding, and to allege other parts of scripture in his own
defence. Pray, sir, replied Hind, make no reflec-
tions against men of my profession, for Solomon
plainly said, 'do not despise a thief.' But it is to
little purpose for us to dispute ; the substance of
what I have to say is this, deliver thy money presently, or else I shall send thee out of the world to
thy master, the devil, in an instant. These terrible
words of the captain's so terrified the old Presbyterian, that he forthwith gave him thirty broad pieces
of gold and then departed.

But Hind was not satisfied with allowing so
bitter an enemy to the royal cause to depart in such

a manner. He accordingly rode after him at full speed, and, overtaking him, addressed him in the following language:—Sir, now I think of it, I am convinced this misfortune has happened to you because you have not obeyed the words of the scripture, which expressly says, 'provide neither gold, nor silver, nor brass, in your purses, for your journey,' whereas it is evident that you have provided a pretty decent quantity of gold. However, as it is now in my power to make you fulfil another commandment, I would by no means slip the opportunity; therefore, pray give me your cloak. Peters was so surprised that he neither stood still to dispute nor to examine what was the drift of Hind's demand. But he soon made him understand his meaning, when he added, you know, sir, our Saviour has commanded, that if any man take away thy cloak, thou must not refuse thy coat also; therefore, I cannot suppose that you will act in direct contradiction to such an express command, especially as as you cannot pretend to have forgot it, seeing that now I remind you of that duty. The old Puritan shrugged his shoulders some time before he proceeded to uncase them; but Hind told him that his delay would be of no service to him, for he would be implicitly obeyed, because he was sure that what he requested was entirely consonant with the scripture. He accordingly surrendered, and carried off the cloak.

The following sabbath, when Hugh ascended the pulpit, he was inclined to pour forth an invective against stealing, and selected for his subject these words: I have put off my coat, how shall I put it on? An honest plain man, who was present, and

knew how he had been treated by the robber, prompt-
ly cried out, upon my word, sir, I believe there is
nobody here can tell you, unless captain Hind were
here. Which ready answer to Hugh's scriptural
question put the congregation into such an outrage-
ous fit of laughter, that the parson was made to
blush, and descended from his pulpit without pro-
secuting the subject farther.

The captain, as before mentioned, indulged a
rooted hatred against all those who were concerned
in the murder of the late king; and frequently these
men fell in his way.

He was one day riding on the road when presi-
dent Bradshaw, who sat as judge upon the king, and
passed the sentence of death upon him, met with
the captain. The place where they came into col-
lision was on the road between Shaftsbury and Sher-
bourne. Hind rode up to the coach, and demanded
Bradshaw's money, who, supposing that his very
name would convey terror along with it, informed
him who he was. Marry, cried Hind, I neither fear
you nor any king killing villain alive. I have now
as much power over you, as you lately had over the
king, and I should do God and my country good
service, if I made the same use of it; but live, villain, to suffer the pangs of thine own conscience,
till justice shall lay her iron hand upon thee, and
require an answer for thy crimes, in a way more
proper for such a monster, who art unworthy to die
by any hands but those of the common hangman, or
at any other place than Tyburn. Nevertheless,
though I spare thy life as regicide, be assured, that
unless thou deliver up thy money immediately, thou
shalt die for thy obstinacy.

Bradshaw began to perceive that the case was not now with him as it was when he sat at Westminster Hall, supported by all the strength of the rebellion. A horror took possession of his soul, and discovered itself in his countenance. He put his trembling hand into his pocket, and pulled out about forty shillings in silver, which he presented to the captain, who swore he would that minute shoot him through the heart, unless he found him coin of another species. To save his life, the serjeant pulled out that which he valued next to it, and presented the captain with a purse full of Jacobuses.

But though Hind had got possession of the cash, he was inclined to detain the serjeant a little longer, and began the following eulogium upon the value of money :—

This, sir, is the metal that wins my heart for ever? O precious gold; I admire and adore thee as much as either Bradshaw, Prynne, or any other villain of the same stamp, who, for the sake of thee, would sell his Redeemer again, were he now on earth. This is that incomparable medicament, which the republican physicians call the wonder-working plaster; it is truly catholic in operation, and somewhat of kin to the Jesuit's powder, but more effectual. The virtues of it are strange and various; it maketh justice deaf as well as blind ; and takes out spots of the deepest treasons as easily as Castile soap does common stains; it alters a man's constitution in two or three days, more than the virtuoso's transfusion of blood can do in seven years. It is a great alexipharmic, and helps poisonous principles of rebellion, and those that use them ; it miraculously exalts and purifies the eye sight,

and makes traitors behold nothing but innocence
in the blackest malefactors; it is a mighty cordial
for a declining cause; it stifles faction and schism
as certainly as rats are destroyed by common arse-
nic; in a word, it makes fools wise men, and wise
men fools, and both of them knaves. The very colour of this precious balm is bright and dazzling.
If it be properly applied to the fist, that is, in a decent manner, and in a competent dose, it infallibly
performs all the above-mentioned cures, and many
others too numerous to be here mentioned.

The captain, having finished his panegyric on the
virtues of the glittering metal, pulled out his pistol,
and again addressed the serjeant, saying, you and
your infernal crew have a long while run on, like
Jehu, in a career of blood and impiety, falsely pretending that zeal for the Lord of Hosts has been
your only motive. How long you may be suffered
to continue in the same course, God only knows.
I will, however, for this time, stop your race in a
literal sense of the word. And without farther delay, he shot all the six horses that were in the carriage, and left Bradshaw to ponder upon the lesson
he had received.

Hind's next adventure was with a company of
ladies, in a coach upon the road between Peters-
field and Portsmouth. He accosted them in a po-
lite manner, and informed them that he was a protector to the fair sex, and it was purely to win the
favour of a hard hearted mistress that he had travelled the country. But, ladies, added he, I am at
this time reduced to the necessity of asking relief,
having nothing to carry me on in the intended prosecution of my adventures. The young ladies, who

had read many romances, could not help concluding that they had met with some Quixote or Amandis de Gaul, who was saluting them in the strains of knight errantry. Sir knight, said one of the most jocular of the company, we heartily commiserate your condition, and are very much troubled that we cannot contribute towards your support; for we have nothing about us but a sacred *depositum*, which the laws of your order will not suffer you to violate.

The captain was much pleased at having met with such a pleasant lady, and was much inclined to have permitted them to proceed; but his neces-sities were at this time very urgent. May I, bright ladies, be favoured with the knowledge of what this sacred depositum, which you speak of, is, that so I may employ my utmost abilities in its defence, as the laws of knight errantry require. The lady who had spoken before told him, that the depositum she had spoken of was £3000 the portion of one of the company, who was going to bestow it upon the knight who had won her good will by his many past services. Present my humble duty to the knight, said he, and be pleased to tell him that my name is Captain Hind; that out of mere necessity I have made bold to borrow part of what, for his sake, I wish were twice as much; that I promise to ex-pend the sum in defence of injured lovers, and in the support of gentlemen who profess knight-er-rantry.

Upon the name of Captain Hind, the fair ones were sufficiently alarmed, as his name was well known, all over England. He, however, requested them not to be affrighted, for he would not do them the least injury, and only requested £1000 out of the £3000. As the money was bound up in several parcels, the request was instantly complied with, and our adventurer wished them a prosperous journey, and many happy days to the bride.

The transactions of Hind were now become so numerous, and made him so well known, that he was forced to conceal himself in the country. During this cessation from his usual industrious labours, his funds became so exhausted, that even his horse was sold to maintain his own life. Impelled by necessity, he often resolved to hazard a few movements upon the highway; but he had resided so long in that quarter, that he durst not risk any such adventure.

Fortune, however, commiserated the condition of the captain, and provided relief. He was informed that a doctor, who resided in the neighbourhood, had gone to receive a handsome fee for a cure which he had effected.

The captain then lived in a small house which he had hired upon the side of a common, and which the doctor had to pass in his journey home. Hind, having long and impatiently waited his arrival, ran up to him, and in the most piteous tone and suppliant language, told the doctor his wife was suddenly seized with illness, and that unless she got some assistance she would certainly perish, and entreated him just to tarry for a minute or two and lend her his medical assistance, and he would gratefully pay him for his trouble as soon as he had it in his power.

The tender hearted doctor, moved with compassion, alighted and accompanied him into his house, assuring him that he should be very happy to be of any service in restoring his wife to health. Hind showed the doctor up stairs ; but they had no soon-er entered the door, than he locked it, presented a pistol, showing, at the same time. his empty purse, saying, this is my wife; she has so long been un-well, that there is now nothing at all within her. I know, sir, that you have a sovereign remedy in your pocket for her distemper, and if you do not ap-ply it without a word, this pistol will make the day-light shine into your body !

The doctor would have been content to have lost his fee, upon condition of being delivered from the importunities of his patient ; but it required only a small degree of the knowledge of symptoms to be convinced, that obedience was the only thing which remained for him to observe ; he therefore emptied his own purse of forty guineas into that of the cap-tain, and thus left our hero's wife in a convalescent state. Hind then informed the doctor, that he would leave him in possession of his whole house to reimburse him for the money he had taken from him. So saying, he locked the door upon the doc-tor, mounted that gentleman's horse, and went in quest of another county, since this had become too hot for him.

Hind has been often celebrated for his generosity to the poor ; and the following is a remarkable in-stance of his virtue in that particular. He was on one occasion remarkably destitute of cash, and had waited long upon the road without receiving any supply. An old man, jogging along upon an ass, at length appeared. He rode up to him, and very politely inquired where he was going. To the market, at Wantage, said the old man, to buy me a cow, that I may have some milk for my children. How many children have you? The old man answered, ten. And how much do you mean to give for a cow? said Hind. I have but forty shillings, master, and that I have been scraping together these two years. Hind's heart ached for the poor man's condition; at the same time he could not help admiring his simplicity; but, being in absolute want himself, he thought of an expedient which would serve both himself and the poor old man. Father, said he, the money which you have is necessary for me at this time; but I will not wrong your children of their milk. My name is Hind, and if you will give me your forty shillings quietly, and meet me again this day se'nnight at this place, I promise to make this sum double. The old man reluctantly consented, and Hind enjoined him to be cautious not to mention a word of the matter to any body, between this and that time. The old man came at the appointed time, and received as much as would purchase two cows, and twenty shillings more, that he might thereby have the best in the market.

Though Hind had long frequented the road, yet he carefully avoided shedding blood; and the following is the only instance of this nature related of him. He had one morning committed several robberies, and among others, had taken more than £70 from colonel Harrison, the celebrated parliamentary general. As the Roundheads were Hind's inveterate foes, the colonel immediately raised the hue and cry after him, which was circulated in that part of the country before the captain was aware of it. At last, however, he received intelligence at one of the inns upon the road, and made every possible haste to fly the scene of danger. In this situation the captain was apprehensive of every person he met upon the road. He had reached a place called Knowl Hill, when the servant of a gentleman, who was following his master, came riding at full speed behind him. Hind, supposing that it was one in pursuit of himself, upon his coming up, turned about, and shot him through the head, when the unfortunate man fell dead upon the spot. Fortune favoured the captain at this time, and he got off in safety.

The following adventure closes the narrative of Hind's busy life. After Charles I. was beheaded, the Scots remained loyal, proclaimed his son Charles II., and resolved to maintain his right against the usurper. They suddenly raised an army, and entering England, proceeded as far as Worcester. Multitudes of English joined the royal army, and among these captain Hind, who was loyal from principle, and brave by nature. Cromwell was sent by parliament with an army to intercept the march of the royalists. Both armies met at Worcester, and a desperate and bloody battle ensued. The king's army was routed. Captain Hind had the good fortune to escape, and, reaching London, lived in a retired situation. Here, however, he had not remained long, when he was betrayed by one of his intimate acquaintances. It will be readily granted that his actions merited death by the law of his country, but the mind recoils with horror from the thought of treachery in an intimate friend.

Hind was carried before the speaker of the house of commons, and, after a long examination, was committed to Newgate, and loaded with irons; nor was any person allowed to converse with him without a special commission. He was brought to the bar of the session house at the Old Bailey, indicted for several crimes, but for want of sufficient evidence, nothing worthy of death could be proved against him. Not long after this, he was sent down to Reading under a strong guard, and being arraigned before Judge Warburton, for killing George Symson, at Knowl Hill, as afore said, he was convicted of wilful murder. An act of indemnity for all past offences was issued at this time, and he hoped to have been included; but an order of council removed him to Worcester jail, where he was condemned for his treason, and hanged, drawn, and quartered, on the 24th of September, 1652, aged thirty four years. His head was stuck upon the top of the bridge over the Severn, and the other parts of his body placed upon the gates of the city. The head was privately taken down and interred, but the remaining parts of his body remained until consumed by the influence of the weather.

CAPTAIN RICHARD DUDLEY

Was born at Swepston in Leicestershire. His father once possessed a large estate, but through extravagance lost the whole except about sixty pounds per annum. In these reduced circumstances he went to London, intending to live in obscurity, corresponding to the state of his finances.

Our hero had a promising genius, and received a

liberal education at St. Paul's school. But a naturally vicious disposition baffled all restraints. When
only nine years old he showed his covetous disposition, by robbing his sister of thirty shillings, and
absconding with it. In a few days, however, he was
found, brought home, and sent to school, where his
vicious propensities were only strengthened by indulgence. Impatient of the confinement of a school,
he next robbed his father of a considerable sum of
money, and absconded. His father, however, discovered his retreat, and found him a little way from
town, in the company of two loose women.

Despairing of settling at home, his father sent
him on board a man of war, in which he sailed up
the Straits, and behaved gallantly in several actions.
Upon his arriving in England, he left the ship, under the pretence that a young officer had been preferred before him, upon the death of one of the
lieutenants. In a short time he joined a band of
thieves, and assisted them in robbing the country-
house of admiral Carter, and escaped detection.
Having at length commenced robber, the first remarkable robbery in which he was engaged, was
that of breaking into the house of a lady at Black-
heath, and carrying off a large quantity of place.

He and his associates were successful in selling
the plate to a refiner; but in a short time he was
apprehended for the robbery, and committed to
Newgate. While there he sent for the refiner, and
severely reproached him in the following manner:
It is, said he, a hard matter to find an honest man
and a fair dealer: for, you cursed rogue, among the
plate you bought, there was a cup with a cover,
which you told us was but silver gilt, buying it at

the same price with the rest; but it plainly appeared, by the advertisement in the gazette, that it was
a gold cup and cover; I see you are a rogue, and
that there is no trusting anybody. Dudley was
tried, convicted for this robbery, and sentenced to
death : but his youth, and the interest of his friends,
procured him a royal pardon.

For two years he conducted himself to the satisfaction of his father, so that he purchased for him a
commission in the army. In that situation he also
acquitted himself honourably, and married a young
lady of a respectable family, with whom he received
an estate of a hundred and forty pounds a year.
This, with his commission, enabled him to live in
a genteel manner. Delighting, however, in company, and having become security for one of his
companions for a debt, and that person being arrested for it, one of the bailiffs was killed in the
scuffle, and he was suspected of being the murderer.

Being hardened in vice, he robbed on the highway, broke into houses, picked pockets, or performed any act of violence or cunning by which he could
procure money. Fortune favoured him long, and he
went on with impunity, but was at last apprehended for robbing Sir John Friend's house. Upon
trial the evidence was decisive, and he received
sentence of death.—His friends again interposed,
and through their influence his sentence was changed for that of banishment. Accordingly, he and several other convicts were put on board a ship for
Barbadoes. But they had scarcely reached the Isle of
Wight, when he excited his companions to a con-
spiracy, and having concerted their measures while

the ship's crew were under hatches, they went off
in the longboat.

No sooner had he reached the shore than he
abandoned his companions, and travelled through
the woods and bye paths. Being in a very mean
dress, he begged when he had no opportunity to
steal. Arriving, however, at Hounslow heath, he
met with a farmer, robbed him, seized his horse,
and having mounted, set forward in quest of new
spoils. This was a fortunate day, for Dudley had
not proceeded far on the heath, when a gentleman,
well dressed, and better mounted than the farmer,
made his appearance. He was commanded to halt
and to surrender. Dudley led him aside into a retired thicket, exchanged clothes and horse, rifled
his pockets, and then addressed him, saying, that
he ought never to accuse him of robbing him, for
according to the old proverb, exchange was no robbery; so bidding him good day, he marched of for
London. Arrived there, he went in search of his
old associates, who were glad to see their friend;
and who, in consequence of his fortunate adventures and high reputation among them, conferred
upon him the title of captain, all agreeing to be
subject to his commands. Thus, at the head of
such an experienced and desperate band, no part of
the country was secure from his rapine, nor any
house sufficiently strong to keep him out. The natural consequences were, that he soon became
known and dreaded all over the country.

To avoid capture, and to prevent all inquiries, he
paid a visit to the north of England, and, being one
day in search of plunder, he robbed a Dutch colonel
of his horse, arms, and fine laced coat. Thus

equipped he committed several other robberies. At length, however, he laid aside the colonel's habit, only using his horse, which soon became dexterous at his new employment. But one day meeting a gentleman near Epsom, the latter resisted the captain's demands and discharged his pistol at Dudley. In the combat, however, he was victorious, and wounded the gentleman in the leg, and, having stripped him of his money, conveyed him to the next village, that he might receive medical assistance, and then rode off in search of new adventures. The captain and his men were very successful in this quarter. No stage, nor coach, nor passenger, of which they had intelligence, could escape their depredations, and scarcely a day passed without the commission of some notorious robbery.

Captain Dudley and his men went on in a continued course of good fortune, acquiring much wealth, but amassing little, as their extravagance was equal to their gains. One ill fated day, however, having attacked and robbed the Southampton coach, they were keenly pursued, and several of them taken; but Dudley escaped. Deprived of the chief part of his own forces, he now attached himself to some housebreakers, and with them continued to commit many robberies; in particular with three others, he entered the house of an old woman in Spitalfields, gagged her, bound her to a chair, and rifled the house of a considerable sum of money, which the good woman had been long scraping together. Hearing the money clink that was going to be taken from her, she struggled in her chair, fell down upon her face, and was stifled to death, while the captain and his companions went off with impunity.   But when the old woman came to be interred, a grandson of her's, who had been one of the robbers, when about to be fitted with a pair of mourning gloves changed his countenance, was strongly agitated, and began to tremble.   He was suspected, charged with the murder, confessed the crime, and informing upon the rest, two of them were taken, tried, and condemned, and the three hanged in chains.

Yet, though Dudley's name was published as accessary to the murder, he long escaped detection. At length, however, he was apprehended, and charged with several robberies, of which he, by dexterous management, evaded the deserved punishment.   He was also called to stand trial for the murder of the old woman; but the principal evidence, upon whose testimony the other three were chiefly condemned, being absent, he escaped suffering for that crime.   The dexterous manner in which he managed that trial, the witness that he suborned, and the manner in which he maintained his innocence before the jury were often the cause of his boast and amusement.

The profligate Dudley was no sooner released from prison, than he hastened to join his old companions in vice.   Exulting to see their captain at their head, they redoubled their activity, and committed all manner of depredations.—Among other adventures, they robbed a nobleman at Hounslow heath of £1500, after a severe engagement with his servants, three of whom were wounded, and two had their horses shot under them.   They next directed their course along the west country road, and having robbed a parson, enjoined him, under the

most terrific threats, to preach a sermon in praise
of thieving. He was forced to comply, and the
sermon being ended, they returned him his money,
and gave him four shillings to drink their health
and success.

After this adventure, they left off infesting the
highways, and rode for London. Arrived in the
capital, the captain's brother employed his dexterity
about town in several adventures, which go so far
to show how well the brother profited by the example and instructions of the captain. He first
dressed himself as a countryman, with a pair of
dirty boots on, and a whip in his hand, and went to
Bartholomew fair, where he wandered all the fore-
noon without meeting any prey. But as he was
returning, he accosted a plain countryman, saying,
have a care, honest friend, of your money, for we
are going into a cursed place, full of thieves, rogues,
and pickpockets. I am almost ruined by them, and
am glad that they have not pulled the teeth out of
my head. Let one take never so good care, they
will be sure of his money; the devil certainly must
help them.

The face of the countryman glowed with courage
as he replied, I defy all the devils to rob me of any
thing I value. I have a round piece which I'll secure; and thrusting it into his mouth he rushed
confidently into the fair. Will was only desirous
to ascertain the fact that he had money about him;
therefore, giving his instructions with a few six-
pences and groats to a hopeful boy, he immediately
ran after the countryman, while Will followed at a
distance. The boy coming up with the countryman, fell down before him, scattering the money all

around; and starting up a most hideous noise, crying that he was undone, and that he must run away from his apprenticeship, that his master was a furious man, and that he would certainly be killed. The countryman and others flocked around, and endeavoured to assist the boy to gather up his lost money. Then one of them said, have you found all? Yes, all the silver, but that is of no avail; there is a broad piece of gold which I was carrying to my master for a token sent from the country, and for the loss of it I shall be killed. Alas! I am undone, what will become of me? Will now advanced among the crowd, and was equally concerned for the unhappy boy; and, seeing the countryman standing by, he gravely observed that he had seen him put a piece of gold into his mouth. The mob instantly seized him, and while one opened his mouth by force, another extracted the broad piece of gold; and when he attempted to speak in his own defence, he was kicked and pinched, and so tossed about that he was glad to escape with his life. Meanwhile, the boy slipped away among the crowd, and at an appointed place met Will to surrender to him his booty.

Having changed his clothes, Will went into the market, and mingling with the crowd, learned that the countryman was gone to an inn, where he had sent for his master, a knight of a large estate, and some other respectable person to attest his character. Will knew this person well, and hastened to the Exchange, in full hopes of meeting him. Having reconnoitred the gentleman, and followed him until he perceived an opportunity, he robbed him of every guinea he had, except one, which he considerately left him to pay for his dinner. The knight, repairing to the inn, laughed heartily when the poor countryman informed him that he also had, in like manner, been just fleeced upon the Exchange. The countryman laughed in his turn, and said, sir, let us make our escape from this roguish place; adding with a shrug of the shoulders, sir, they'll steal our small guts to make fiddle strings of them.

The gentleman having recruited his purse, went out the next day to the Exchange. Will paid him the same compliment the second day. The knight was surprised how it was possible for any man to rob him when he was forewarned, and so upon his guard; but, looking hastily about, his eyes fixed upon Will, whom he suspected to be the delinquent. He went up to him, and, taking him by the button, informed him that he strongly suspected he was the person who had robbed him; but, as he was a gentleman of a large fortune, he did not regard the money, upon condition that he would inform him by what means he had done so. This, said he, I promise upon my honour. Your word of honour, said Will, is sufficient: I know the greatness of your fortune; I am the man, I will wait on your worship at the tavern, and there shew you some of my art more freely than I would to my fellow rogues. In their way to the inn, the gentleman informed Will, that as he wished to make a frolic of the matter, he would send for some other gentlemen to be present, assuring him, at the same time, that he should sustain no damage from any discovery that he might make to them. I know you're a gentleman, said Will, and men of honour scorn to keep

base company. Call as many as you please; I'll
take their word, and I know that I am safe.

When the gentlemen had arrived, Will told them
many things which greatly astonished and pleased
them; and when he pulled out the piece of gold,
and informed them how he had used Roger, the
gentleman's tenant, he was immediately sent for to
increase the amusement. What would you say,
cried the knight, as he entered, if you saw your gold
again? Oh! said he, I wish I could; but if my
mouth can't keep it, where shall I put it? Shud;
I'd rather see the rogue; I'd make a jelly of his
bones! There he is, said the knight, and there's
your broad piece. As Roger began to heave and to
bully, his master commanded him to take his piece
of gold, and sit down by him: upon which the paci-
fied Roger, seeing how things went, drank to his
new acquaintance.

One of the gentlemen pulled out a curious watch,
said, he wondered how it was possible to take a
watch out of a fob; that it certainly must be from
carelessness on the part of the owner. No, said
Will, if the gentleman will take a turn in Moorfields I'll wager a guinea I'll have the watch before
he returns let him take what care he pleases, and I
shan't stir out of the room. Done, cried the gentleman; and every gentleman in the room laid down
his guinea, while Roger staked his broad piece. The
gentleman went out, and was careful not to suffer
man, woman, nor child to come near him. When
the time approached that he should return, a boy
came pretty near him, but, to avoid suspicion, ran
past him, and at the same time looking on his back,
informed the gentleman that it swarmed with ver-

min. The gentleman observing them, and loathing the sight, said, good boy, take them off and I'll give you a shilling. The boy did so, and at the same time stealing his watch; and, having received his shilling, ran off. The gentleman returned to the tavern, wondering all the way how he could possibly come by such vermin, and taking the greatest care that no person should approach him.

Upon his return to the tavern, Will asked him what o'clock it was. He attempted to pull out his watch, but, to his utter astonishment and confusion, it was gone. Upon this, Will produced it, and asked him if that were his. The gentleman was struck dumb, casting up his hands and eyes, and, full of amazement, addressed Will, saying, you must have had the assistance of the devil. Of a boy, said Will. Did not a boy pick you clean? There's the devil, said the gentleman; and he threw them on, too, I suppose. Aye, through a quill, said the other.

All present were astonished at the ingenuity of the trick, but particularly plain Roger, who could not, at times, restrain his laughter. Alas! said Will, this trick is not worth talking about: it is only one of those we commit to our boys. There is a nobleman just passing the window, with a rich coat on his back: I'll wager as before, to steal it from him before all his followers, and bring it here on my own back. The gentlemen all staked their guineas, and were seconded by Roger. Come, now, said Will, this matter must not be entrusted to a boy; you will give me leave to go myself, nor must you restrict me any particular time to return. So out he ran, and followed the nobleman from street to street, until he saw him enter a tavern.

The nobleman was conducted up stairs. Will bustling in after him, hastened to the bar-keeper, and desired him to lend him an apron, as his master would be served only by his footman. He is a very good customer, and expects the very best wine: I must go to the cellar and taste it for him. The apron being given, he went to the cellar, and returned with some of the best of each wine for his pretend-ed master. He ran so quick up and down stairs, and was so alert at his work, that none of the other servants could equal him. Meanwhile, the com-pany up stairs taking him for the servant of the house, were highly satisfied with his attendance. He was also careful to give full cups to the servant who should have waited in his place, with some money which the other was very glad to receive for doing nothing. He seldom also went into the room without passing some merry jest to amuse the com pany. They were so highly pleased with him, that they said one to another, this is a merry, witty fel-low; such a man as he is fit to make a house; he deserves to have double wages. When Will saw his plan ripe for execution, he came into the room with some wine, and by the the aid of a knife made a slit in my lord's coat. Returning with a bottle in one hand, and his other hand full of glasses, before he approached his lordship, he started and stared, saying, what fellows are those who have made that coat? with other imprecations against the tailor. Then some of the company rising up, saw the rent in my lord's coat, and cried, my lord, the tailor has cheated you. Will, drawing near, said, such things may happen; but give me the coat, and I'll carry it privately under my master's cloak to an acquaintance of mine, who will presently make it as good as if it had not been torn. Borrowing a great coat of a gentleman present, the nobleman gave Will his coat to carry to the tailor, who, coming down stairs, informed the landlord of the disaster, received his cloak, and, putting the rent coat below it, seized a good beaver hat off one of the cloak pins and hastened from the tavern. Arriving at the inn where the gentlemen were anxiously waiting his return, he went into another room, dressed himself, and went with the cloak and beaver on. What! said one of them, instead of a coat, you come with a cloak, and great need for it: for there's a great deal of knavery under it. Will then opened the cloak, and showed them the coat, saying that he had received the cloak, and the beaver into the bargain; and related the foregoing adventure.

Meanwhile, my lord and his company had waited long in expectation of the servant, whom they supposed to have been one of the waiters of the house. The landlord also wondering that they were so long in calling for more wine, one of the servants was sent up stairs, to force trade. He entered the room, saying, 'Call here, call here, gentlemen?' 'Yes, (said one of them) where is your fellow-servant who waited upon us?' 'My fellow-servant (exclaimed the other), he said he was my lord's servant, and that his master would be served by none but himself, and I should have good vails nevertheless.' My lord, replied, 'How can that be? I have only one gentleman of my own retinue: the rest are with my lady. He that served us came in with an apron, and in the character of one of the servants of the house: call up the landlord!' Bo-

niface instantly waited upon them, when one of the
gentlemen asked him if he kept sharpers in his
house, to affront gentlemen and to rob them. 'Nay,'
replied the vintner, who was a choleric man, 'do
you bring sharpers along with you, to affront me
and rob my house? I am sure I have lost a new
cloak and beaver; and, for aught I know, though
you look like gentlemen, you may be sharpers your-
selves; and I expect to be paid by you for the losses,
as well as for the reckoning.' One of the company instantly drew upon him, enraged at his inso-
lent language; but the landlord ran down stairs in
affright, and alarmed the whole house, entreating
them not to suffer such rogues to escape. In the
meantime, he seized a sword, and the servants armed themselves with spits, pokers, and such other
weapons as the house afforded. A great uproar was
soon raised; and the nobleman coming first out to
make his way past the crowd, made a thrust at the
landlord, but was beaten back by a fire shovel in
the hand of one of the waiters, and very narrowly
escaped being run through with a long spit by the
hands of a cook maid. His lordship, seeing the
door so completely guarded, shut himself up in the
room, and began to consult with the rest of the
company, what was best to be done.

Fortunately, however, the gentleman who was in
the other tavern with Will, conjecturing that a quarrel might ensue, between the nobleman and the
vintner, who had lost his cloak and beaver, sent his
own landlord to inform him that the rogue was
caught, and in safe custody.

He was admitted up stairs, waited on his lordship, and communicated to him the whole affair.

A cessation of arms took place. They drank to the health of the landlord, assuring him, that in future, they would be friendly to his house: but, in the meantime, they attended their peacemaker to the tavern, where Will was exhititing his dexterity. The vintner went along with them, when, after common compliments, Will restored the coat, the cloak, and the beaver, and continued to amuse them during the remainder of the evening with the recital of his adventures.

But to return, at length, to the captain, his brother. He had, along with his companions, committed so many robberies upon the highway, that a proclamation was issued against them, offering a reward to those who should bring them, either dead or alive. This occasioned their detection in the following manner: having committed a robbery, and being closely pursued to Westminster ferry, the wherryman refused to carry any more that night. Two of them rode off, and the other four gave their horses to a waterman to lead to the next inn. The horses foaming with sweat, the waterman began to suspect they were robbers who had been keenly pursued, and communicated his suspicions to the constable, who secured the horses, and went in search of the men.

He was not long in seizing one of them, who confessed; and the constable, hastening to the inn, secured the rest, and having placed a strong guard upon them, rode to Lambeth, and making sure of the other two, led them before a justice of the peace, who committed them to Newgate.

At the next sessions, Captain Dudley, his brother, and three other accomplices were tried, and condemned to suffer death.

After sentence, Captain Dudley was brought to Newgate, where he conducted himself agreeably to his sad situation. He was conveyed from Newgate with six other prisoners. He appeared pretty cheerful, but his brother lay all the time sick in the cart. The ceremonies of religion being performed, they were launched into another world on the 22d of February, 1681, to answer for the numerous crimes of their guilty lives.

The bodies of the captain and his brother having been cut down, were put into separate coffins, to be conveyed to their disconsolate father, who at the sight was so overwhelmed, that he sank upon the dead bodies, and never spoke more, and buried at the same time, and in the same grave with his two suns.

TIMOTHY BUCKLEY,

Was reared to the useful occupation of a shoemaker, but leaving his master, he came to London, and soon found out companions suited to his disposition. He and his associates frequented an alehouse at Wapping ; and one day being run short of cash, Tim asked the landlord for ten shillings, which he refused. Tim was so exasperated, that, along with some of his associates, he broke into his house, and bound him, his wife, and maid. When Tim was about this operation, the landlord conjured him to be favourable. ' No, no, you must not expect any

favour from my hands, whose prodigality makes you
lord it over the people here like a boatswain over a
ship's crew; but I will go to another part of the
town, where I will be more civilly used, and spend
a little of your money there.' Accordingly, Tim and
his companions robbed the house of forty pounds,
three silver tankards, a silver watch, and three gold
rings.

Upon another day Tim was airing in Hyde park-
corner, and met with Dr. Catesby the famous moun-
tebank. At the words 'stand and deliver!' the Doctor went into a long harangue about the honesty of
his calling, and of the great difficulty with which he
made a living. Tim laughed heartily, saying,
' Quacks pretend to honesty, there is not such a
pack of cheating knaves in the nation. Their impudence is intolerable for deceiving honest simple
people, and pretending that more men were not slain
at the battle of the Boyne, than they have recovered
from death or beckoned their souls back when they
have been many leagues from their bodies : therefore, deliver ! or this pistol shall put a stop to your
further ramblings and deception.' The doctor preferring his life to his gold, presented Tim with six
guineas, and a watch, to show him how to keep time
while spending the money.

Tim was once apprehended by a baker, in the character of a constable, and sent to Flanders as a soldier. He deserted, and returning to London, one
day met with the baker's wife. He presented a pistol, and demanded her money; she exclaimed, ' Is
this justice or conscience, sir !' ' Don't tell me of
justice, for I hate her as much as your husband can
because her scales are even : And as for conscience,

I have as little of that as any baker in England, who cheats other people's bellies to fill his own! Nay, a baker is a worse rogue than a tailor : for, whereas the latter commonly pinches his cabbage from the rich, the former, by making his bread too light, robs all without distinction, but chiefly the poor, for which he deserved hanging more than I, or any of my honest fraternity.' Then he took from her eleven shillings and two gold rings, and sent her home to relate the adventure to her husband.

Tim next stole a good horse and commenced upon the highway, and meeting with a pawnbroker, by whom he had lost some articles, he commanded him to stand and deliver. The pawnbroker entreated for favour, saying ' that it was a very hard thing that people could not go about their lawful business, without being robbed.' 'You talk of honesty, who live by fraud and oppression—your shop, like the gates of hell are always open, in which you sit at the receipt of custom, and having got the spoils of the needy, you hang them up in rank and file, like so many trophies of victory. To your shop all sorts of garments resort, as on a pilgrimage. Thou art the treasurer of the Thieves' Exchequer, for which purpose you keep a private warehouse, from whence you ship them off wholesale, or retail, according to pleasure. Nay, the poor and oppressed have often to pay their own cloth, before they can receive them back by your exorbitant exactions. Come, come, blood sucker, open your purse strings, or this pistol shall send you where you are sure to go sooner or later.' The pawnbroker did not, however, wish to visit his old friend before his time; he therefore ransomed his life at the expense of twenty eight guineas, a gold watch, a silver box, and two gold rings.

Upon another occasion, Tim fortunately met with a stock jobber (who had prosecuted him for felony,) and robbed of forty eight guineas. He requested something to carry him home. Tim refused, saying, ' I have no charity for you stock jobbers, who rise and fall like the ebbing and flowing of the tide, and whose paths are as unfathomable as the ocean. The grasshopper in the Royal Exchange is an emblem of your character. What! give you something to carry you home out of the paltry sum of forty eight guineas! I won't give you a farthing.' He bade him farewell till next meeting.

Though unexpected and unwished, it was not long before the stock jobber reconnoitered Tim, and caused him to be apprehended, and committed to Newgate. He was tried and received sentence of death; but obtaining a reprieve, and afterwards a pardon, he was determined to be revenged of the man who would not give him rest to pursue his honest employment; he therefore set fire to a country house belonging to him. To his no small chagrin, however, it was put out before much harm was done.

Tim went to Leicestershire, broke into a house, seized eighty pounds, purchased a horse, and took to his former mode of life. Thus mounted, he attacked a coach in which were three gentlemen, and two footmen attending. Tim's horse being shot under him, he killed one of the gentlemen and a footman, but being overpowered, was committed to Nottingham jail, and suffered the due reward of murder and robbery, at the age of twenty-nine, in the year 1701.

THOMAS JONES.

Tom was a native of Newcastle-upon-Tyne. His father was a clothier, whose business he followed until he was two and twenty years of age. In that period, however, the prominent dispositions of his mind were displayed, by extravagance, and running in debt. In order therefore, to retrieve his circumstances, he went upon the highway.

Out of gratitude to his father's kindness, he commenced by robbing him of eighty pounds and a good horse. Unaccustomed to such work, he rode, under the impression that he was pursued, and in danger of being taken, no less than forty miles. Arriving in Staffordshire, he attacked and robbed the stage coach of a considerable booty. During the scuffle, several shots were fired at the passengers, but no injury was done.

A monkey belonging to one of the passengers being tied behind the coach, was so frightened with the firing, that he broke his chain, and ran for his life. At night, as a countryman was coming over a gate, pug leaped out of the hedge upon his back, and clung very fast. The poor man, who had never seen such an animal, imagined that he was no less a person than the devil; and when he come home, thundered at the door. His wife looked out of the window, and asked him what he had got. 'The devil!' cried he, and entreated she would go to the parson and beg his assistance. 'Nay,' quoth she, 'you shall not bring the devil in here. If you

belong to him I don't; so be content to go without
my company.' Poor Hob was obliged to wait at his
door until one of his neighbours, wiser than the
rest, and with a few apples and pears, dispossessed
him of the devil, and got him for his pains. He
accordingly carried him to the owner, and received
a suitable reward.

Tom's next adventure was with a Quaker, who
formerly kept a button shop, but, being reduced in
his circumstances, he was going down to the country to avoid an arrest. In this situation he was
more afraid of a bailiff than a robber. Therefore,
when Tom took hold of him by the coat, broad-brim
very gravely said, At whose suit dost thou detain
me? I detain thee on my own suit, and my demand is for all thy substance. The Quaker having
discovered his mistake, added, Truly, friend, I don't
know thee, nor can I indeed imagine that ever thee
and I had any dealings together. You shall find
then, said Jones, that we shall deal together now.
He then presented his pistol. Pray, neighbour, use
no violence, for if thou carriest me to jail, I am undone. I have fourteen guineas about me, and if
that will satisfy thee, thou art welcome to take
them. Here they are, and give me leave to assure
thee, that I have frequently stopped the mouth of a
bailiff with a much less sum, and made him affirm
to my creditors that he could not find me. Jones
received the money, and replied, Friend, I am not
such a rogue as thou takest me to be: I am no bailiff, but an honest, generous highwayman. I shall
not trouble myself, cried the Quaker, about the distinction of names; if a man takes my money from
me by force, it concerns me but little what he

calls himself, or what his pretences may be for so doing.

At another time Tom met with lord and lady Wharton, and though they had three men attending, demanded their charity in his usual style. His lordship, said, Do you know me, sir, that you dare be so bold as to stop me upon the road? Not I; I neither know or care who you are. I am apt to imagine that you are some great man, because you speak so big; but, be as great as you will, sir, I must have you to know, that there is no man upon the road so great as myself; therefore pray be quick in answering my demands, for delays may prove dangerous. Tom then received two hundred pounds, three diamond rings, and two gold watches.

Upon another day, Tom received intelligence that a gentleman was upon the road with 100 pounds. He waited upon the top of a hill to welcome his approach. The steward of the gentleman discovered him, and suspecting his character, desired that the money might be given to him, and he would ride off with it, as the robber would not suspect him. This was done; Tom came forward, stopped the coach, and the gentleman gave him ten pounds. He was greatly enraged, and mentioned the sum he knew the gentleman carried along with him. In an instant however, suspecting the stratagem, he rode after the steward with all possible speed; but the latter observing him in pursuit, increased his pace, and reached an inn before Tom could overtake him.

After many similar adventures, Tom was apprehended for robbing a farmer's wife. He was so habituated to vice, that nothing but the gallows could arrest his course, and in the forty second year of his age he met with that fate, on the 25th of April, 1762.

ARTHUR CHAMBERS.

Arthur Chambers was of low extraction, and destitute of every amiable quality. From his very infancy he was addicted to pilfering; and the low circumstances of his parents being unable to support his extravagances, he had recourse to dishonest practices. It is even reported, that before he was dressed in boy's clothes, he committed several acts of theft.

The first thing which he attempted was, to learn, from an experienced master, all those cant words and phrases current among pickpockets, by which they distinguish one another. Chambers was soon an adept in this new language; and being well dressed, he was introduced to the better sort of company, and took occasion, when opportunities offered, to rob his companions.

In a short time he was confined in Bridewell, to answer with hard labour for some small offence. Having obtained his liberty, he left the town, where he again begun to be suspected, and went to Cornwall. His social turn gained him reception in genteel companies, and he became a memorable character in the place. Before he left London, he provided himself with a large quantity of base crowns and half crowns, which he uttered wherever he went. After many had been deceived, strict search was

made, and Chamber detected.   For this offence he
was committed to jail, where he remained a year
and a half.

As he could no longer abide in Cornwall, he returned to London.   Upon his arrival, he went to an
alehouse, and called for a pot of beer and a slice of
bread and cheese.   Having refreshed himself, he
entered into conversation with some persons in a
neighbouring box.   The conversation turned on the
great advantages of a country life, but was insensi-
bly directed to that of robbery.   Chambers, improving the hint, regretted that no better provision was
made for suppressing such villanies; for, added he,
death is too scarce a punishment for a man even if
he robbed the whole world.   But why do I talk
thus? continued he, if great offenders are suffered,
well may the poor and necessitous say, we must
live, and where is the harm of taking a few guineas
from those that can spare them, or who, perhaps,
have robbed others of them?   For my own part, I
look upon a dexterous pickpocket as a very useful
person, as he draws his resources from the purses
of those who would spend their money in gaming,
or worse.   Look ye, gentlemen, I can pick a pocket
as well as any man in Britain; and yet, though I
say it, I am as honest as the best Englishman
breathing.   Observe that country gentleman passing
by the window there; I will engage to rob him of
his watch, though it is scarcely five o'clock.

A wager of ten shillings was instantly taken, and
Chambers hastened after the gentleman.   He accosted him at the extremity of Long lane, and pulling of his hat, asked him the nearest way to Knave's
acre.   The stranger replied that he himself wished

to know the way to Moorfields, which Chambers pointed out ; and while the other kept his eyes fixed on the places to which he directed him, he embraced the opportunity to rob him of his watch, and hastening back to the alehouse, threw down his plunder and claimed the wager.

He next exerted his ingenuity upon a plain countryman, newly come to town. The rustic had got into the company of sharpers, and stood gazing at a gambling table. Our adventurer stepping up, tapped him on the shoulder, and inquired what part of the country he came from, and if he was desirous to find a place as a gentleman's servant. Robin answered that his very errand to town, was to find such a place. Chambers then said that he could fit him to a hair. I believe I can afford you myself four pounds a year, standing wages, and six shillings a week board wages, and all cast clothes, which are none of the worst. This was sufficient to make Robin almost jump out of his skin, for never before had such an offer been made to him. Having arranged every thing to his wish, Robin entered upon his new service. He received Chambers's cloak, threw it over his arm, and followed his master. Chambers ordered a coach, and Robin being placed behind, they drove off to an inn. Dinner being ordered, Robin sat down with his master, and made a hearty meal, the former in the meanwhile instructing him in all the tricks of the town, and inculcating the necessity of always being upon his guard. He informed him also, that the servants of the inn would be requesting him to join in play at cards, and that he was in danger of being imposed upon; therefore, if he had any money upon

him, it would be proper to give it to him, and he
would receive it back when necessary. Robin, accordingly pulled out his purse, and delivered all he
had, with which Chambers paid for his dinner, and
went off, leaving Robin to shift for himself, and to
lament the loss of his money and his new master.

The next adventure of Chambers was directed
against the innkeeper of the Greyhound, St. Alban's.
His wife was rather handsome, and exceedingly
facetious; and Chambers being often there, was on
terms of the greatest familiarity with the household.
Directing his steps thither, and pretending to have
been attacked by three men near the inn, he went
in with his clothes all besmeared. The travellers
who were in the inn condoled with him on his misfortune, and gave him clothes until his own should
be cleaned. To make amends to himself for the
sad disaster, he invited six of his fellow travellers,
with the landlord and his wife, to supper. The
glass circulated pretty freely, and the wife entertained them with several songs. Chambers was careful
that her glass never remained long empty. In a
short time he saw with pleasure that all his companions, with the solitary exception of the landlord,
were sunk in the arms of sleep, and he proposed
that they should be conveyed to bed; whereupon
two or three stout fellows came to perform that
office. Chambers was so obliging as to lend his assistance, but took care that their money and watches
should pay him for his trouble.

Left alone with the landlord, he proposed that
they should have an additional bottle. Another
succeeded before the landlord was in a condition
to be conveyed to rest. In aiding the servants with

the corpulent innkeeper, he discovered the geography of his bed room, and finding that the door was opposite his own, he retired, not to rest, but to plot and to perfect his villany.

When he was convinced that the wine would work its full effect on the deluded pair, he revisited the bed chamber, waited some time, and extracted what property he could conveniently carry away; by the dawn of the day he dressed himself in the best suit of clothes his bottle companions could afford, called for the horse of the person whose clothes he now wore, left two guineas with the waiter to pay his bill, gave half a crown to the ostler, and rode off to London.

His first enterprise after his arrival was attacking an Italian merchant upon the Exchange. He took him aside, eagerly inquired what goods he had to dispose of, and entering into conversation, one of Chamber's companions approaching, joined the conversation. Meanwhile, our adventurer found means to extract from his pocket a large purse of gold and his gold watch, which he delivered to his accomplice. Not satisfied with his first success, and observing a silk handkerchief suspended from his pocket, he walked behind him to seize it, but was detected in the act, and kept fast hold off by the merchant, who called out lustily, 'Thief! thief!' In this dilemma, Chamber's accomplice ran to the crier, and requested him to give public proclamation, that if any body had lost a purse of gold, upon giving proper information, it would be restored. With the expectation of finding his money the merchant let go his hold; and in the crowd, Chambers and his friend retired with their booty.

But Chambers was now resolved to perform an action worthy of his talents. He hired the first floor of a house, and agreed with the landlord, for fourteen shillings a week. Having, in the first instance, been mistaken for a man of fortune, both from his appearance and style of living, a mutual confidence was gradually established. When his plot was matured, he entered with a very pensive and sorrowful look the apartment of his landlord, who anxiously inquired the cause of his great uneasiness; when Chambers, with tears in his eyes, informed him that he was just returned from Hampstead, where he had witnessed the death of a beloved brother, who had left him sole heir, with an expressed injunction to convey his dear remains to Westminster Abbey. He therefore entreated the favour of being allowed to bring his brother's remains at a certain hour to his house, that from thence they might be conveyed to the place of their destination, which very reasonable request was readily granted by his unsuspecting landlord.

Chambers went off the next morning, leaving word, that the corpse would be there at six o'clock in the evening. At the appointed hour the hearse, with six horses, arrived at the door. An elegant coffin with six gilded handles, was carried up stairs, and placed upon the dining room table, and the horses were conveyed by the men to a stable in the neighbourhood. They informed the landlord, that Chambers was detained on business, and would probably sleep that night in the Strand.

The artful rogue was, however, confined in the coffin, in which air holes had been made, the screw nails left unfixed, his clothes all on, with a winding sheet wrapped over them, and his face blanched with flour. All the family were now gone to bed, except the maid servants. Chambers arose from his confinement, went down stairs to the kitchen wrapped in his winding sheet, sat down and stared the maid in the face, who, overwhelmed with fear, cried out, 'a ghost! a ghost! and ran up stairs to her master's room, who chid her unreasonable fears, and requested her to return to bed, and compose herself. She, however, obstinately refused, and remained in the room.

In a short, time however, in stalked the stately ghost, took his seat, and conferred a complete sweat and a mortal fright upon all three who were present. Retiring from his station when he deemed it convenient, he continued by the moving of the doors, and the noise raised in the house, to conceal his design: in the meantime, he went down stairs, opened the doors to his accomplices, who assisted him to carry off the plate, and all that could be removed, not even sparing the kitchen utensils. The maid was the first to venture from her room in the morning, and to inform her master and mistress of what had happened, who, more than the night before, chid her incredulity in believing that a ghost could rob a house, or carry away any article out of it. In a little time however the landlord was induced to rise from his bed, and move down stairs, and found, to his astonishment and chagrin, that the whole of his plate, and almost the entire of his moveables, were gone, and for which he had only received in return an empty coffin.

A great many other stories of the like nature, are told of Chambers; and it is well known, that for the few years he was permitted, by singular good fortune, to go at large, he committed as many artful and daring actions as was ever committed by one man.

At length, however, one Jack Hall, a chimney sweeper, being apprehended, to save his own life, made himself an evidence against Chambers, who, being cast upon that information, was with two other notorious offenders, executed at Tyburn, in 1703, in the twenty eighth year of his age.

JOHN OVET

Was born at Nottingham, and, after serving an apprenticeship to a shoemaker, for some time gained his bread by that useful employment: but his licentious dispositions inclining him to profligate and abandoned company, he soon took to the highway.

After having purchased a horse, pistols, and every necessary utensil proper to his projected profession, he rode towards London, and on the way robbed a gentleman of £20. That gentleman, however, was not destitute of courage, and told Ovet, that if he had not taken him unawares, he would not so easily have plundered him of his property. The son of Crispin was not destitute of the essential qualifications of his new profession; he, therefore, replied, that he had already ventured his life for his £20. But, continued he, here's your money again, and whoever is the better man, let him win it and wear it. The proposal was then accepted, each employed his sword, the gentleman fell, and Ovet seized the money.

But having now stained his hands with blood, he not long after killed another man in a quarrel. He, however, escaped from justice, and continued his depredations. One day, being greatly in want of money, and meeting one Rodgers with some pack horses, he turned one of them off the way, opened the pack, and extracted about two hundred and eighty guineas, with three dozen of silver knives, forks, and spoons. Then he tied the horse to a tree, and made off with the spoil.

Another time, when Ovet was drinking at the Star Inn in the Strand, he overheard a soap boiler contriving with a carrier how he should send £100 to a friend in the country. At length it was concluded to put the money into a barrel of soap: which project was warmly approved off by the carrier, who answered, if any scoundrels should rob my waggon, (which they never did but once,) the devil must be in them if they look for any money in the soap barrel. Accordingly the money and the soap were brought to the inn, and the next day the carrier went out of town. Ovet followed him, and overtook him in the afternoon, and commanded him to stop, otherwise he would shoot him and his horses too; he was therefore compelled to obey the word of command, and to stop. Then, cried the honest highwayman, I must make bold to borrow a little money out of your waggon; therefore, if you have any, direct me to it, that I may not lose any time, which you know is always precious. The carrier told him he had nothing but cumbersome goods in his waggon, that he knew of; but, however, if he would not believe him, he might search every box and bundle there, if he pleased.

Ovet soon got into the waggon, and threw all the boxes and bundles about, till, at last, he came to the soap barrel, which feeling somewhat heavy, he said to the carrier, what do you do with this nasty commodity in your waggon? I'll fling it away. So throwing it on the ground, the hoops burst, out flew the head, and the soap spreading abroad, the bag appeared; then jumping out of the waggon, and taking it up, said he again, is not he that sells this soap a cheating rascal, to put a bag of lead into it to make the barrel weigh heavy? If I knew where he lived, I'd go and tell him my mind. However, that he may not succeed in his roguery, I'll take it and sell it at the next house I come to, for it will wet one's whistle to the tune of two or three shillings.

He was going to ride away when the carrier cried after him. Hold, hold, sir! that is not lead in the bag; it is a hundred pounds, for which (if you take it away) I must be accountable. No, no, replied Ovet, this cannot be money; but if it is, tell the owner that I will be answerable for it if he will come to me. Where, sir, said the carrier, may one find you? Why truly, replied Jack, that is a question soon asked, but not so easily to be answered; the best direction I can give is, it is likely that you may find me in a jail before night, and then, perhaps, you may have again what I have taken from you, and forty pounds to boot.

Another time, Ovet meeting with the Worcester stage coach on the road, in which were several young gentlewomen, he robbed them all; but one of them being a very handsome person, he was struck with admiration, and when he took her money from her, said, madam, cast not your eyes down, neither cover your face with those modest blushes; your charms have softened my temper, and I am no longer the man I was: what I have taken from you (through mere necessity at present) is only borrowed; for as no object on earth ever had such effect on me as you, assure yourself, that if you please to tell me where I may direct to you, I will, upon my honour, make good your loss to the very utmost. The young gentlewoman told him where he might send to her; and then parting, it was not above a week after that Ovet sent a letter to the young lady, who had gained such an absolute conquest over his soul that his mind now ran as much upon love as robbery.

Unfortunately, however, the sentimental attachment of our too susceptible highwayman was doomed to suffer a defeat; and still more unfortunately, he was quite as unsuccessful in his profession : for, committing a robbery in Leicestershire, where his comrade was killed in the attempt, he was closely pursued by the county, apprehended, and sent to jail; and at the next Leicester assizes condemned. Whilst under sentence of death, he seemed to feel no remorse at all for his wickedness, nor in the least to repent of the blood of two persons which he had shed. So being brought to the gallows, on Wednesday the 5th of May, 1708, he was justly hanged, in the 32nd year of his age.

THOMAS DORBEL

WAS bred a glover; but before he had served one half of his time, ran off from his master, and coming to London, soon became acquainted with men of dispositions similar to his own. About the age of seventeen, Tom ventured to appear upon the highway, but was outwitted in his first attempt.

Meeting a Welchman, he demanded Taffy's money, or he would take his life. The Welchman said, hur has no money of hur own, but has threescore pounds of hur master's money; but, Cot's blood! hur must not give hur master's money,—what would hur master say for hur doing so? Tom replied, you must not put me off with your cant; for money I want, and money I will have, let it be whose it will, or expect to be shot through the head. The Welshman then delivered the money, saying, what hur gives you is none of hur own; and that her master may not think hur has spent hur money, hur requests you to be so kind as to shoot some holes in hur coat lappets, that hur master may see hur was robbed. So suspending his coat upon a tree, Tom fired his pistol through it, Taffy exclaiming, Gots splatter a nails! this is a pretty pounce; pray give hur another pounce for hur money! Tom fired another shot through his coat. By St. Davy, this is a better pounce than the other! pray give hur one pounce more! I have never another pounce left cried Tom. Why then, replied the Welshman, hur has one pounce left for hur, and if hur will not give hur hur money again, hur will pounce hur through hur body. Dorbel very reluctantly but quietly returned the money, and was thankful that he was allowed to depart.

But this narrow escape did not deter Dorbel, and he continued his villanies for the space of five years.

It happened, however, that a gentleman's son was taken for robbing on the highway, and as he had been formerly pardoned, he now despaired of obtaining mercy a second time. Tom undertook, for the sum of five hundred pounds, to bring him off.

The one half was paid in hand, and the other half was to be paid immediately the deliverance was effected. When the young gentleman came upon his trial, he was found guilty, but just as the judge was about to pass sentence, Tom cried out, Oh! what a sad thing it is to shed innocent blood! Oh! what a sad thing it is to shed innocent blood! And continuing to reiterate the expression, he was apprehended, and the judge interrogating him what he meant by such an expression, he said, may it please your lordship, it is a very hard thing for a man to die wrongfully; but one may see how hard mouthed some people are, by the witnesses swearing that this gentleman now at the bar robbed them, on the highway at such a time, when indeed, my lord, I was the person that committed the robbery.

Accordingly, Tom was taken into custody, and the young gentleman liberated. He was brought to trial at the following assizes; and being asked whether he was guilty or not, he pleaded not guilty. Not guilty, replied the judge; why, did not you, at the last assizes, when I was here, own yourself guilty of such a robbery ?   I don't know, said Tom, how far I was guilty then, but upon my word, I am not guilty now; therefore if any person can accuse me of committing such a robbery, I desire they may prove the same.   No witness appearing, he was ac-quitted.

Tom, living at such an extravagant rate in the prison, had scarcely any part of the five hundred pounds remaining when he obtained his liberty; therefore, endeavouring to recruit his funds, by rob-bing the duke of Norfolk near Salisbury, his horse was shot and he himself taken, and condemned at the next assizes.   While under sentence he found a lawyer who engaged, for the sum of fifty guineas, to gain his pardon. He accordingly rode to London, was successful, and just arrived in time with the pardon, when Dorbel was about to be thrown off, having rode so hard that his horse immediately drop-ped down dead.   Such, however, was Tom's ingrati-tude, that he refused to pay the lawyer, alleging, that any obligation given by a man under sentence of death was not valid.

Dorbel was so much alarmed upon his narrow escape from a violent death, that he resolved to abandon the collecting trade, and obtained a situa-tion in several families as a footman. He also served six or seven years with a lady in Ormond street, who had a brother, a merchant in Bristol, whose only daughter, a girl sixteen years of age, prevailed upon her father to allow her to come to London to perfect her education.   Dorbel being a person to whom her aunt thought she could place unlimited confidence, was sent to convey the young lady to London. In the last stage he was left alone with her, when the miscreant first shockingly abused her, then robbed her of her gold watch, diamond ring, jewels to the amount of one hundred pounds, and cutting a hole in the back of the coach, escaped, leaving the young lady in a swoon. It was with difficulty she recovered, to inform her relations how she had been treated. Her mother hastened to town to see her, and after speaking a few words to her, the poor girl breathed her last. The disconsolate father soon after lost his senses.

Dorbel was pursued in different directions, and apprehended just as he had robbed a gentleman of three pounds five shillings. He was tried, and condemned to be executed and hung in chains; which well merited sentence was put in force against this hardened villain, on the 23d of March, 1708.

DICK ADAMS.

THE parents of this worthless fellow lived in Gloucestershire, and gave him an education suited to his station. Leaving the country, and coming to London, the abode of the most distinguished virtue as well as the most consummate villany, he was introduced into the service of a great duchess at St. James's, and stayed there two years. He was at last dismissed for improper conduct; but while he remained there, he had obtained a general key which opened the lodgings in St. James's. Accordingly, he went to a mercer, and desired him to send, with all speed, a parcel of the best brocades, satins, and silks, for his duchess, that she might select

N

some for an approaching drawing-room. Having often gone on a similar errand, the mercer instantly complied. His servant, and a porter to carry the parcels, accompanied Dick, and when arrived at the gate of some of the lodgings, he said, let's see the pieces at once, for my duchess is just now at leisure to look at them. So receiving the parcel, he conveyed it down a back stair, and went clear off. After waiting with great impatience for two or three hours, the porter and the man returned home, much lighter than when they came out.

About a month after, one evening when Dick had taking his glass pretty freely, he unfortunately came by the mercer's shop, while the mercer was standing at the door; the latter recollected and instantly seized him, saying, oh, sir, have I caught you! you're a fine spark, indeed! to cheat me out of two hundred pounds' worth of goods! but before I part with you, I shall make you pay dearly for them! Adams was not a little surprised at being so unexpectedly taken; but instantly seeing the bishop of London coming up in his carriage, he said to the mercer, I must acknowledge I have committed a crime to which I was forced by extreme necessity; but I see my uncle, the bishop of London, coming this way in his coach; therefore, I hope, that you'll be so civil as not to raise an hubbub of a mob about me, by which I should be exposed and utterly undone: I'll go and speak to his lordship about the matter, if you please to step with me; and I'll engage he shall make you satisfaction for the damage I have done you.

The mercer eager to receive his money, and considering his proposal a better method than sending

him to jail, consented. Adams went boldly up, desired the coachman to stop, and requested a word
or two with his lordship. When he saw him in the
dress of a gentleman, he was pleased to listen to
him, upon which Adams said, asking your lordship's
pardon for my presumption, I make bold to acquaint
your reverence that the gentleman who stands behind me is an eminent mercer, and keeps a house
hard by, and is a very upright man; but he is a
great reader of books of divinity, especially pole-
mical pieces, and he has therein met with some intricate cases, which very much trouble him, and his
conscience cannot be at rest until his doubts and
scruples are removed about them; I humbly ask,
therefore, that your lordship would vouchsafe him
the honour of giving him some ease before he runs
utterly to despair.

The bishop, always ready to assist any person
troubled with scruples of conscience, requested
Adams to bring his friend to him the following day:
but, said Adams, deferentially, it will be more satisfactory to the poor man, if your lordship will speak
to him yourself. Upon which the bishop bowing
to the mercer, the latter approached the coach, when
the bishop said, the gentleman has informed me of
all the matter about you, and if you please to give
yourself the trouble of coming to my house at Ful-
ham, I will satisfy you in every point. The mercer
made many thankful bows, and taking Adams to a
tavern, gave him a good entertainment.

The next morning, Adams waited upon the mercer, who was making out his bill to present to the
bishop, and his pretending that his coming in haste
to attend him to the bishop's house, had made him

forget to bring money with him, entreated him to lend him a guinea, and put it down in the bill. They went off to wait upon the bishop at the time appointed. After they were cheered in the parlour with a bottle of wine, the mercer was introduced to the bishop, who addressed him, saying, I understand that you have been much troubled of late; I hope that you are better now, sir? The mercer answered, my trouble is much abated since your lordship has been pleased to order me to wait upon you. Upon this he pulled out his pocket book, and presented his lordship with a bill containing several articles, and the borrowed guinea, amounting in all to two hundred and three pounds nineteen shillings and twopence.

His lordship stared upon the bill, and examining its contents, said, what means all this? The gentleman yesterday might very well say, that your conscience could not be at rest, and I wonder why it should, when you present a bill to me of which I know nothing. Your lordship, said the mercer with a bow and a scrape, was pleased last night to say, that you would satisfy me to-day. Yes, replied the prelate, and I would with respect to what the gentleman told me; who said that you were much troubled about some points in religion, and desired to be resolved therein, in order to which, I appointed that you should come to-day. Truly, your worship's nephew told me otherwise; for he said you would pay *me* this bill of parcels, which, upon my word, he had of me, and in a very clandestine manner too, if I were to tell your lordship all the truth; but out of respect to your lordship, I will not disgrace your nephew. My nephew! he is none of my nephew! I never, to my knowledge, saw the man before in my life.

Dick, a short time after went into the life-guards, but as his pay would not support his expenditure, he sometimes resorted to the highway. In company with some of his companions upon the road, they robbed a person of a gold watch and a purse of a hundred and eight pounds. Not content with this booty, Adams went after the gentleman, saying, sir, you have a very fine coat on; I must make bold to exchange with you. As the gentleman rode onwards, he felt as if something was too heavy in his pockets, and to his inconceivable joy, found his watch and his money, which Adams, in his hurry, had forgot to remove out of the pocket of his own coat, when he made the exchange. But when Adams and his associates came to an inn, and sat down to examine their booty, to their unspeakable chagrin, they found that all was gone.

Adams and his companions went that very day to repair their loss, and attacked the stage coach, in which were several women, with whom, irritated by their recent misfortune, they were very rough and urgent. While Dick was searching the pockets of one of the women, she said, have more compassion on our sex? Certainly, you have neither Christianity, nor conscience, nor religion in you! Right, we have not much Christianity or conscience in us; but, for my part you shall soon find a little religion in me. So falling next upon her jewels and ear rings, indeed, madam, said Adams, supposing you to be an Egyptian, I must beg the favour of you, being a Jew, to borrow your jewels and earrings; and having robbed the ladies to the amount of two hundred pounds in money and other property, allowed them to proceed. After a course of depredations, Dick, in robbing a man between London and Brentford, was so closely pursued by the person who was robbed, and a neighbour he met upon the road, that in a little time afterwards he was apprehended, carried before a magistrate, committed to Newgate, tried, condemned, and executed, in March, 1713. Though rude and profligate before, he was penitent and devout after receiving his sentence.

WILLIAM GETTINGS,

Commonly called the Hereford Boy. His father was a grazier in Herefordshire; and he lived with him until he was sixteen years of age, and then came to London. Sometimes in the capacity of a footman and sometimes that of a butler, he spent five years in a very irreproachable manner. Unfortunately, however, he became acquainted with evil company, and was soon corrupted in principle, and became a rogue in practice.

He began his course under the name of William Smith, and traded in the smaller matters of pilfering. In the dress of a porter he one evening went into the house of a doctor of medicine, took down a rich bed and packed it up. In carrying it off, he fell down stairs, and had almost broke his neck. The noise alarmed the old doctor and his son, and they ran hastily to see what was the matter; whereupon Gettings, puffing and blowing as if he was quite of breath, perceiving them nearer than they should be, said to the doctor, Is not your name so and so? Yes, replied the doctor; and what then? Why, then, sir, said Gettings, there's one Mr. Hugh Hen Penhenribus has ordered me to carry these goods here (which have almost broken my back,) and take them away to a new lodging, which he has taken somewhere hereabouts. Mr. Hugh Penhenribus! replied the doctor again; and pray who is he? for, to the best of my knowledge, I don't know such a gentleman. I can't tell, said Gettings, but, indeed, the gentleman knows you, and ordered me to leave the goods here. I don't care, said the doctor, how well he knows me! I tell you I'll not take the people's goods, unless they were here themselves; therefore I say, carry them away! Nay, pray sir, said Gettings, let me leave the goods here, for I am quite weary already in bringing them hither. I tell you, replied the doctor, there shall be none left here; therefore take them away, or I'll throw them into the street! This was sufficient for Gettings: he asked the doctor to assist him in lifting them on his back, which he did, and the thief bore away his prize.

Scarcely was William gone, when the doctor's wife coming home from the market, and going into the room, she saw the bed taken down, and came running in a passion to her husband, exclaiming, why, truly, this is a most strange business, that I cannot stir out of doors, but you must be making some whimsical alteration or other in the house! What's the matter, replied the doctor, with the woman? Are you beside yourself? No, said the wife, but truly you are, in thus altering things a s you do, almost every moment! Certainly, my dear, replied the doctor, you must have been spending your market penny, or else you would not talk at that rate as you do, of alterations, when not the smallest have been made since you have been gone out. I am not blind, I think, retorted the wife, for I am sure the bed is taken out of the two-pair-of-stairs back room; and pray, husband, where do you design to put it now? The doctor and his son then went up stairs, and not only found that the bed was stolen, but that they had assisted the thief to carry it off.

Our hero next resolved to try his fortune upon the highway, and meeting with a sharper on the road, commanded him to stand and deliver! He robbed him of two pence half penny, when the sharper remarked, that the world was come indeed to a very sad pass, when one rogue must prey upon another.

He next robbed a man of twelve shillings and a pair of silver buckles. From thence he proceeded to rifle a stage coach, and took away some money and a silver watch. Not long after, he robbed Mr. Dashwood and his lady of a gold watch and some money.

These, however, were only smaller exhibitions of his dexterity. One evening, well mounted, he passed through Richmond, and perceiving a gentleman walking in the gardens, inquired of the gardener if he might be permitted to view the gardens, of which he had heard such favourable accounts.

The gardener well acquainted with the harmless vanity and benevolence of his master, granted his request. Giving his horse to the gardener, Gettings walked forward, and in a very respectable manner accosted the gentleman, who received him very courteously; when sitting down together in an arbour, Gettings said, your worship has got a fine diamond ring upon your finger.—Yes, replied the owner, it ought to be a very fine one, for it cost me a very fine price.—Why, then, said Gettings, it is the fitter to bestow upon a friend; therefore, if your worship pleases, I must make bold to take it and wear it for your sake. The gentleman stared at his impudence, but Gettings presented a pistol, and made a short process of the matter. Having taken the ring, the villain added, I am sure you do not go without a gold watch too. Making free with that also, and some guineas, he bound the gentleman, and went off with his booty, after requesting him to be patient, and he would send some person to set him at liberty.

When he came to the gate, he gave the gardener a shilling, informing him that Sir James wanted to speak to him. The botanical retainer accordingly went and untied his master, who with a grim smile returned him thanks for sending a robber into his own garden to plunder him.

Upon another day, Gettings undertook a long journey, for the express purpose of robbing the house of a friend: and being well acquainted with all parts of the house, was successful, and brought off money, plate, and goods, to a considerable amount.

He at last, in an unlucky moment, robbed a Mr. Harrison of four guineas, some silver, and a watch;

and being detected, was tried, condemned, and executed, on the 25th of September, 1713, at the age
of twenty-two.

EDWARD BONNET

WAs born of respectable parents in the isle of Ely,
in Cambridgeshire, received an education superior
to many of his companions, and when he was only
ten years old, gave the following proof of his promising genius :—

He was sent to the parson with a present of a
spare-rib of pork, wrapped up in a cloth in a basket.
He knocked with some degree of importance at the
door, which a servant answered, inquiring his business. I want to speak with your master. The
master came. Well, my dear, what is your business? Why, only my father has sent you this,
said young Ned; and gave him the basket, without
moving his hat. O fie! fie! child, have you no
manners? you should pull off your hat, and say,—
sir, my father gives his service to you, and desires
you to accept this small token. Come, go you out
again with the basket, and knock at the door, and
I'll let you in, and see how prettily you can perform
it. The parson waited within until his impatience
to receive and examine the contents of the basket
incited him to open the door. But Ned was at a
considerable distance, walking off with the present.
So ho! so ho, sirrah! where are you going? Home
sir, replied Ned, in an equally loud voice. Hey,
but you must come back and do as I bade you first

Thank you for that, sir, I know better than that; and if you teach me manners, I'll teach you wit. The father smiled at the story, and retained his spare-rib.

At the age of fifteen, Bonnet was sent apprentice to a grocer, served his time with credit, was afterwards married to a young woman in the neighbourhood, and continued in business till he had acquired about six hundred pounds.

Unfortunately, however, he was reduced to poverty by an accidental fire. Unable to answer the pressing demands of his creditors, he left the place, and came up to London. Here he soon became acquainted with a band of highwaymen, and began with them to seek from the highway what had been lost by fire.

Nor did he long continue in the inferior walks of his new profession, but providing himself with a horse which he taught to leap over ditch, hedge, or toll-bar, and to know all the roads in the country, whether by day or night, he quickly became the terror of Cambridgeshire.

Upon this horse, he one day met a Cantabrigian, who was possessed of more money than good sense, morality, or wit, in a calash with a dashing courtesan. Ned commanded the student to stand and deliver. Unwilling to show his cowardice before his companion, he refused. Without any respect for the venerable university to which he belonged, Ned by violence took from him about six pounds, and presenting a pair of pistols, constrained the hopeful pair to strip themselves, then bound them together, and giving the horse a lashing, the animal went off

at full trot with them to the inn to which he belonged.

No sooner did these Adamites enter the town,
than men, women, and children, came hallooing,
shouting, and collecting the whole town to behold
such an uncommon spectacle. The student was
expelled for disgracing the university, and the courtesan was sent to the house of correction.

Humerous Ned next met with a tailor and his
son, who had arrested him for five pounds. He
commanded him to surrender, and received thirty-
five pounds in place of his five. I wonder, said the
innocent son, what these fellows think of themselves? Surely they must go to the place below
for committing those notorious actions. God for-
bid, replied the tailor, for to have the conversation
of such rogues there, would be worse than all the
rest.

Ned's next adventure was with an anabaptist
preacher, whom he commanded to deliver up his
purse and scrip. The latter began by reasonings,
ejaculations, and texts, to avert the impending evil.
Ned instantly put himself in a great passion, and
replied, pray, sir, keep your breath to cool your por-
ridge, and don't talk of religions matters to me, for
I'll have you to know, that, like all other true bred
gentlemen. I believe nothing at all of religion;
therefore deliver me your money, and bestow your
laborious cant upon your female auditors, who never scold their maids without cudgelling them with
broken pieces of scriptures. Whereupon, taking a
watch and eight guineas, he tied his legs under his
horse, and let him depart.

On another occasion, Bonnet and a few associates met a nobleman and four servants in a narrow pass, one side of which was enclosed by a craggy and shattered rock, and the other by an almost impenetrable wood, rising gradually considerably higher than the road, and accosted him in his usual style. The nobleman pretended that he supposed they were only in jest, and said, 'that if they would accompany him to the next inn, he would give them a handsome treat.' He was soon informed that they preferred the present to the future. A sharp dispute ensued, but the nobleman and his men were conquered; and the lord was robbed of a purse of gold, a gold watch, a gold snuff box, and a diamond ring.

Being conducted into the adjacent wood, and bound hand and foot, the robbers left them, saying, 'they would bring them more company presently. Accordingly they were as good as their word, for in less than two hours they increased the number to twelve, on which Ned said, 'there are now twelve of you, all good men and true; so bidding you farewell, you may give in your verdict against us as you please, when we are gone, though it will be none of the best; but to give us as little trouble as possible, we shall not now stay to challenge any of you. So once more, farewell.'

Ned Bonnet and his comrades now going to the place of rendezvous, to make merry with what they had got, which was at a by sort of an inn standing somewhat out of the high-road between Stamford and Grantham, it happened at night to rain very hard, so that Mr. Randal, a pewterer, living near Marygold alley in the Strand, before it was burnt down, was obliged to put in there for shelter.

Calling for a pot of ale, on which was the innkeep-er's name, which was also Randal, the pewterer asked him, being his namesake, to sit and bear him company.

They had not been long chatting, before Ned and one of his comrades came down stairs, and placed themselves at the same table; and under-standing the name of the stranger, one of the rogues, fixing his eyes more intently than ordinary upon him, in a seeming joy leaped over the table, and embracing the pewterer, exclaimed, ' dear Mr. Randal, who would have thought to have seen you here ? it is ten years, I think, since I had the hap-piness to be acquainted with you.'

Whilst the pewterer was recollecting whether he could call this to mind or not, for it came not into his memory that he had ever seen him in his life, the highwayman again cried out, ' Alas, Mr. Ran-dal, I see now I am much altered, since you have forgotten me.' Here, being arrived at a *ne plus ultra*, up started Ned, and with as great apparent joy, said to his companion, ' Is this Harry, the ho-nest gentleman in London, whom you so often used to praise for his great civility and liberality to all people ? Surely then we are very happy in meet-ing thus accidentally with him."

By this discourse they would almost have per-suaded Mr. Randal that they perfectly knew him, but being sensible of the contrary, he very serious-ly assured them that he could not remember that he had ever seen any of them in his life. ' No, said they, struck with seeming astonishment; it is strange that we should be so altered within these few years.

But to evade further ill-timed questions, the rogues insisted upon Mr. Randal's supping with them, which invitation he was by no means permitted to decline.

By the time they had supped, in came four more of Ned's comrades, who were invited also to sit down, and more provisions were called for, which were quickly brought, and as rapidly devoured.

When the fury of consuming half a dozen good fowls and other victuals was over, besides several flasks of wine, there was not less than three pounds in money to pay. At this they stared on each other, and held a profound silence, whilst Mr. Randal was fumbling in his pocket. When they saw that he only brought forth a mouse from the mountain of money the thieves hoped to find piled in his pocket, which was only as much as his stake, he that pretended to know him started up, and protested that he should be excused for old acquaintance sake; but the pewterer, not willing to be beholden, as indeed they never intended he should, to such companions, lest for this civility they should be expecting greater obligations from him, pressed them to accept his dividend of the reckoning, saying, if they thought it equitable he would pay more.

At last one of them, tipping the wink, said, 'Come, come, what needs this ado? Let the gentleman, if he so pleases, present us with this small treat, and do you give him a larger at his taking farewell in the morning.' Mr. Randal not liking this proposal, it was started that he and Ned should throw dice to end the controversy; and fearing that he had got into ill company, to avoid mischief, Randal acquiesced to throw a main who should pay the whole shot, which was so managed that the lot fell upon Randal, having the voice of the whole board against him, was deputed to pay the whole reckoning; though the dissembling villains vowed and protested that they had rather it had fallen to any of them, that they might have had the honour of treating him.

Mr. Randal concealed his discontent at these objectionable tricks as well as he could; and they perceiving he would not engage in gaming, but counterfeited drowsiness, and desired to be abed, the company broke up, and he was shown to his lodgings, which he barricadoed as well as he could, by putting old chairs, stools, and tables against the door. Going to bed and putting the candle out, he fell asleep; but was soon awakened by a strange walking up and down the room, and an outcry of murder and thieves.

At this unusual noise he leaped out of bed and run to the door, to see whether it was fast or not: and finding nothing removed (for the thieves came into a chamber by a trap door which was behind the curtains) he wondered how the noise should be there in his apartment, unless it was enchanted; but as he was about to remove the barricade to run and raise the house, he was surrounded by a crew who tied and gagged him, and then took away all his clothes, and left him to shift for himself as well as he could.

One day having the misfortune to have his horse shot under him. Bonnet embraced the first opportunity to select a gelding from the man who kept the Red Lion Inn He was now equipped in a first style, and rode into Cambridgeshire, where he met with a gentleman, who informed him that he had nearly been robbed, and requested him to ride with him for protection. As a highwayman is never

out of his way, he complied, and, at a convenient place
levied a contribution, as protector of his companion,
by emptying his pocket of ninety guineas. He,
however, had the kindness to leave him half a crown
to carry him to the next town.

After committing about a hundred robberies, another thief was apprehended, who in order to save
his own life, informed against Bonnet, who was apprehended at his own residence, and sent to Newgate, and at the next assizes carried down to Cambridge, sentenced and executed before the Castle, on
the 28th March, 1713, to the great joy of the county, which had suffered severely by his depredations.

JOHN PRICE.

THE depravity of human nature was exemplified in
its full extent in the character of John Price. The
indigence and profligacy of his parents were such,
that he received no education, and he was sent into
the world to shift for himself at the age of seven.
Before this period, he was a proficient both in curs-
ing and lying. It is rather a singular fact, that his
habitual lying was once the means of saving his life.

About the age of eighteen, he was serving a gentleman in the country, who turned him off for his
notorious falsehoods. In going to London, he robbed a woman of eighteen shillings, was apprehended
in the act, and convicted. But his late master, who
was sheriff, took pity upon his situation, and saved
his life. Informed of this, the judges at the next
assizes blamed the gentleman's conduct for allowing

o

a man to escape who had pleaded guilty. The
sheriff acknowledged that such a man had been condemned at the last assizes; but then, he knew the
fellow to be such an unaccountable liar, that there
was no believing one word he said; so his pleading
guilty to what was laid to his charge, was in his
opinion a sufficient reason for his being believed innocent of the fact, and he would not hang an innocent man for the world. This reply made the
judges smile; he was dismissed with a severe re-
primand, and cautioned not to come before them
again.

When Price obtained his liberty, he went to London; associated with a band of robbers, and in a
short time was apprehended for diving into another
person's pocket instead of his own, and for that
crime committed to Newgate. He was sentenced to
be severely whipped, and sent on board a man of
war; but after he had received the punishment
awarded to theft from the sailors, he was dismissed
from the ship.

He hastened forthwith to London, joined another
gang of thieves, and abandoned himself to all manner of wickedness. On one occasion the crew divided themselves into three companies. They first
met an attorney, whom they robbed of eight guineas.
The unfortunate lawyer had not gone far when he
was attacked by the second party, to whom he related his misfortunes, and into what cruel hands he
had fallen. 'Cruel?' cried one of them; 'how
dare you use these terms? And who made you
so bold as to talk to us with your hat on? Pray,
sir, be pleased henceforward, to learn more manners.' They then snatched off his hat and wig,

and took a diamond ring from his finger. As
he was plodding his way home, uncertain which
road was safest, the third division came up with
him near Kentish Town, bringing with them a man
whom they pretended to have completely stripped,
and constrained the lawyer to clothe naked with his
own coat and waistcoat; they told him he might be
thankful to get off with his life, which he employed
in sowing division amongst society.

In a short time after this, Price and a companion
one evening entered a garret, in which there was
nothing but lumber, with the intention of robbing
the house when all was silent. But in the dark, as
Price was laying his hand upon a pistol which he
had placed upon a table, it went off, and alarmed
the people of the house. His comrade instantly
ran to the window, where they fastened a ladder of
ropes for their escape, and his companion attempting to slide down, the rope soon broke, though he
was not so much injured but that he got away.
Price seeing the extreme danger of being caught,
removed the rope to another window, and it conveyed him to a balcony. He was however, scarcely
there, when all the people in the house were alarmed; on which he leaped into a large basket of eggs
which a man was carrying on his head from Newgate market; so that the fall being broken, he was
able to make his escape, amid the cry of ' thieves!'

Jack now began to be so well known about town
that he found it necessary to remove to the country. He was there most industrious in stripping
the hedges of all the linen he found upon them.
Putting up at an inn, the landlord soon understood
from his discourse that he was a servant who would

suit him, and therefore hired him as his tapster. It was this miscreant landlord's custom to murder travellers who put up at his house ; but one gentleman being warned by a maid of his danger, provided for his safety.

Among other things the maid informed him that it was usual for the landlord to ring a bell, on which an assassin, pretending to be a servant, entered the chamber and snuffed out the candle, when the other villains rushed in and murdered the stranger. The gentleman caused the maid to place a lantern with a candle in it under a stool, and he laid his arms ready, and stood upon his guard. Scarcely had he sat himself down, when it happened as the girl had mentioned ; but the gentleman, with the assistance of his servant, killed two of the villains, and put the rest to flight. He then seized the innkeeper and his wife, carried them before a magistrate, and they were indicted to stand trial at the next assizes. From the maid's desposition it appeared that fourteen strangers had been murdered by them, and that their bodies were concealed in an arched vault in the garden, to which there was a passage from the cellar. Both were executed, and the innkeeper hung in chains.

Jack having once more escaped death, returned to his pilfering trade, was committed to Newgate, and was whipped for his crimes. But Jack was now determined to follow the examples of the great ones of the earth, and to better his circumstances by marriage. Accordingly, he married one of the name of Betty, who gained her livelihood by running errands to the prisoners of Newgate. Nor was Jack, like too many, disappointed in his matri-

monial connexion, for he was soon elevated to be
hangman to the county of Middlesex. In this station he assumed great importance, and held a levee
every day that he did business at Tyburn; but
though he sometimes ran in debt, yet he was always very willing to work in order to pay his obligations. But envy reached even him, and he lost
his place by means of one who had great ministe-
rial interest. But Jack could never be destitute
while he had hands to lay hold of whatever was
within his reach.

He at last suffered for having assaulted a watchman's wife, whom he met in Bunhill Fields, and
used in such a barbarous manner that she died in
a few days of her wounds. Two men suddenly
came up to him, and, being seized, he was secured
in Newgate. After his trial and condemnation he
remained impenitent, and endeavoured, by intoxication, to stifle the forebodings of conscience. He
was hanged on the 31st of May, 1711.

HENRY SIMMS, *alias* THE YOUNG GENTLE-
MAN HARRY.

WE give the life of this person in his own language :—

I am now thirty years of age, was born in London,
October 19, 1716, of honest industrious parents, in
the parish of St. Martin's in the Fields. Having
the misfortune to lose my father and mother when
very young, I was left to the care of an indulgent
grandmother, who tenderly loved me, had me edu-

cated with maternal fondness, and early began to instil into me sentiments of virtue, honour, and honesty, from which I too early swerved. My grandmother having been many years in the service of a nobleman, was an old servant much respected, and on that account indulged not only with a permission to have me with her, but was likewise indulged with my being permitted to go to Eton school with the two sons of the noble lord. I remained at Eton school some time, and even there began to show an early inclination to vice, without an opportunity of committing it. When I arrived at the age of fourteen, my grandmother put me apprentice to a breeches-maker, but a life of servitude ill suited my constitution. I stayed with him no longer than a month, in which time I procured to myself several choice acquaintances, particularly two, (since hanged) and was easily persuaded to accompany them in many robberies, which we committed in and about Mary-le-bone fields, and the money we got riotously, we spent among thieves and bullies, and when that was gone, turned out (as we called it) for more.

Thus some months passed on in a round of wickedness which not all the counsel in the universe could restrain. My poor grandmother, with tears in her eyes, entreated {me to leave off my wicked course and to follow her advice. But I little regarded her instructions, and still pursued my own schemes.

There was hardly a place round London famed for wickedness, but I was there. Tottenham Court fair, when it came I rejoiced at, for there I lived riotously, and there too I became a proficient in the dexterous art of picking pockets, by which I gained for some time pretty handsomely. But at length that business grew dead, and, as I lived at a large rate, money was wanting. Accordingly, having mustered up a sufficient quantity of cash, I purchased a pair of pistols, and a horse, and set out; and in Epping forest, near Woodford, I stopped two gentlemen in a chaise and pair, from whom I only took a little silver, and proceeded to Newmarket, were I arrived that night, and early next morning set out again, stopped the Norwich coach, and took from the passengers thirty guineas, a gold watch, and a diamond ring, and then rode away; and about three hours after, near Littlebury, met the Cambridge coach, from the passengers of which I took about five pounds and came on for London. I now began to frequent a celebrated gaming house in Covent garden, where, for several nights, I had a prodigious run of good luck, and won a considerable sum of money. I bought a silver-hilted sword for myself, had several new suits of clothes made, particularly one suit of black velvet, and appeared at my usual haunts with my surprising eclat. It was at this time I gained the name of gentleman Harry, for though I was before only called plain Harry, yet, on this my sudden grand appearance, I was styled gentleman Harry, which name I retained for ever. But fortune not continuing her favours to me at the gaming table, I was now reduced, and obliged to take up again my old trade. Hitherto, what business I had done was by myself; but being out one day with a companion of mine, we agreed to attack the first person with powder and shot. We saw nothing for some days that we either cared or dared to attack, till we came to a place called Eversley bank, where we met a collector of Shrewsbury; we ordered him to stand and deliver, and took from him near three hundred pounds. For this robbery two men were taken up a short time after, tried at the assizes, capitally convicted, and executed; and I cannot but own, that notwithstanding my hardened villany, so often as I remember it, I felt great sorrow at being the cause of shedding innocent blood, which I always avoided and abhorred.

About a month after this, I robbed a lady in her coach, on Blackheath. After this robbery, riding down the hill that leads to Lewisham wash, I was overtaken by six or seven butchers, one of whom, seizing the cape of my coat, pulled me off my horse, and the cape giving way, he tore it quite off. I then pulled out my pistols, swearing I would shoot the first man that dared to advance; which none of them cared to do. I retreated into the fields, and got off with the loss of my horse, which cost me seventeen pounds. But I was not long without a horse, for, going towards Bromley, I met a gentleman on horseback, to whom I presented my pistols, ordering him to dismount or I would shoot him through the head, which he did, and I took from him eight guineas and seventeen shillings in silver, and, mounting the horse left him to pursue his journey on foot. I sold the horse the next day, at the George, in Farnham, and bought another, which cost me thirteen guineas. From thence I proceeded to Tunbridge, at which place I stayed a day or two, and then came to London, where I found an old companion, a sailor, who agreed to turn out with me. At the bottom of Shooter's hill, we robbed a gentleman of his gold watch, and about seventeen pounds; the watch I afterwards sold for nine pounds at the gaming-table in Covent garden, and lost the money when I had done.

Being by this time pretty well known, I ran numerous hazards; it was but a few days after I lost my money as above, I was attacked by several soldiers in Drury-lane, and had been carried to the Savoy, had I not been rescued by some friends from Covent garden; and in about a week after that, I was taken out of a tavern for the robbery of a gold watch which I had about me, and was again rescued by my companions. Some little time after this I was attacked by about nine gentlemen thief takers, in Bridewell walk, Clerkenwell, but having my pistols about me, I soon dispersed the cowardly rascals and walked off. Another time, riding through Covent-garden, I was pursued by a party of thief takers, but got clear.

Being in this manner continually beset on all sides, I was at length, by the perfidy of some ladies with whom I was in company at Goodman's Fields' Wells, taken by a parcel of thief takers, and conducted to Clerkenwell Bridewell, where several prosecutions were commenced against me, and I was obliged to come to a composition with divers of them, which drained me very low. One gentleman, in particular, whom I had robbed of eleven shillings and a medal, made me pay him forty-seven guineas. By these means, I god rid of my several prosecutors, but was, by the order of the court of justice, confined in Clerkenwell Bridewell two months for an assault, at the end of which time I

was set at liberty, giving sureties for my good behaviour for two years. Shortly after my release
from confinement I was pressed and sent on board
his majesty's ship the Rye, where I continued for
about three months, though much against my inclination. I was continually forming some scheme
for an escape, not one of which took an effect till
the following was hit upon. Whilst we were at
Leith, we had pressed several hands out of some
collieries, who, I found by talking to, were as little
desirous of staying on board as myself; I therefore
proposed to eight of them this scheme ;—that when
the cutter, which had been on shore pressing, came
alongside at night, one of them should fall out of
the main chains into the river, and the rest of us
should immediately jump into the boat, and take
the man up, and row away, which we put in practice with success, only, just as we got up our man,
the boatswain jumped on board and threatened us.
My companions were for throwing him overboard,
but as he promised to be quiet they were overruled,
and he was suffered to sit still ; several guns were
fired after us, but we rowed safe to shore, and took
leave of each other ; they set out for Scarborough,
and I for Edinburgh, in which city I staid about a
week, and during that time I became acquainted
with a Scotch lass, who not only furnished me with
money to purchase my former implements, but lent
me seven guineas to bear my expenses to London,
which lasted me no farther than Grantham; and
between Grantham and Stamford I was compelled
to *speak* with the York stage, from the passengers
of which I took eight guineas, about a pound in

silver, a silver watch, and three plain rings, with which I came to London.

In a short space of time after this I committed many robberies by myself, which I did not exactly minute down. My general rendezvous was about Epping Forest, where I robbed the Harwood coach, the Cambridge coach, &c., to a very considerable amount, but which I spent as fast as I received it. About this time, I kept company with another man's wife, who was so fond of me, that I could persuade her either out of cash or any valuables she had, to supply my present necessities ; as was the case when I persuaded her out of her gold watch, and some other things which her husband had me taken up for, and I was committed to Newgate, tried at the Old Bailey, and acquitted by the court, who very justly saw through the prosecution. Shortly after I was discharged on this affair, I unluckily, in a quarrel, ran a crab stick into a woman's eye in the New Prison. In the meantime, I was informed that the wife was arrested on an action, and sent to a sponging house. Being determined to relieve her, if possible, I contrived in what manner I could make my escape, and, accordingly, by the help of sheets I let myself down out of my room, and so escaped. I went to a friend of mine in Leather-lane, who furnished me with two pistols, with which I went to the above mentioned house in Gray's Inn Lane, expecting to find my lady ; but when I arrived there I found she had been removed to Newgate. As I was disappointed, and no hopes of releasing her from Newgate, I determined to pursue my old trade.

In Broad street, St. Giles', about nine at night, I

stopped a coach which contained a single gentleman, from whom I took about seventeen shillings, and from thence went to my old haunts in Covent Garden, and after drinking pretty freely, I had a quarrel with a gentleman, who calling the watch to his assistance, I was taken and carried to Covent Garden round house.

Being very much fuddled, I soon went to sleep; but when I awaked next morning, and found myself in a prison, after having escaped from one but the night before, I was almost distracted, and began to contrive to escape, but to no purpose : for after calling for the keeper of the round house, under pretence of being hungry, I got some toast and ale and therewith a knife, with which I hoped once more to make a breach whereby to escape. But I was doomed to be disappointed : for notwithstanding my cutting down the plaster and lath of the ceiling, the joists were so firm that I could not make any opening. I then grew desperate, broke all the things I could find in the room, cut the sheets to pieces, pulled off some tiles from the roof, and did every offensive act in my power, till at length the constable with a large posse of myrmidons arrived, who carried me before Sir Thomas De Veil, where, after a long examination, I laid my information of robbery of Mr. Smith in Southwark, which robbery I was actually concerned in, though not with the persons I swore against at Croydon assizes, but with three others.

We committed the robbery in December, 1745, getting in at the two pair of stairs window by a Jacob, that is, a ladder of ropes, which was fixed to the sign-post first, drawn afterwards into the balcony, and then attached to the two pair of stairs window.

We took from Mr. Smith's house, after having frightened Mrs Smith almost to death, two bags of money, containing £514. and a 20l. bank note, and carried off in bags, goods to the value of 800l.

The cash we divided equally amongst us at a house in the mint: the plate we sold; and we carried the goods to a house near the Pindar of Wakefield, near Pancras; but for my share of the goods I never received one penny: they were carried to Ireland by my three accomplices, who promised to remit me my part, but were never so good as their words. After my examination I was removed to the New Gaol, Southwark, to give evidence at the assizes at Croydon.

After this affair at Croydon, I was removed by habeas to Newgate, on the oath of a barber at Westminster, whom I had robbed, which barber was found out by some of my enemies to prosecute me; and upon this indictment I was tried, found guilty, and sentenced to transportation; and, about two months after, was with several other convicts put on board the Italian Merchant, which carried us to Maryland.

On our passage I had formed several plans for an escape, one of which had nearly been successful, and was agreed upon between me and the rest of the transports. We were at a certain time to have secured the captains and sailors, as well as the fire arms, and to have run away with the ship, but one of them discovered it to the captain, who put us under arrest during the remainder of the voyage. When we arrived at Maryland, I was disposed of to the mas-

ter of the Two Sisters, who was in want of sailors,
and with whom I went to sea. We had not been out
many days before we were taken by a privateer of
Bayonne, and carried into Spain. We were all sent
on shore, and had papers given us to go to Portugal.
When I arrived at Oporto, I was pressed on board
his majesty's ship the King Fisher, where I remained about four months, in which time we took several
prizes. But not liking my station, I left her at
Oporto, travelled to Lisbon, and got in the Packet
to Falmouth, where I stayed about a month. My
companions endeavoured to persuade me to go a
privateering with them in the Warran gallery; but
I refused, and leaving Falmouth travelled to St.
Ives, where I found a vessel ready to sail for
Bristol, on board of which I went, and arrived at
Bristol in two days. I was not 'long there before I
determined to set up my old trade, and procured a
pair of pistols, though I still wanted a horse; but
having observed several horses in a field near Law-
ford's gate, I soon marked out one for myself, and
that night got into a stable, from whence I stole a
saddle and a bridle, and without much difficulty
caught my horse, and set out for London.

When I reached London, I was soon informed
the thief takers were after me. That night I came
to town, I put my horse up at the White Swan, in
Whitechapel, but went no more near him, fearful,
as I had stolen him, he might be advertised. But,
I was not long without a horse, for one Saturday
night, about eight o'clock, coming from St. James's,
where I had been regaling with some friends, I perceived a boy in Rider street, walking a horse about,
apparently waiting for somebody. I called and per-

suaded him to step on an errand into Duke-street,
while I held the horse, and, as soon as the boy was
gone, I mounted and rode away, and crossing the
country, reached Harrow on the Hill, where I passed the night, and the next day set out towards
London, in hopes of meeting some of the farmers
returning from the hay markets, after having sold
their hay.

I had drunk pretty freely at dinner, and was
somewhat elevated. I had not ridden far before I
met three gentlemen, whom I commanded to stand
and deliver their money, which they did very quietly. From the first I got about three pounds, from
the second I received about five pounds, and from
the third only thirteen or fourteen shillings.

The next person I robbed was Mr. Sleep, my
prosecutor, and though neither he nor I recognised
each other at that time, yet he, it seems, has known
me from childhood. I took from him his watch
and six shillings, and immediately made off.

After robbing Mr. Sleep, I still kept travelling
towards London, in hopes of meeting the farmers.
At length, five of them made their appearance; I
boldly commanded them to stand, and took from
them about fifteen pounds in silver. I felt in their
pockets for watches, but they had none.

Next I met three men, whom I ordered to stand,
but they, not regarding my orders, refused, and rode
off at full speed, and I alongside of them, for at
least five or six minutes, presenting my pistol,
swearing I would shoot if they did not stop: but
they still rode on; and I turned from them, giving
them a hearty d—, not caring to let off my pistol;
for I had determined to shoot no man, unless he

attempted to take me. But after this, on the same road, I robbed two other men; from one I took about fifteen shillings, and about seven shillings from the other. Turning from them, I let off one of my pistols in the air, and went on for London.

That night I made a sort of perambulation among the thief-takers, determining to do mischief to some of them, if possible, especially to those who, I heard, had been after me. The first I went to, was W. H. in Chancery-lane. Being on horseback, I knocked at the door, which his wife opened, and demanded my business. I told her to speak with her husband. She replied, he was gone to bed, at the same time desiring to know my name and business. I am a gentleman of his acquaintance, said I; he will know me when he sees me. My blunderbuss, which I then carried, being mounted with brass, and having a brass barrel, by the light of her candle she perceived it, and directly slapped to the door, called to her husband and told him (mentioning my name) that I was at the door. I heard him ask for his piece, on which I cried out, you rascal, come to the door, and I'll piece you; and if he had come, I should certainly have killed him, but he thought better of it, and I rode away.

From my friend H. I went to another of the same sort of gentry in Holborn, of I. S. I got off my horse and went into his house threatening destruction; but the moment he saw me enter at one door, he went out at another, and after venting a few oaths, I remounted my horse, and went to the Greyhound inn, in Drury-lane, where I lay that night.

Next morning I set out for Epping Forest, and dined at the Bird-in-hand, at Stratford; after dinner, about two o'clock, I set out on the Romford road. I met in the forest a chaise, and from a man therein took about fourteen shillings. This robbery was done within sight of the Spread Eagle, at the door of which several people were drinking on horseback. From thence I rode through Ilford, then came on the forest again, and stayed till it was almost dark, and rode towards Laytonstone, within half a mile of which I robbed a captain of his gold watch, ten guineas and some silver. After speaking with the captain, I came off the forest towards London.

Perceiving a hurly-burly, and a great mob at Snaresbrook turnpike, I rode up to see what was the matter, and on enquiry amongst the mob, found that they had stopped a gentleman whom they mistook for me. As it was dark they could not distinguish me; I thought it the most prudent to ride through the turnpike, and go directly for London, which I did, and putting up my horse at the Saracen's Head, Aldgate, and calling a coach, I went to a tavern, where I lay that night.

In the morning I began to reflect that, it being well known that I was in England, returned from transportation, and as well known too, that I had committed a great many robberies, there were a many thief takers after me, and I was surrounded with danger; and I therefore determined to set out for Chester immediately, and from thence to Dublin; resolving, as I had now a handsome sum, as well as a parcel of diamond rings and watches, to live entirely upon my stock, and rob no more, at least while that lasted.

P

I dined that day at St. Alban's, and as I generally drank both at and after my meals, I soon grew warm, and after dinner, setting out for Dunstable, I found my resolution to rob no more would not hold, for within a quarter of a mile of Redbourne, I ordered three gentlemen to stand and deliver. Presenting my pistol at the first, he replied, that he would not be robbed, and rode on; the second hit me on the head with his whip, and at the same time the other rode by me.

Having a good beast under me, I was quickly up with them, and putting on one of my terrible countenances, with bitter imprecations I avowed that I would instantly shoot the first man dead who refused to deliver; when the first of them quietly gave me about nine shillings; from the second I took an old-fashioned watch and seventeen shillings; and from the third, two guineas and about five shillings; and taking my leave immediately, attacked two more gentlemen, who likewise rode for it; but their horses being as good as mine, I ran them into Redbourne, and then gave it up.

About an hour after, I stopped a single man on horseback, who told me he had but eighteen-pence, which I bade him keep; but as he seemed to have a better horse than mine, I made him dismount, and tendered mine in return. He had a portmanteau on his horse, which he was very industriously taking off, when I told him to let it remain where it was, which he did, although I had no opportunity to see what was in it; for being now become, perhaps, one of the most industrious of my profession, I could no more let a coach, chaise, or man pass without speaking with them in my way, than I could fly; and perceiving a coach come up, which proved to be the Warrington stage, I directly made to it, and received from the passengers therein about three pounds. The ladies seemed terribly frightened, and requested I would take my pistol away, which I did, and after taking their money I went on for Dunstable, and calling at several houses, before I reached there, I became pretty well fatigued, not only with my business, but also with the liquor I had drank. Being very much fuddled, I was so cunning as to think of putting up at the Bull Inn, at Dunstable, the very house where the Warrington coach went to. After dismounting my horse, and calling for a quartern of brandy, I saw some of the passengers in the kitchen, belonging to the coach I had just then robbed, on which, I never waited for my brandy, but went out of the house, mounted my horse, and rode as fast as I could make him go, till I came to Hockliffe, and as it rained very hard, I resolved to put up, and accordingly went into the Star Inn.

After I had been there about an hour, and had drank very freely, I became intoxicated, and fell asleep by the kitchen fire; but was soon awakened by three troopers and some others with pistols at my head, swearing they would shoot me if I offered to put my hand to my pockets. Being half asleep as well as drunk, they soon disarmed me.

They took from me one gold watch, two silver ones, four diamond rings, forty-seven guineas in gold, and four pounds in silver; three of the best diamond rings I had secreted in my neck-cloth. I desired them to give me my money again, and let me go to bed; they gave me about nine pounds in gold and silver back, and then conducted me to a chamber, where I went to bed, after putting my money under my pillow, and fell asleep, guarded by the troopers, who took my money from under my head, which, when I awoke and missed, I charged them with, telling them it was using me extremely ill indeed, as they had gotten so much from me already, to take that from me too; whereupon, they returned it to me. Presently, I got up and sat by the fireside, a good deal chagrined at my unfortunate fate.

I resolved in my mind a thousand different methods of escape, but none appeared feasible even to myself. At length a thought came into my head, of which I was resolved to make a trial. As I knew these troopers from their behaviour, to be hungry hounds, and having two seals, the one gold and the other silver, about me; as I sat over the fire, I determined to throw them in, naturally supposing from their eagerness after plunder, they would endeavour to get them out, and I might thus, by some means or other, become master of their fire arms.

It happened as I had imagined; eager for their prey they soused down to rake them from the ashes, when I, at the same time, snatched a pistol from one of their hands, and snapped it at his head; it missed fire, I was immediately overpowered by the rest of the troopers, the landlord and others coming to their assistance; and I was the next day carried before the justice at Dunstable, where I insisted upon the troopers returning me my money and watches, before I would answer any questions, and, accordingly, I undressed their pockets both of money and watches, asking them if they thought I had nothing else to do than venture my life to dress the pockets of such fellows as they, who knew not how to wind up a watch ; for in the attempt to wind up one of the watches they had broken it.

I was eventually committed to Bedford jail for the robbery of the Warrington stage coach, where I remained about four months, till I was removed by habeas corpus to Newgate, and in February last was tried at the Old Bailey for robbing Mr. Francis Sleep of his watch and six shillings, of which I was found guilty, and received sentence of death.

The above is an abstract containing all the most interesting or prominent transactions in the life of Henry Simms, who seems to have laboured in his vocation with a zeal worthy of a better calling, and with a wantonness deserving of the gallows, to which, at length, he was compelled to ascend.

Young Gentleman Harry was executed at Tyburn in June, 1747 ; and after hanging till he was dead, his body was cut down by a mob appointed for that purpose, and carried to a surgeon's in Covent Garden.

JAMES MACLAINE.

JAMES MACLAINE called in his own time by the distinguished title of ' the gentleman highwayman.' seemed at his birth to be far removed from the common temptations which too frequently lead to an infamous death. Until the decease of his father, which took place when he was about eighteen years of age, a fair prospect of prosperity was presented to him; which entitled him, by a slight straining of courtesy, to the designation of a gentleman ; he imbitbed, together, with an inordinate vanity, an aversion from business, and an immoderate desire to appear a gay young fellow.

Lauchlin Maclaine, the father of our adventurer, was a Presbyterian divine, and pastor of a congregation of that communion at Monaghan, in the North of Ireland. He designed James, his second son, for a merchant, and bestowed upon him a sound education, but died before he could put his intentions into effect of sending him to Rotterdam to be placed in the counting house of a Scotch merchant of his acquaintance.

Young Maclaine, the instant his father's breath was out of his body, proceeded to take possession and to dispose of his father's substance ; and treated with perfect contempt the remonstrances of his friends and relations, and the exhortations of his aunt, who, finding all her entreaties ineffectual took his only sister into her charge, and left him to pursue what course he pleased.

Thus left to himself, Maclaine forgot, altogether, the projected Dutch counting house, and equipped himself in the gayest apparel that part of the country could afford, and purchasing a gelding, set up fine gentleman at once, and in a twelvemonth dissipated almost the whole of his property. During his extravagancies, however, his ear had been frequently troubled with the remonstrances of his aunt and his other relations, which at length he found so disagreeable, that he was fain to set out for Dublin without communicating his intention to any one. It was here, it appears, that he first conceived the notion of making his fortune by marriage ; and having no disagreeable person, he gratuitously gave himself credit for more excellencies than, unfortunately, other people could discover in him. The demands for the maintenance of such an appearance as would realise his hopes of a rich marriage, soon swept away the small remainder of his property; and he had now full time to reflect on his folly and vanity, and to regret not a little having despised the advice of his relations, who had for some time turned a deaf ear to his entreaties by letter for a supply of money. But upon them, nevertheless, he felt was now his sole dependence. He had long spent his all—he was an entire stranger to a single individual of worth or substance in the place, and his credit and clothes, even to the last shirt, were gone. Selling his sword, therefore, the last piece of splendour that remained to him, he raised as much as would bear his charges on foot, and with a heavy heart set out to return to Monaghan, his native place.

Not a hand was outstretched to welcome the prodigal home again; his aunt refused to see him, all his other relations followed her example, and the companions of his former riots not only refused him relief but rendered him the sport and ridicule of the town. His sister, however, sometimes contrived to see him by stealth to give him her pocket money, but that could not long support him. Here, then, he must have inevitably starved, had not a gentleman on his way to England, passing through the town compassionately offered him the place of a servant who had recently died. Want, and the dread of starving, had by this time entirely banished all unnecessary or superfluous pride, and our young gentleman accepted the offer with joy. But, unhappily, the extreme pressure of want once removed, old thoughts return, old vanities are renewed; and so it was with Mr. Maclaine. His master's commands though uniformly softened by good-nature and benevolence, appeared to him as so many insults offered to his birth and breeding; it is no wonder, therefore, that in a few months he was discharged from his service. Depending on his sister, who was about to be married to a man of some wealth, he set out once more for Ireland, to endeavour to obtain enough from his relations to fit him out for America, or the West Indies; but here again he was doomed to disappointment. His sister's marriage had been broken off—she was unable to do any thing for him;—and his other relations, deeming themselves scandalised by his having been a footman, were even less tractable than before, treated him with great indignity, and finally refused all manner of assistance.

Again reduced to starvation, he was obliged to think of service as his only resource. With much difficulty he obtained a situation as butler to a gentleman near Cork, with whom he did not live long, being discharged for some breach of trust. Here he remained for many months out of place, wandering about, without any settled abode or means of subsistence, except occasional remittances from his elder brother, a pastor of the English congregation at the Hague, whose friendly assistance was less relished, because it was accompanied by warm remonstrances on the past, and wholesome advice on the future conduct of his life.

Fortune was at length favourable; his old master, though he refused him a character to another family; generously paid his passage to England, and also allowed him, for a limited period, after his landing, a shilling a day for subsistence.

Once again on this side of the water, his notions of gentility returned; he scorned being a menial servant; and valuing the minimum of his ambition at a pair of colours, he actually had the impudence to attempt to borrow the purchase money on the bond he had obtained from his master. This absurd scheme failing, he threw up his shilling a day in disgust, and heroically cast himself for support on a celebrated courtesan, a countrywoman of his own, who maintained him for some months in great magnificence, and enabled him to attend the public places with something like splendour.

But having disgusted this lady by his pusillanimous conduct in a rencontre with a certain peer,—who bestowed upon him a severe castigation, and very nearly ran him through the body, though he was much stronger, and as well armed,—he was once more without resources. His grandeur now suffered an eclipse for two or three months, and his last suit had been laid up in lavender, or in other words, pawned, when he inspired the regard of a lady of quality, the consequence of which was that for five or six months longer he flourished away as an idle fellow in the public places.

But Maclaine inwardly was not idle. He was extremely anxious for an independent settlement, and the thought of inveigling some woman of fortune by the charms of his person was still uppermost in his mind. Among other schemes to this

end, there was one he built upon as a very hopeful
and grateful plot he had laid for the daughter of his
patroness and benefactress, who had a considerable
fortune. But the young lady's waiting maid, who
had either more honesty than the Abigails in general are furnished with, or had not received the price
with which they are generally awarded, discovered
the affair to the old lady, who forthwith dismissed
Maclaine from her service; but when, in a few
months after, he was much reduced, she privately
bestowed upon him fifty pounds in order to fit him
out for Jamaica, where he had proposed to go and
seek his fortune, and where the lady was willing
enough that he should retire, that she might be free
from fears on her daughter's account.

But Maclaine was no sooner possessed of this
sum than he forgot his Jamaica expedition, and returned to his favourite scheme of fortune hunting:
for he never could rid himself of the idea that one
day or other he should succeed in the main object
of his existence. He released, therefore, his best
clothes from the durance vile into which they had
been plunged, and after various treaties with match
makers and chambermaids, relating to ladies of
great reputed fortunes, all which treaties ended in
disappointment, he reluctantly contracted his ambition, and made suit to the daughter of a considerable innkeeper and dealer in horses, with whom he
was fortunate enough to succeed, and whom he
married with her parents' consent and £500.

Here it would seem that Maclaine had laid aside
all thoughts of the fine gentleman, and had really
determined to make the best of his wife's fortune
by industry and diligence. He took a house in

Welbeck street, and set up a grocer and chandler's shop : was very obliging to his customers, punctual in his dealings, and while his wife lived, was esteemed by his neighbours a careful and industrious man. However, though at times, and while he was in his shop, he appeared to like his business, yet in parties of pleasure, which he made but too often, and on holy days, he affected the dress of a gentleman, and thus created expenses which only a gradual encroachment on his capital enabled him to meet; insomuch that when his wife died, which was about three years after their marriage, he resolved to leave off business, and converted his furniture and goods into the miserable sum of eighty-five pounds, which perhaps, with frugality might have supported him in business, but which was at all times too small a sum for Maclaine.

His mother in law consenting to take charge of his only daughter, and once more in a manner a single man, with eighty pounds in his pocket, again did the desire of appearing the gay fine gentleman obtrude itself upon his mind, and his old project of marrying a rich fortune engrossed all his faculties. For this purpose, Mr. Maclaine, who but a few weeks before was not ashamed to appear in his patched coat, or to carry a half-penny worth of coal or sand to his customers, now hired handsome apartments near Soho square, and resumed his laced clothes and a hat and feather.

But, however unreasonable to others this sudden transition from the grub to the butterfly might appear, Mr. Maclaine had very good private reasons for his actions. It appears that during his wife's last illness, she had been attended by one Plunket, as a surgeon and apothecary; this Plunket, after the decease of the poor woman, opened his mind to Maclaine, saying, that though the latter had lost a good wife, yet, seeing that she was gone, it was of no use to despond or to repine, particularly as it might turn out the most lucky circumstance in all his life. He added at the same time, that if Mr. Maclaine would agree to share the fortune with him he could help him to a lady worth £10,000 at least in her own right.

This motion was too agreeable to Mr. Maclaine to be rejected. It is hardly necessary to detail with what zeal this affair was followed up, or how often they flattered themselves with the deceitful prospect of success. The young lady having been taken to Wells, Maclaine followed her, passing for a man of fortune, and in every part of his dress and equipage appearing in that character. Plunket acted as his partner, and was a sort of under agent, while Maclaine himself was ogling, dancing and flirting with the young lady. But an ill timed quarrel with an apothecary, one evening in the public room, placed a quietus upon his hopes for ever, for the disciple of Galen enlisting a gallant son of Mars' in his quarrel, had the effrontery to kick our young adventurer down stairs, declaring publicly that he knew the rascal a footman a few years ago. This statement, which was believed by every body present, amongst whom was his mistress, whose credulity he had ascertained before, and was not therefore in a situation to doubt, compelled him and his footman Plunket to decamp without the ceremony of leave taking, and, indeed without any ceremony at all.

Returning to town from this woeful expedition, and examining the state of their cash, these faithful friends discovered that five guineas were the whole that remained,—a sum too little to support them, or to enter into any new project, or to keep up their assumed grandeur. Maclaine now found himself in a worse plight than he had brought himself to for some years past, without any visible hope of a supply, and yet engaged in a mode of life highly expensive, which it went to his heart either to retrench or relinquish. He now thought seriously of embarking for Jamaica, where he hoped to find employment as an accountant, and flattered himself that his person might be turned to account amongst the rich planter's daughters or widows. But no money was there for this purpose, nor could he think of any possible scheme whereby it might be raised.

Certainly, never had any man less cause to complain of fortune than Maclaine, and it would seem throughout his life, that he was determined to make his ruin entirely the work of his own hand, and leave him at last utterly without any excuse or palliation ; for meeting on 'Change with a gentleman, a countryman of his own, to whom he had formerly related his hopes of making a fortune in the manner we have related, he told him his situation at the present moment, adding that he was now undone, that he had spent his whole in the unhappy project, and had not where-withal to subsist on here, or to carry him from a place where he felt he was cutting a very ridiculous figure. Hereupon the gentleman spoke in his behalf to some others of his countrymen ; and as his conduct heretofore, according to the notions of the age, had been rather imprudent than vicious, they actually raised fifty guineas to fit him out for Jamaica, which they gave him, promising him letters of recommendation from some merchants of respectability to their own correspondents. Here then, was a prospect at once opened to him of future happiness and prosperity.

He had agreed for the passage, paid part of the passage money in advance, and bespoke some necessaries fitted for the climate, when, unhappily for the infatuated man, he was prompted to go to a masquerade, to take leave, as he said, for the last time, of the bewitching pleasures of London, and to bid a final farewell to this species of enjoyment, which he should have no hope of partaking in the West Indies. He went with the whole of his money in his pocket. The strange appearance of the place and of the company amused for a while, but the noise of the gamesters, drew his attention to the gaming table, where the quick transition of large sums from one hand to another awakened his avarice, and lulled his prudence asleep. In short, he ventured, and in half an hour possessed himself of one hundred guineas, with which he resolved, according to their phrase, 'to tie up;' but avarice had now attacked him; and after taking a turn or two round the room, he again returned, and in a very short time was stripped to the very last guinea.

It is needless to describe his agony on this occasion. His money gone, his expedition utterly disconcerted, and his friends lost past redemption! What was now to be done?

In this extremity, his evil genius, now in the ascendant, prompted him to send to Plunket to advise with, and from that moment his ruin commenced.

This was a favourable moment for Plunket. Himself a man of no honour, an utter stranger to all ties or principles of religion or honesty, an old sharper, and a daring fellow also, this was an opportunity, when his friend was agitated almost to madness, to propose, at first by distant hints, and at last in plain English, going on the highway.

Had he approached him in a calm hour, it is more than probable that his proposal had been rejected with horror; but the former strongly represented the necessity of a speedy supply before his friends could discover that his money was gone, which, he said would expose him to universal scorn and contempt. A strange infatuation, the dread of shame—the shame of appearing a fool, diminished the horror of being a villain, and decided him to recruit his losses by means the most hazardous and wicked.

Having agreed upon a plan of copartnership, and hired two horses, Plunket furnishing the pistols, for this was not his first entrance upon business of that nature, they set out on the evening after the masquerade, to lie in wait for some passengers coming from Smithfield market. They met on Hounslow heath with a grazier, next morning about four o'clock, from whom they took, without opposition, between sixty and seventy pounds.

In this, and other expeditions of the same kind, they wore Venetian masks; but this covering could not stifle conscience in Maclaine, nor animate him into courage. He accompanied Plunket it is true, and was by at the robbery, but, strictly speaking, had no hand in it; and his fears were so great, that he had not power to utter a word, or to draw a pistol. The least resistance on the part of the coun-

tryman would have given wings to his heels, and
have caused him to leave his more daring accomplice in the lurch.

Even when the robbery was over, and the countryman out of sight, Maclaine's fears were intolerable. He followed Plunket for some miles without
speaking a word ; and when they put up at an inn,
nearly ten miles from the place of the robbery, he
called for a private room, fearful of every shadow,
and terrified at every sound. His agonies of mind
were so great, that Plunket was fearful that his folly
would rise suspicions in the house, and he would
fain have persuaded him to return immediately to
London ; but he would not stir till it was dusk, and
then would not appear at the stables from which
they had hired the horses, but left the care of them
to Plunket.

He was now, by his share of the ill-acquired
booty, very nearly reimbursed for his losses at the
masquerade, and might easily have undertaken his
voyage ; but he had lost all peace of mind, and was
become entirely void of prudence. So great was
his dread of a discovery, though Plunket represented the impossibility of it, that he would not stir out
of his room for some days, and even then did not
think himself safe, but proposed going down to the
country for a week or two. Plunket did not oppose
his departure, especially as he was to direct the
route, and had gotten some intimation of a prize
coming that day from St. Alban's, towards which
place they set out. When they had gone a few
miles, Plunket imparted to him his design, which
Maclaine promised to second with a great deal of
reluctance. When they came within the sight of

the coach, in which was their expected booty,
Maclaine would have persuaded Plunket to desist;
but the other turning his qualms of conscience into
ridicule, and dropping some hints of cowardice,
Maclaine prepared for the attack, crying, ' He needs
must whom the devil drives. I am over shoes, and
must over boots ;' but, notwithstanding, conducted
himself in so distracted a manner as went nigh to
lose them their prey. They took, however, from a
gentleman and lady in the coach, two gold watches
and about twenty pounds in money, with which
they got clear off; but did not think fit to keep that
road any longer, but turned off, and before morning
put up at an inn at Richmond, where Maclaine was
as much in the horrors as in London; had no rest,
no peace of mind, and stayed there two or three days
sulky, sullen and perplexed as to what course he
was to pursue. His wish however, to be in town
in time for the ship's departure for Jamaica, determined him to return to London in a fortnight, when
he found that the ship had sailed two days before,
—a disappointment that added to his former per-
plexity. Nevertheless, having money in his pocket
he contrived to excuse himself to his friends for his
untoward absence, and promised, and seriously designed, to set out on the very next opportunity.

But the expensive company he kept in the in-
terim, and his further losses at play, once more
stripped him of his money, and his evil genius,
Plunket, was ever at his elbow, ready to suggest the
former method of supply, with which he complied
much less reluctantly than before. The bounds of
honour once overstept, especially when success and
security attend the villany, the habits of vice grow

strong ; and the checks of conscience, gradually less regarded, at length pass without notice. In a word, Maclaine hardened himself by degrees to villany, left the company of his city acquaintances, that they might not tease him about his voyage to Jamaica, and took apartments in St. James-street, a place excellently suited to his purpose, for his appearance glanced off all suspicion, and he had a favourable opportunity, when the gentlemen came to town, of knowing all their motions, and consequently of following and waylaying them on the road.

In the space of six months, he and Plunket, sometimes in company and sometimes separately, committed fifteen or sixteen robberies in Hyde Park, and within twenty miles of London, and obtained some valuable prizes. But still the money went as it came, for Plunket loved his bottle and intrigue, and Maclaine was doatingly fond of fine clothes, balls, and masquerades, at all which places he made a conspicuous figure. As he still had fortune hunting in view, he was very assiduous in his attentions to women, and was not altogether unsuccessful ; but we imagine he made sincere return to none but such as had money in their own hands, or could be useful in helping him to an introduction to such as had.

And here it were needless and not productive of much interest to recount several intrigues in which Maclaine was engaged, and it were not a little painful to narrate two instances of wanton seduction on his part, which were there no other counts in the moral indictment against him, would be sufficient to consign him to eternal infamy.

Mr. Maclaine applied himself also to his old profession of fortune-hunting, and in company with his old and worthy coadjutor Plunket, made several attempts to entrap heiresses, all of which proved abortive. While he was intent upon these schemes he had no opportunity of making excursions on the road, and to defray his expenses had borrowed from a citizen's wife, with whom he had an intrigue, about twenty pounds, which he promised faithfully to repay before her husband should return from the country. The time of the citizen's arrival being at hand, the good wife became exceedingly anxious about the coin; and as a similar favour might be wanted some other time, Mr. Maclaine made it a point of conscience to keep his word with her, and appointed her to come to him at his country lodgings at Chelsea, where he paid her the money. He, however, took care that his friend Plunket should ease her of the trouble of carrying it home, by waylaying her in the Five-fields.

Soon after this a supply of cash being wanted, Plunket and he prepared for an expedition, and took the road to Chester; and in three days committed five robberies between Stony Stratford and Whitchurch, one of which was upon an intimate acquaintance, by whom Maclaine had been handsomely entertained but two days before. However, the booty in the whole five robberies did not amount to thirty pounds in cash, but they had watches, rings, &c. to a much greater amount. On the very evening of their return to town, they obtained information that an officer in the East India company's service had received a large sum of money, with which he was about to return to Greenwich. They waylaid and robbed him of a very considerable sum, and it would seem that on this occasion they were under some dread of a discovery; for, in a few days after the commission of it, Maclaine set out for the Hague, and Plunket for Ireland.

On the arrival of the former at the Hague, he pretended a friendly visit to his brother, who received him with cordiality and affection, and as honesty is never suspicious, he was easily induced to give credit to the specious tale which his brother related to him. He told him that he had got a considerable fortune with his late wife, and that her father, who died some few months before had left him a valuable legacy, with which he designed to purchase a commission in the army. Upon that and the interest of his other funds he said, he hoped to live at ease for the remainder of his life. His worthy brother, rejoicing at his prosperity, introduced him to his acquaintance and friends, amongst whom Mr. Maclaine behaved with great politeness, and held balls and large parties; to pay for which, it is surmised, he had the art to extract the gold watches and purses of his guests without suspicion.

However, upon his arrival in London, to which place he had been induced to return by a letter from Plunket, informing him of another rich matrimonial prize, which was, as usual, beyond his reach or above his ingenuity to ensnare, he again appears to have taken up his old thoughts of preparing for Jamaica as a last resource. But these thoughts did not long possess him; for though by the sale of his horses and furniture he might have fitted himself for the West Indies in a very handsome manner, and had still reputation sufficient left to have procured recommendations from home; yet he was prevailed on to try his fate once more, and was but too successful, having in some of his illegal despresation, succeeded in obtaining several rich prizes. Amongst the rest, he and Plunket robbed Horace Walpole, and on a reward being advertised for the watch which they had taken from him, Plunket had the impudenc to go and receive it himself, choosing to run the risk rather ther than trust a third person with their hazardous secret. But all human prudence is in vain to stop the hand of justice, when once the measure of our iniquity is full; our closest secrets take wind we know not how; and our own folly acts the part of an informer to awaken offended justice. The crisis of Maclaine's fate was at hand. It was he who proposed his last excursion to Plunket, who was ill at the time, and was very unwilling to turn out; but Maclaine, impelled by some uncommon impulse, urged him so earnestly that he at last complied. They came up, about two o'clock in the morning, near Turnham green, with the Salisbury stage coach, in which were five men and a woman. Though this was Maclaine's expedition, yet Plunket was the acting man, and compelled all the men to come out of the coach, one by one, and rifled them; and then he put his pistol into his pocket, lest he should too much alarm the lady, and took from her what she offered without further search. Plunket would now have gone off; but Maclaine, full of his fate, demanded the cloak-bags out of the boot of the coach; each of them took one before him and rode off.

On the same morning they met and robbed lord

Eglington, who was the prize for whom they chiefly went out. They effected this by manœuvre, as his lordship was armed with a blunderbuss. One of them screened himself behind the post boy, so that if his lordship fired he must shoot his servant; while the other with a pistol cocked, demanded his money, and ordered him to throw his blunderbuss on the ground. But it appears that the prize obtained at this hazard was but seven guineas, with which and the bags they returned to Maclaine's residence, before the family were risen, and there divided their spoil.

But though the clothes were described in the public papers, yet so infatuated was Maclaine, that he sold his share of the booty to a salesman, who instantly knew them to be the property of a Mr. Higden, and the latter immediately had Maclaine taken into custody.

On his first examination he denied the fact, but afterwards, that he might leave himself no room to escape, he formed the project of saving his life by impeaching his companion Plunket, foolishly supposing that justice would promise life to a villain she had in custody, for the impeachment of another that was out of her reach. For though he was forewarned that a confession, without impeaching a number of his accomplices, would not avail him, he still insisted upon taking that step, not from compunction or remorse, but with the intention of saving his own life at the expense of that of his friend.

On his second examination he delivered his confession in writing, and behaved in a most dastardly manner: he whimpered and cried like a whipped school boy. This conduct, contemptible as it was, drew sympathetic tears from, and opened the purses of his fair audience, whose bounty maintained him in affluence while he remained in the Gatehouse, and whose kind offers of intercession gave him hopes of getting free pardon.

On his trial, he saw fit to retract his confession, and pretended that he was flurried, and in some measure delirious, when he made it, and that he had received the clothes from Plunket in payment of a debt. But this evasion had no influence with the jury, who found him guilty, without retiring from court.

On receiving sentence, guilt, shame, and dread, deprived him of the power of speech, and disabled him from reading a paper, pathetically enough composed, in which he prayed for mercy.

He was carried to Tyburn in a cart, like the rest of the criminals, and not as was expected, in a coach. He stood the gaze of the multitude (which on this occasion was very great) without the least concern; his thoughts were stedfast in his devotion, and when he was about to be turned off, he exclaimed, O God, forgive my enemies, bless my friends, and receive my soul: His execution took place on Wednesday, October 3rd, 1750.

EUGENE ARAM.

THE accounts of the life of this man have become of late so widely circulated, and the particulars respecting the murder of which he was the perpetrator, so generally known, that any notice of him in this work would appear almost supererogatory, were it not that a charge of oversight and omission could, without injustice, be reasonably advanced against it, were we to slight over or leave unmentioned a name so notorious. We shall, therefore, give a summary of his history, commencing with an account of his family and early life, furnished by himself at the request of the two gentlemen, who, at his own particular request, attended him at his condemnation.

I was born at Ramsgill, a little village in the Netherdale, in 1704. My maternal relations had been substantial and reputable in that dale, for a great many generations; my father was of Nottinghamshire, a gardener, of great abilities in botany, and an excellent draughtsman, he served the right reverend bishop of London, Dr. Compton, with great approbation: which occasioned his being recommended to Newby, in this county, to Sir Edward Blackett, whom he served in the capacity of gardener, with much credit to himself, and satisfaction to that family, for above thirty years. Upon the decease of that baronet, he went, and was retained in the service of Sir John Ingilby, of Ripley, bart., where he died; respected when living, and lamented when dead. My father's ancestors were of great antiquity and consideration in the country, and originally British. Their surname is local, for they were formerly lords of the town of Haram, or Aram, on the southern banks of the Tees, and opposite to Sockburn, in Bishopric; and appear in the records of St. Mary's, at York, among other charitable names, early and considerable benefactors to that abbey. They, many centuries ago, removed from these parts, and were settled under the fee of the lords Mowbray, in Nottinghamshire, at Haram or Aram Park, in the neighbourhood of Newark upon Trent; where they were possessed of no less than three knight's fees in the reign of Edward the Third. Their lands, I find not whether by purchase or marriage, came into the hands of the present lord Lexington. While the name existed in the country, some of them were several times high sheriffs for the county: and one was professor of divinity, if I remember right, at Oxford, and died at York. The last of the chief of this family was Thomas Aram, Esq. of Gray's Inn, and one of the commissioners of the salt office, under queen Anne. He married one of the co-heiresses of Sir John Coningsby, of North Mimms, in Hertfordshire, where I saw him, and where he died without issue.

I was removed very young, along with my mother, to Skelton, near Newby; and thence at five or six years old, my father making a little purchase at Bondgate, his family went thither. There I went to school; where I was made capable of reading the Testament, which was all that I was ever taught, except, a long time after, for about a month, in a very advanced age for that, with the reverend Mr. Alcock of Burnsal.

After this, at about thirteen or fourteen years of age, I went to my father at Newby, and attended him in the family there, till the death of Sir Edward Blackett. It was here my propensity to literature first appeared, for being always of a solitary disposition, and uncommonly fond of retirement and books, I enjoyed here all the repose and opportunity

I could wish. My study at that time was engaged in the mathematics; I know not what my acquisitions were, but I am certain my application was intense and unwearied. I found my father's library there, which contained a very great number of books in most branches, Kersey's Algebra, Leybourn's Cursus Mathematicus, Ward's Young's Mathematician's Guide, Harris's Algebra, &c., and a great many more; but these being the books in which I was ever most conversant, I remember them the better. I was even then equal to the management of quadratic equations, and their geometrical constructions. After we left Newby, I repeated the same studies in Bondgate, and went over all parts I had studied before, I believe not altogether unsuccessfully.

But about the age of sixteen, I was sent for to London, being thought, upon examination by Mr. Christopher Blackett, qualified to serve him as book-keeper in his counting house. Here after a year or two, I took the small-pox and suffered most severely under that distemper. I returned home again, and there with leisure on my hands, and a new edition of authors to those brought me from Newby, I renewed not only my mathematical studies, but began to prosecute others of a different turn, with much avidity and diligence. These were poetry, history, and antiquities; the charms of which quite destroyed all the heavier beauties of numbers in lines, whose applications and properties I now pursued no longer, except occasionally in teaching.

'I was, after some time employed in this manner, invited into Netherdale, my native air, where I first engaged in a school, and where unfortunately enough for me, I married. The misconduct of the wife which that place afforded me, has procured me this prosecution, this prison, this infamy, and this sentence.

'During my marriage here, perceiving the deficiencies in my education, and sensible of my want of the learned languages, and promoted by an irresistible covetousness of knowledge, I commenced a series of studies in that way, and undertook the tediousness and the intricacies and the labour of grammar; I selected Lilly from the rest, all of which I got and repeated by heart. The task of repeating it all every day was impossible while I attended the school; so I divided it into portions; by which method it was pronounced thrice every week, and this I performed for years.

'I next became acquainted with Camden's Greek Grammar, which I also repeated in the same manner *memoriter.* Thus instructed I entered upon the Latin classics, whose allurements repaid my assiduities and my labours. I remember to have, at first, overflung five lines for a whole day; and never in all the painful course of my reading, left any one passage, till I did, or thought I did perfectly understand it.

'After I had accurately perused every one of the Latin classics, historians and poets, I went through the Greek Testament, first parsing every word as I proceeded; next I ventured upon Heriod, Homer, Theocritus, Heroditus, Thucydides, and all the Greek tragedians: a tedious labour was this; but my former acquaintance with history lessened it extremely, because it threw light on many passages, which without that assistance must have appeared obscure.

In the midst of these literary pursuits a man and horse from my good friend William Norton Esq., came for me from Knaresborough, bearing that gentleman's letter, inviting me thither; and accordingly I repaired there in some part of the year 1734, and was, I believe, well accepted and esteemed there. Here, not satisfied with my former acquisitions, I prosecuted the attainment of Hebrew, and with indefatigable diligence. I had Buxtorff's Grammar, but that being perplexing, or not explicit enough, at least in my opinion at that time, I collected no less than eight or ten different grammars; and thus one very often supplied the omission of the others, and was, I found, of extraordinary advantage. Then I purchased the Bible in the original, and read the whole Pentateuch, with an intention to go through the whole of it, which I attempted, but wanted time.

In April, I think the 18th, 1744, I went again to London, and agreed to teach the Latin and writing, for the Rev. Mr. Painblanc in Piccadilly, which he, along with a salary, returned, by teaching me French; wherein I observed the pronunciation the most formidable part, at least to me, who had never before known a word of it. By continued application every night and every opportunity, I overcame this, and soon became a tolerable master of French. I remained in this situation upwards of two years.

Some time after this I went to Hays, in the capacity of writing master, and served a gentlewoman there, since dead; and stayed, after that, with a worthy and reverend gentleman. I continued here between three and four years. To several other places I then succeeded, and all that while used every occasion for improvement. I then transcribed acts of parliaments to be registered in chancery; and afterwards went down to the free-school, at Lynn.

From my leaving Knaresborough to this time is a long interval, which I had filled up with the farther study of history and antiquities, heraldry and botany; in the last of which, I was very agreeably entertained, there being in that study such an extensive a display of nature. I well knew Tournefort, Ray, Miller, and Linnæus, &c. I made freqent visits to the botanic garden at Chelsea; and traced pleasure through a thousand fields : at last, few plants, domestic or exotic, were unknown to me. Amidst all this I ventured upon the Chaldee and Arabic; and, with a design to understand them, supplied myself with Erpenius, Chappelow, and others; but I had not time to obtain any great knowledge of the Arabic; the Chaldee was easy enough, because of its connexion with the Hebrew.

I then investigated the Celtic, as far as possible, in all its dialects; began collections, and made comparisons between that, the English, the Latin, the Greek, and even the Hebrew. I had made notes, and compared above three thousand of these together, and such a surprising affinity, even beyond my expectation or conception, that I was determined to proceed through the whole of these languages, and form a comparative lexicon, which I hoped would account for numberless vocables in use with us, the Latins, and Greeks, before concealed and unobserved: this, or something like it, was the design of a clergyman of great erudition in Scotland; but it must prove abortive, for he died before he executed if, and most of my books and papers are scattered and lost.

Such is the account Eugene Aram has given of himself, until the commission of the fatal act that brought down upon him the execration of the world and the vengeance of the law. Of all the crimes man is capable of committing, there is none so offensive to Omnipotence as murder; and, the Almighty, therefore, seems to be more intent to expose that heinous and accursed offence to mankind; to warn and admonish them, to shew them that rocks cannot hide, nor distance secure them from the inevitable consequences of the violation of that law, which nature dictates and man confirms. The extraordinary means by which this murder was brought to light, is one of the many instances of the divine interposition.

Daniel Clark was born at Knaresborough, of reputable parents, where he lived and followed the business of a shoemaker. About the month of January, in 1744 or 5, he married, and became possessed of property to the amount of two or three hundred pounds. He was at that time in very good credit at Knaresborough, and it is supposed that a scheme was then laid by Eugene Aram, at that time a schoolmaster in the town, and one Houseman, a flax-dresser, to defraud several tradesmen of great quantities of goods and plate. Clark having been the fittest person to carry their plan into execution; for, as he then lived in very good reputation, and, moreover, was lately married, he was the person of all others best calculated to effect the in-

tended purpose. Accordingly, Clark for some days
went about to various tradesmen in the town, and
under the pretext that, as he was newly married, it
was not altogether irrational to suppose that cloth,
and table and bed linen, would considerably contribute to his matrimonial comfort, he took up a great
quantity of linen and woollen drapery goods; the
worthy dealers of Knaresborough, rendering up
their commodities with the utmost zeal and expedition on so interesting an occasion. After this, he
went to several innkeepers and others, and borrowed a silver tankard of one, a silver pint of another,
and the like, under the pretence that he was to have
company that night, and should be glad of the use
of them at supper; and in order to give a colour
to his story, he procured of the innkeepers (of
whom he had borrowed the plate) other liquors to
regale his visitors.

Some suspicious circumstances, however, appearing that night and the following morning, it was
rumoured that Clark had absconded; and upon inquiry, most certainly he was not to be found. An
active search was immediately made for the goods,
and the plate with which he had provided himself,
when some part of the goods was found in Houseman's house, and another part dug up in Aram's
garden: but as no plate could be found, it was concluded, somewhat naturally, that Clark had decamped with it. The strictest inquiry was instantly set
on foot, to discover his retreat; persons were dispatched to all parts; advertisements describing his
person, inserted in all the newspapers; but to no
purpose.

Eugene Aram being suspected to be an accomplice, a process was granted against him by the steward of the honour of Knaresborough to arrest him for a debt due to a Mr. Norton, with a view to detain him till such time as a warrant could be obtained from the justice of the peace to apprehend him upon that charge. To the surprise of all, however, the money was instantly paid, moreover, at the same time, a considerable mortgage upon his house at Bondgate was also discharged. Soon afterwards, Aram left the town, and was not heard of till the month of June, 1758, when the murder of Clark being traced to him, he was found residing at Lynn.

Upwards of thirteen years after Clark's disappearance, it happened that a labourer employed in digging for stone to supply a lime-kiln, at a place called Thistle hill near Knaresborough, striking about half a yard and half a quarter deep, turned up an arm bone and the leg of a human skeleton. His curiosity being excited, he carefully removed the earth round about the place, and discovered all the bones of a human body, presenting an appearance from their position, as if the body had been doubled at the hips, though the bones were all perfect. This remarkable occurrence was rumoured in the town, and gave rise to a suspicion that Daniel Clark had been murdered and buried there; for no other person had been missed thereabouts for sixty years and upwards. The coroner was instantly informed, and an inquest summoned.

The wife of Eugene Aram, who had frequently before given hints of her suspicions, was now examined. From her evidence it appeared that Clark was an intimate acquaintance of Aram's before the

8th of February, 1744 or 5, and they had frequent transactions together, and with Houseman also. On the morning of February 8, 1744, 5, as early as two o'clock, Aram, Clark, and Houseman came to Aram's house, and went up stairs, where they remained about an hour. They then went out together, and Clark being last, she observed he had a sack or wallet on his back. About four, Houseman and Aram returned, but without their companion, Clark. Where is Clark? she inqiured; but her husband only returned an angry look in reply, and desired her to go to bed, which she refused, and told him, she feared he had been doing something wrong. Aram then went down stairs with the candle, and she, being desirous to know what they were doing, followed them, and from the top of the stairs heard Houseman say, she's coming; if she does, she'll tell. What can she tell, poor simple thing? replied Aram; she knows nothing. I'll hold the door to prevent her coming. It's of no use, something must be done, returned Houseman; if she don't split now, she will some other time. No, no foolish, her husband said; we'll coax her a little till her passion is off, and then—what! said Houseman, sullenly. Shoot her, whispered Aram, shoot her! Mrs. Aram, hearing this discourse, became very much alarmed, but remained quiet. At seven o'clock the same morning they both left the house, and she immediately their backs were curned, went down stairs, and observed there had been a fire below, and all the ashes taken out of the grate. She then examined the dunghill, and perceived ashes of a different kind lying upon it, and turning them over, found several pieces of linen and woollen cloth

R

very nearly burnt, which had the appearance of wearing apparel. When she returned into the house, she found a handkerchief that she had lent to Houseman the night before, and a round spot of blood on it about the size of a shilling. Houseman returned soon afterwards, and she charged him with having done something dreadful to Clark; but he pretended total ignorance, and added, she was a fool, and knew not what she said. From these circumstances she fully and conscientiously believed that Daniel Clark was murdered by Houseman and Eugene Aram, on the 8th of February, 1744-5.

Several other witnesses were examined, all affirming that Houseman and Eugene Aram were the last persons who were with Clark, especially on the night of the 7th of February, being that after which he was missing. Upon hearing these testimonies, Houseman, who was present, was observed to become very restless, discovering all the signs of guilt, such as trembling, turning pale, and faltering in his speech. Few men guilty of the crime of murder have the strength of heart and self-command to conceal it; by some circumstance or other, the truth will out; a look, a dream, and not unfrequently, as in this case, their own unfaithful tongue, is the involuntary agent that brings at last the blackened culprit to that punishment which unerringly awaits the man that sheds his brother's blood. Accordingly, upon the skeleton being produced, Houseman taking up one of the bones, dropped this most unguarded expression : this is no more Daniel Clark's bone than it is mine. What! remarked the coroner instantly—what?—how is this? How can you be so sure that that is not Daniel Clark's bone? Because I can produce a witness, who saw Daniel Clark upon the road two days after he was missing at Knaresborough. This witness was instantly summoned, and stated that he had never seen Clark after the 8th of February; a friend, however, had told him (and this only had he mentioned at first) that he met some one very like Clark; but, it being a snowy day, and the person having the cape of his coat up, he could not say with the least degree of certainty who it was. This explanation, so far from proving satisfactory, increased the suspicion against Houseman; and accordingly a warrant was issued against him, and he was apprehended and brought before William Thornton, Esq., who examining him, elicited a full acknowledgment of the fact of his having been with Clark on the night in question, on account of some money, (twenty pounds) that he had lent him, and which he wanted at the time very pressingly. He further stated that Clark begged him to accept the value in goods, to which proposition he assented, and was necessarily therefore, several times between Clarke's house and his own, in order to remove the goods from one to another. When he had finished, he left Clark at Aram's house, with another man whom he had never seen before. Aram and Clark, immediately afterwards, followed him out of the house of the former, and the stranger with them. They then went in the direction of the market place, which the light of the moon enabled him to see, and he lost sight of them. He disavowed most solemnly that he came back to Aram's house that morning with Aram and Clark, as was asserted by Mrs. Aram; nor was he with Aram, but with Clark, at the house of the former on that night, whither he only went to see Clark in order to obtain from him the note.

Being then asked if he would sign his examination he said he would rather wave it for the present, for he might have something to add, and therefore desired to have time to consider it. The magistrate then committed him to York castle, when expressing a wish to explain more fully, he was again brought before Mr. Thornton, and in his presence made the following confession :—That Daniel Clark was murdered by Eugene Aram, late of Knaresborough, a schoolmaster, and, as he believed, on Friday the 8th of February, 1744-5; for that Eugene Aram and Daniel Clark were together at Aram's house early that morning, and that he (Houseman) left the house and went up the street a little before, and they called to him, desiring that he would go a short way with them ; and he accordingly went with them to a place called St. Robert's Cave, near Grimble bridge, where the two former stopped, and there he saw Aram strike Clark several times over the breast and head, and saw him fall as if he were dead ; upon which he came away and left them: but whether Aram used any weapon or not to kill Clark he could not tell, nor did he know what he did with the body afterwards, but believed that Aram left it at the mouth of the cave ; for that, seeing Aram do this, lest he might share the same fate, he made the best of his way to the bridge-end, where, looking back, he saw Aram coming from the cave side, (which is in a private rock adjoining the river,) and could discern a bundle in his hand, but did not know what it was: upon this he hastened away to the town, without either joining Aram or seeing him again till the next day, and from that time he had never had discourse with him. He stated, however, afterwards, that Clark's body was buried in St. Robert's cave, and that he was sure it was there, but desired it might remain till such time as Aram was taken. He added further, that Clark's head lay to the right, in the turn at the entrance of the cave.

Proper persons were instantly appointed to examine St. Robert's cave, when, agreeably to Houseman's confession, the skeleton of a human body (the head lying as he had described) was found. A warrant was instantly issued to apprehend Eugene Aram, who was discovered to be living at Lynn in the capacity of usher at a school. He confessed before the magistrate that he was well acquainted with Clark, and, to the best of his remembrance, about or before the 8th of February, 1744 5, but utterly denied any participation in the frauds which Clark stood charged with at the time of his disappearance. He also declared that he knew nothing of the murder, and that the statements made by his wife were without exception false : he, however, declined to sign his examination, on the same plea preferred by Houseman, that he might recollect himself better, and lest any thing should be omitted which might afterwards occur to him. On being conducted to the castle, he desired to return, and acknowledged that he was at his own house when Houseman and Clark came to him with some plate, of which Clark had defrauded his neighbours. He could not but observe that the former was very diligent in assisting ; in fact, it was altogether Houseman's business ; and there was no truth whatever

in the statement that he came there to sign a note
or instrument. All the leather which Clark had
possessed himself of, amounting to a considerable
value, was concealed under flax at Houseman's
house, with the intention of disposing of it little by
little, to prevent any suspicion of his being concerned in the robbery. The plate was beaten flat
in St. Robert's cave.

At four o'clock in the morning, they, thinking
that it was too late to enable Clark to leave with
safety, agreed that he should stay there till the next
night, and he accordingly remained there all the
following day. In order, then, the better to effect
his escape, they both went down to the cave, Houseman only entering, while he watched without, lest
any person should surprise them. On a sudden he
heard a noise, and Houseman appeared at the mouth
of the cave, and told him that Clark was gone. He
had a bag with him, containing plate, which he said
he had purchased of Clark, money being much more
portable than such cumbersome articles.

They then went to Houseman's house, and concealed the property there, he fully believing that
Clark had escaped. He never heard anything of
Clark subsequently, and was as much surprised to
hear there was a suspicion of his being murdered,
as that he (Eugene Aram) should be considered to
be the murderer. Notwithstanding this surprise,
however, his examination having been signed, he
was committed with his companion to York castle,
there to await the assizes.

On the third of August, 1759, they were both
brought to the bar. Houseman was arraigned on

the former indictment, acquitted, and admitted evidence against Aram, who was thereupon arraigned.

Houseman was then called, and deposed to the same effect as that which has already appeared in his own confession. Several witnesses were called who gave evidence as to finding several kinds of goods buried in Aram's garden, Aram's knowledge of the fact of Clark's possessing two hundred pounds, and to show that they had both been seen together on the evening of the 7th of February. After which the skull was produced in court; on the left side there was a fracture, from the nature of which it was impossible to have been done but by the stroke of some blunt instrument. The skull was beaten inwards, and could not be replaced but from within. The surgeon gave it as his opinion, that no such breach could proceed from natural decay; that it was not a recent fracture made by the spade or axe by which it might have been dug up; but seemed to be of some years' standing.

Augene Aram's defence, which he read, was marked with an undoubted manifestation of very considerable powers. It was learned and argumentative: and in some passages, glowing and eloquent. He attempted to show, that no rational inference can be drawn that a person is dead who suddenly disappears;—that hermitages such as St. Robert's cave were the constant repositories of the bones of the recluse; that the proofs of this were well authenticated; and, that therefore the conclusion that the bones found were those of some killed in battle, or some ascetic, remained no less reasonably than impatiently expected by him. A verdict of guilty was however returned, and he was condemned to be hanged accordingly.

On the morning after his condemnation, he confessed the justice of his sentence to the two gentlemen who attended him, and acknowledged that he had murdered Clark. He told them, also, that he suspected Clark of having an unlawful commerce with his wife ; and that at the time of the murder he felt persuaded that he was acting right, but since he had thought otherwise.

It was generally believed, as he promised to make a more ample confession on the day he was executed of every thing prior to the murder, that the whole would have been disclosed; but he put an end to any farther discovery, by an attempt upon his own life.

When he was called from his bed to have his chains taken off, he refused, alleging that he was very weak. On moving him, it was found that he had inflicted a severe wound upon his arm, from which the blood was flowing copiously. He had concealed a razor in the condemned hold some time before. By proper and prompt applications he was brought to himself, and though weak from the loss of blood, conducted to Tyburn in York, where, being asked if he had anything to say, he answered, ' No.'

He was then executed, and his body conveyed to Knaresborough Forest, and hung in chains, pursuant to his sentence.

That Eugene Aram murdered Clark is beyond all question, since we have his confession, that he committed the murder actuated by the cause he alleges, is open to suspicion. The solicitude which all men, even the most vicious, manifest to leave behind a memory mingled with some little good, prompted him, doubtless, to give his crime the mitigatory motive to which he attributes it. That the perpetration of a murder is unjustifiable, even urged by the wrong which Aram states himself to have suspected, must be obvious to every rightly constituted mind; and whether the horrible act can be extenuated by a deliberate and foul attack on the virtue and character of a woman, whom he upon all occasions used with infamous barbarity, is a question we can confidently leave to the common sense of every man. That Eugene Aram was leagued with Clark and Houseman in their fraud at Knaresborough, there can be little doubt; that he plundered his unhappy victim after he had murdered him, there can be less; that no sense of domestic injury would urge a man to rob another who had wronged him after he had slain him, needs only to be mentioned to be admitted; and therefore believing conscientiously from these facts that the charge against his wife was not sustained, a double indignation is entailed upon the wretch who could add to the measure of his crime this gratuitous calumny.

GEORGE BARRINGTON

WAS originally a native and inhabitant of Ireland; and, as it will appear in the sequel that the name of Barrington was assumed, let it suffice to remark that his father's name was Henry Waldron, and that he was a working silversmith; while his mother, whose maiden name was Naish, was a mantuamaker, and occasionally a midwife.

Our adventurer was born in the year 1755, at the village of Maynooth, in the county of Kildare. His parents, who bore a good character for industry, integrity, and general good behaviour, were, however, never able to rise to a state of independence, or security from indigence, because of a law suit with a more opulent relative, in order to the recovery of a legacy, to which they conceived they had a lawful right. To the narrowness of their circumstances the neglect of their son's education is imputed; and, therefore, they were incapable of improving, or of giving a proper bias to those early indications of natural abilities, and a superiority of talents, which must most inevitably have unfolded themselves ever in the dawn of young Barrington's existence. He was, notwithstanding these obstacles, instructed to read and write at an early age, at their expense; and afterwards, through the bounty of a medical gentleman in the neighbourhood, he was initiated in the principles of common arithmetic, the elements of geography, and the outlines of English grammar

This ill-fated youth, however, enjoyed but for a short time the benefits derived from the kindness of his first patron, a dignitary of the church of Ireland; for the violence of his passions, which equalled at least the extent of his talents, precipitated him into an action by which he lost his favour for ever, and which, in its consequences, finally proved his ruin When he had been about half-a-year at the grammar school in Dublin, to which he had been sent by his patron, he unluckily got into a dispute with a lad much older, larger, and stronger than himself; the dispute grew into a quarrel, and some blows ensued, in which young Waldron suffered considerably; but in order to be revenged, he stabbed his opponent with a pen knife; and had he not been seasonably prevented, he would in all probability have then murdered him. The wounds which he gave did not prove so dangerous as to render the several circumstances of the quarrel which occasioned them a subject of legal investigation. The discipline of the house, (flogging,) however, was inflicted with proper severity on the perpetrator of so atrocious an offence, which irritated the unrelenting and vindictive temper of the young man to such a degree that he determined at once to run away from school, from his family, and from his friends; thus abandoning the fair prospects he had before him, and blasting all the hopes that had been fondly, though vainly, formed of the great things that might be effected by his genius when matured by time and improved by study.

His plan of escape was no sooner formed than it was carried into execution; but previously to his departure, he found means to steal ten or twelve pounds from the master of the school, and a gold watch from Mrs. Goldsborough, the master's sister. With this booty, a few shirts, and two or three pair of stockings, he silently but safely effected his retreat from the school house, in the middle of a still night in the month of May, 1771; and pursuing the great northern road all that night, and all the next day, he late in the evening arrived at the town of Drogheda, without interruption, without accident, and in a great measure without halting, without rest, and without food.

The first place of safety at which young Waldron thought proper to halt, was at an obscure inn in Drogheda, where a company of strolling players happening to be at the time, it was the occasion of a new series of acquaintance, which, though formed on precipitation, and on the spur of the occasion, was retained from choice and affection for a number of years.

One John Price, the manager of the strolling company, became quickly the confidant, and from the confidant the sole counsellor of the fugitive Waldron, who, influenced by the ardour, the natural and unguarded ingenuousness of a youthful mind, communicated to his new friend, without reserve, all the circumstances of his life and story. By his advice this young man renounced his paternal name, assumed that of Barrington, entered into the company, and in the course of four days became so absolutely and formally a strolling son of Thespis, that he performed the part of Jaffier in *Venice Preserved*, with some applause, to a crowded audience, in a barn in the suburbs of Drogheda; and this without the assistance of a prompter.

Though the reception he met with on his debut was very flattering to a mind like his, Price, as well as himself, thought it would not be proper for him to appear in public so near the scene of his late depredations in the capital. It was, therefore, resolved on by them, that the whole company should without delay move to the northward, and, if possible, get to the distance of sixty or eighty miles from Dublin before they halted for any length of time. In order that so numerous a body might be enabled to move all their baggage, it was necessary to raise money; and in doing this, Barrington's assistance being the first that offered, was indispensably necessary. He was therefore applied to, and acquiesced with a good grace, and gave Price Mrs. Goldsborough's gold repeater, which was disposed of for the general benefit of the strollers.

As soon as the necessary funds were procured, all these children of Thespis set out for Londonderry, which was the place at which they first designed to play. Travelling but slowly, they were a considerable time on their journey; and during the course of it, the penetrating eyes of the experienced actresses discovered that Barrington had made a tender impression on the heart of Miss Egerton, the young lady who played the part of Belvidera when he acted that of Jaffier at Drogheda. The poor girl was the daughter of an opulent tradesman at Coventry. She was young and beautiful, sweet-tempered and accomplished, but now friendless; and though like the rest, inured to misfortune, she was destitute of the experience which is generally acquired during a series of sinister untoward events. At the age of sixteen she was seduced by a lieutenant of marines, with whom she fled from her father's house to Dublin, where in less than three months he abandoned her, leaving her a prey to poverty, infamy, and desperation.

Having been thus deceived in the simplicity of innocence by the cunning and falsehood of one of the vilest and most profligate of human beings, she had no other resource from the most extreme want than closing with Price, who proposed to her to join his company; which, situated as she was, she readily agreed to do, and had been with him but a very short time when she saw Barrington, of whom, being of a warm constitution, she became rather suddenly enamoured. But to the credit of our adventurer, although his affection was as ardent as her own, it was not of that brutal and profligate cast that so frequently disgraces the devious paths of youthful imprudence and indiscretion. On the part of Miss Egerton, the symptoms of her affection for him were so obvious, that, inexperienced as he then was in matters of gallantry and intrigue, he not only perceived her passion, but was sensible of her merit, and returned her love with perfect sincerity.

It was not long before Price, urged a second time by want of money, found it expedient to insinuate to the unfortunate Barrington, that a young man of his address and appearance might very easily find means to introduce himself into some of the public places to where the merchants and chapmen of that commercial city generally resorted: and that he there might, without any great difficulty find opportunities of picking their pockets unnoticed, and of escaping undetected, especially at that time, when the fair being held, a favourable juncture afforded itself of executing a plan of such a nature with safety and facility. The idea pleased our needy adventurer, and the plan formed on it was carried into execution by him and his trusty confidant John Price, the very next day, with great success; at least, such it appeared to them at that time, their acquisitions having amounted, on the close of the evening, to about forty guineas in cash, above one hundred and fifty pounds, Irish currency, in bank notes; which, however, they artfully determined not, on any account, to circulate in the part of the kingdom in which they were obtained. This precaution became peculiarly necessary for several gentlemen having been robbed, the town took the alarm, which was the greater, or at least made the more noise, from the rarity of such events in that part of the kingdom, where the picking of pockets is said to be very little practised or known. But whatever the alarm was, or whatever noise it made, neither Barrington nor his accomplice was suspected. They, however, resolved to leave Derry as soon as they could with any appearance of propriety depart from thence; so that, having played a few nights as usual, with more applause than profit, they and their associates of the sock and buskin removed from Londonderry to Ballyshannon, in the county of Donegal, and never more returned into that part of the kingdom, where George Barrington may be considered to have commenced the business of a regular and professed pickpocket, in the summer of 1771, being at that time little more than sixteen years of age, and having just laid by the profession of a strolling player.

This wretched company having now become thieves as well as vagrants in the eye of the law, and compelled to subsist entirely upon the plunder above mentioned, after travelling about a fortnight arrived at Ballyshannon. Here Barrington, with the company to which he belonged spent the whole of autumn and the winter of the year 1771, playing generally on Tuesdays and Saturdays, and picking pockets with John Price every day in the week, whenever opportunity offered; a business which, though attended with danger and certain infamy, he found more lucrative and more entertaining than that of the theatre, where his fame and proficiency were by no means equal to the expectations he had raised, or to the hopes that had been formed of him on his first appearance at Drogheda.

From Ballyshannon, at length, having left the company of his friend Price, he moved to the southward, with his faithful Miss Egerton, whom he had the misfortune to lose for ever, in crossing the river Boyne, in which she was drowned, through the ignorance, or the more culpable carelessness of a ferryman.

Barrington, however, virtuous in his attachment to Miss Egerton, was for some time inconsolable for the loss which he had just sustained; but being neither of an age nor a temper propitious to the continuance of sorrowful sensations, he hastened to Limerick, where he hoped to meet Price, his old accomplice. On his arrival in that city, he learned that the person after whom he inquired had set out for Cork ten days before, and thither our adventurer followed him, and found him within an hour after he had entered the town gates. On their meeting, it was agreed on by them never more to think of the stage; a resolution which was the more easily executed, as the company to which they originally belonged was now broken up and dispersed. It was besides settled between them that Price should pass for Barrington's servant, and that Barrington should act the part of a gentleman of large fortune, and of a noble family, who was not yet quite of age, but, until he should attain that period, travelled for his amusement. In pursuance of this hopeful scheme, horses were purchased, and the master and man, now united as knight errant and esquire, and well equipped for every purpose of depredation, accordingly took their determination to act their several parts in the wide field of adventure; and thus in the summer of 1772, as the race grounds in the south of Ireland presented themselves as the fairest objects, they hastened to those scenes of spoliation, and were successful even beyond their expectation.

Picking pockets being rather new amongst the gentry of Ireland, their want of precaution rendered them a more easy prey to Mr. Barrington and his abandoned accomplice, who found means of retiring to Cork on the setting in of winter, with a booty of nearly two thousand pounds. In this city they found it convenient to fix their residence, at least till the next spring. And now it was that Barrington first determined within himself to become what has been called a gentleman pickpocket, and to affect both the airs and importance of a man of fashion.

In this desperate career of vice and folly, it was the fate of Price, the preceptor of Barrington, to be first detected in the act of picking the pocket of a gentleman of high rank, for which he was tried, convicted, and in a very short period sentenced to transportation for the term of seven years, to America.

Barrington naturally alarmed at the fate of his iniquitous preceptor, without loss of time converted all his moveable property into cash, and taking horse made as precipitate a journey to Dublin as he possibly could.

On his arrival there, he lived rather in a private

and retired manner, only lurking in the darkest
evenings about the playhouses, where he occasionally picked up a few guineas or a watch. But he
was soon weary of the sameness, and disgusted with
the obscurity of a life of comparative retirement,
such as that he had led in the Irish capital; so
that when the spring and fine weather that accompanied it returned, he embarked on board the Dorset yacht, which was then on the point of sailing
with the Duke of Lienster for Parkgate; and before
the expiration of a week, he found himself for the
first time of his life on English ground.

With Sir Alexander Schomberg, who commanded
the Dorset yacht, there were three other persons
embarked, and of some distinction, from whence it
appeared that the connection which our adventurer
formed with them had considerable effect afterwards
in the course of the long succession of transactions
in which he was engaged. A young captain was
one of the three who was most conspicuous, and,
as it will appear, a striking, though an innocent
cause of Barrington's success in his projects of depredation.

It did not require so much sagacity and penetration as Barrington at the time certainly possessed,
to penetrate into the character of this young gentleman, and to predict the consequences that might
follow an intimacy with a young man of his rank,
disposition, and family. Actuated by a sordid sense
of the utility of such a connexion to one in his circumstances, the adventurer employed all those base
arts of flattery and insinuation of which he had
long been a perfect master, to ingratiate himself

with this gentleman; and in this design he succeeded to the utmost extent of his wishes.

Barrington formed an artful tale, which he told as
his own story, the purport of which was, that his
father was a man of noble family in Ireland, and il-
lustrious in England, to which country he himself
now came to study the law in one of the inns of
court, more, however, to avoid the ill-natured severity of a harsh and unrelenting step-mother, which
rendered his paternal mansion in a great measure
intolerable to him, than from any predilection for
the profession to which he intended to apply himself,
but the exercise of which the ample fortune that he
was heir to would render unnecessary.

The story took as well as could be desired by
the inventor of it, and it was settled between him
and his new friend that he should, on his arrival in
town, enter himself of the Middle Temple, where
Mr. H ———n had some relations and a numerous
acquaintance, to whom, he said, he should be
happy to introduce a gentleman so eminently distinguished by his talents and his accomplishments,
as well as by fortune and birth, as Mr. Barrington
was.

It was also further agreed on between them, that
they should travel together to London; and they
accordingly the next day took a post chaise at Parkgate, and continuing their journey by easy stages
through Chester, Nantwich, and Coventry, where
they stopped two or three days, arrived by the end
of the week at the Bath coffee house in Piccadilly,
which, on the recommendation of the captain, who
had been several times before in the metropolis, was

fixed upon as their head quarters for the remaining part of the summer.

But the expensive manner in which he lived with Mr. H————n, and those to whose acquaintance that gentleman introduced him, all of them gay sprightly young fellows, who had money at command, in less than a month reduced the funds which Barrington had brought with him from Ireland to about twenty guineas, which to him, who had been for a few years accustomed to live like a man of affluent fortune, seemed to afford a very inconsiderable resource; he therefore resolutely determined to procure a supply of money by some means or other. One evening, while he was deliberating with himself on the choice of expedients to recruit his finances, he was interrupted in his meditations on the subject by the arrival of a party of his friends with the captain, who asked him to accompany them to Ranelagh, where they had agreed to meet some of their acquaintance, and spend the evening. Their proposal was, with much hesitation, acceded to by Barrington, and they, without further loss of time, ordered coaches to set them down at that celebrated place of amusement.

Walking in the middle of the gay scenes that surrounded them, he chanced to espy the two other companions of his voyage in the Dorset packet, to whom he made only a slight bow of recognition; and in less than a quarter of an hour afterwards, he saw the duke of Leinster engaged deeply in conversation with two ladies and a knight of Bath, who, it afterwards turned out, was Sir William Draper; and near these he placed himself, quitting for a short time the company to which he belonged.

While he was stationed there, an opportunity, which he considered a fair one, offered itself of making a good booty, and he availed himself of it; he picked the duke's pocket of above eighty pounds, Sir William's of five and thirty guineas, and one of the ladies of her watch, with all which he got off undiscovered by the parties, and joined the captain and his party as if nothing had happened out of the ordinary and common routine of affairs in such places of public recreation as Ranelagh.

A degree of fatality, rather unfortunate for Barrington, it seems, occurred during the perpetration of the robbery, just related; that is to say, he was observed in the very act by one of the persons who came with him in the Dorset packet from Ireland to Parkgate; and this man, who was also a practitioner in the same trade of infamy, lost no time in communicating what he had seen.

The consequence of a proposal of this nature presenting a disagreeable alternative, Mr. Barrington, as it may be imagined, naturally chose the least of two evils, and, under the pretence of being attacked with a sudden complaint, immediately retired with his new acquaintance to town, and putting up at the Golden Cross Inn, at Charing-cross, the booty acquired at Ranelagh was in some sense divided, the new intruder contenting himself with taking the lady's watch, chain, &c., which were of gold, and a ten pound note, leaving all the rest of the money and the bank-papers with Mr. Barrington, who, he probably conceived, had run the greatest risk to obtain them at first.

But in order to cement the connection which these two were now on the point of forming, Mr.

James (for by that name this new accomplice called himself), insisted upon Barrington supping with him; and as Mr. James knew the town much better than himself, Barrington thought he would be a real acquisition, particularly in helping him to dispose of the valuables he might acquire. Picking pockets, therefore, was proposed by Mr. Barrington as a joint concern.

The outlines of the future operations of these adventurous colleagues being adjusted, it was further agreed to have another interview the next day at a tavern in the Strand, there to regulate the plan of their future conduct; and affairs being so far arranged, Barrington returned to his lodgings at the Bath coffee-house, where, luckily enough, neither captain H———n nor any of his party were at that time returned from Ranelagh.

The next morning, at breakfast, he informed his friend the captain, that on his return last night, he chanced to meet with an old relation of his, Sir Fitzwilliam Barrington, who engaged him that day to dinner; so that it would be out of his power to make one of the party that were to spend the day with the captain at the Thatched house tavern; but that, however, he would endeavour to contrive matters so as to join them early in the evening, and stay to supper with them, if they were bent upon keeping it up till a late hour.

This apology was received without any suspicion by the gentleman to whom it was made, as it accounted plausibly enough for his fellow-traveller's absenting himself, notwithstanding he had a kind of prior engagement to Mr. H———n.

Afterwards, Barrington being dressed, called a

coach, and drove to the Crown and Anchor tavern, where he found Mr. James, who had been for some time waiting for him. The cloth being removed, and the servants withdrawn, these two worthy gentlemen entered upon business. It was agreed upon, that whatever either acquired, should be equally divided between them; and that, in the sale of jewels, watches, or any other articles they might have to dispose of, both should be present. By this provision, no suspicion of fraud could be entertained; and thus Barrington obtained what he sincerely wished, an introduction to a fence, or a receiver of stolen goods. It was further settled by them, that while the captain remained in town, they should take care not to be seen together, and that Mr. James should resume his long neglected habit of a clergyman. These weighty conditions, and some others of equal magnitude and importance, being ultimately adjusted, to the satisfaction of these systematic plunderers, it was determined on, that they should meet regularly twice a week, that is, on Tuesdays, and on Fridays, to settle with each other! but never, if it could possibly be avoided, twice at the same house. Having then adjourned to the next Tuesday, and fixed on the Devil tavern, at Temple-bar, as their next place of meeting, our adventurers separated for that time, and Barrington went, in accordance with his appointment, to the Thatched-house tavern, and arrived there about eight at night, where he found his friend the captain, and a large party of his acquaintance. Though rather far gone in liquor, most of them knew him personally, and considering him in the light in which he was represented to them by captain H———n, as a young man of condition, they were delighted with his company. He only waited till the bills were called for, and the reckoning paid, when, there being no farther obstacle to a hasty retreat, he plundered those who were most off their guard; or rather those who, as he supposed, were possessed of the most portable kind of property. Still, as the prey then made consisted more of watches and trinkets, than ready money, he was under the necessity of calling upon Mr. James, his new friend, the next morning, who readily introduced him to a man, who was a receiver of stolen property, and who, paying them what they deemed an adequate consideration, they made the first division with as much apparent satisfaction, as if they had been lawful dealers in the commodities, of which they had unjustly deprived the right owners.

So strongly did appearances plead for him at this time, that Barrington's depredation was never imputed to him by those who suffered in consequence of it; and though similar offences were at different seasons, for upwards of two years, committed by him without suspicion or detection, he preserved his fame, and even extended his acquaintance.— With certain superficial qualifications for shining in company, and yet a stranger to honour and honesty. In the summer of 1775, in the course of his depredations, he visited, as his custom was, the most celebrated watering places; and amongst the rest, he paid a visit to Brighton, which at that time, though frequented by genteel company, was very far from having arrived at that celebrity which it has since acquired, especially since the peace with France. But notwithstanding the paucity of num-

bers in this place, he is said to have had the address
to ingratiate himself into the notice and favour of
the late duke of Ancaster, with several other persons of rank and property, who all considered him
as a man of genius and ability, and as a gentleman
of fortune and noble family.

But tracing all Mr. Barrington's very singular
connexions, it is necessary to remark, that about
the conclusion of this winter, he became acquainted with one Lowe, a very singular character, and
one who, like his friend James, he occasionally made
use of to vend his ill-gotten property.

Mr. Barrington's new junction with Mr. Lowe,
having rendered Mr. James rather a dead weight
upon his hands, he began to think about breaking
with him, which he did not find a difficult matter,
as Mr. James, having at bottom some remorse of
conscience for his neglect of the laws of justice and
moral obligation, very easily quitted Mr. Barrington's connexion; and what is more extraordinary,
being a Roman Catholic by profession, retired to a
monastery upon the Continent, there in all probability, to end his days in piety and peace.

Barrington on the other hand, seemed to increase
his temerity and desperation; for, on his forming a
connexion with Lowe, which was but a short time
previous to that evening of the month of January,
which was observed as the anniversary of the queen's
birth-day, it was resolved on between them, that,
habited as a clergyman, he should repair to court,
and there endeavour, not only to pick the pockets
of some of the company, but, what was a bolder
and much more novel attempt, to cut off the diamond orders of some of the Garter, Bath, and

Thistle, who on such days, usually wear the collars
of their respective orders over their coats.   In this
enterprise, he succeeded beyond the most sanguine
expectations, that could have been formed by either
his new accomplice Lowe, or himself; for he found
means to deprive a nobleman of his diamond order,
and also contrived to get away from the palace with·
out suspicion.   This being an article of much value
to dispose of in England, it is reported that it was
sold to a Dutchman, or rather to a Dutch Jew, who
came over from Holland once or twice a year, for
the sole object of buying jewels that had been stolen; and though a stranger, he is generally reported
to have given a much higher price for articles than
could have been obtained from any receivers in
town.

The celebrated Russian Prince Orloff, paid his
first visit to England in the winter of 1775.   The
high degree of estimation in which that nobleman
had long been held by the late empress Catherine,
had ultimately heaped upon him not a few of her
distinguished favours.   Among other things of this
nature, she had expressed her approbation of his
merits, by presenting him with a gold snuff box,
set with brilliants, generally supposed to have been
worth no less a sum than thirty thousand pounds.
This distinguishing trophy having caught the eye
of Barrington, impelled him to contrive means to
get it into his possession, and he thought a fit opportunity presented itself, one night at Covent Garden theatre, where, getting near the prince, he had
the dexterity to convey it out of his excellency's
waistcoat pocket into his own: when, being immediately suspected by the prince, he seized him by

the collar; but, in the bustle that took place, Barrington slipped the box into his hand, which that nobleman gladly retained, though Barrington, to the astonishment of all near, was secured and lodged in Tothill-fields Bridewell, till the Wednesday following, when his examination took place at the public office in Bow-street.

Sir John Fielding being at that time the magistrate, Barrington represented himself to him as a native of Ireland, of an affluent and respectable family. He said that he had been educated in the medical line, and came to England to improve himself by the extent of his connexions. To this plausible representation he added so many tears, and seemed to rest so many upon his being an unfortunate gentleman, rather than a guilty culprit, that prince Orloff declining to prosecute him, he was dismissed with an admonition from the magistrate to amend his future conduct; but this, it will appear, had no manner of influence upon his subsequent proceedings. In fact, Barrington having gone too far to recede, every one now taking alarm at his character and conduct, and the public prints naturally holding him up as a cheat and impostor, he was even forsaken by those who, until that discovery of his practises, generally countenanced him, and enjoyed his company as a young gentleman of no common abilities.

Being in the lobby of the lords one day, when an appeal of an interesting nature was expected to come on, so that Barrington thought to profit by numbers of genteel people that attend; unhappily for Barrington's projects, a gentleman recognised his person, and applying to the deputy usher of

the black rod, Barrington was disgracefully turned
out, and, of course totally disappointed of the
harvest he had promised himself.

Barrington, having by some means heard the name
of the gentleman who had denounced him to the
keeper of the lobby, was so indiscreet as to threaten
him with revenge for what he deemed an unmerited
injury; but the magistrates thinking otherwise, they
granted a warrant upon that gentleman's complaint,
against Barrington, to bind him over to keep the
peace. His credit having sunk so very low, that no
one of all his numerous acquaintance would become
a surety for him, he was compelled to go to Tothill
fields Bridewell, where he remained a considerable
time under confinement from his inability to procure
the bail that was required. However, having obtained release from that unpleasant quarter, he had
no alternative but that of his old profession, and
therefore, in about three months afterwards, we
find him detected in picking the pocket of a low
woman, at Drury lane theatre, for which, being indicted and convicted at the Old Bailey, he was sentenced to ballast heaving, or, in other words, to
three years' hard labour on the river Thames, on
board of the hulks at Woolwich. As soon as it
was convenient, in the spring of 1777, Barrington
was put on board one of these vessels.

A sudden remove from ease and affluence to a
scene of wretched servitude and sorrow, and the
privation of almost every comfort in life, could not
but have a most sensible effect upon a man in his
condition. In short, he was not only harassed and
fatigued with labour to which he had been unaccustomed, but even disgusted with the filthy langu-

age of his fellow convicts, whose blasphemous effusions, which they seemed to make use of by way of amusement, must have been a constant source of the most disagreeable sensations in the mind of almost any persons not totally lost to the feelings and decencies of civilized, or even a savage state of existence. At length the mental, as well as the corporeal suffering of Barrington, did not escape the notice of Messrs. Erskine and Duncan Campbell, the superintendents of the convicts ; for, in consequence of Barrington's good behaviour, and through the interference of these gentlemen, he was set at liberty, after sustaining nearly a twelvemonth's suffering on board the hulks at Woolwich.

Still, nothing that Barrington had yet undergone was sufficient to produce any cordial repentance in his mind. He entered anew into the full practice of his former profession. In six months after his liberation from hard labour, he was detected by one Payne, a very zealous constable in the city, in the very act of picking pockets at St. Sepulchre's church during divine service, and being convicted upon undeniable evidence at the ensuing Old Bailey sessions, he was a second time sentenced to hard labour on board the hulks, and that for five years.

It was upon his trial on this occasion, that Barrington was first noticed in the public prints as an able speaker. He then essayed, with no small degree of artifice, to interest the feelings of the court in his behalf ; but the evidences of his guilt being too forcible and repeated, and all his efforts proving abortive, he was again removed to the hulks, about the middle of the year 1778. Being a second time in this humiliating and disgraceful situation, he found his imaginary consequence so much hurt, that, failing in a variety of plans to effect his escape, his next attempt was to destroy himself. For this purpose, he took an opportunity of being seen stabbing himself with a penknife in the breast, but as the wound, by the immediate application of medical assistance, was slowly healed, he continued to linger in this new state of wretchedness, till happening to be seen by a gentleman who came to visit the hulks, it produced another event in his favour.

The gentleman just alluded to being most sensibly affected by the dejected and squalid appearance of Barrington, made a most successful use of his influence with government to obtain Barrington's release, upon the condition that he should leave the kingdom. To this as Barrington gladly assented, he generously supplied him with a sum of money to defray the expense of his removal to Ireland, where it is understood this unhappy offender always persisted in stating that he had friends and relatives of credit and character. In London he did not think proper to stay longer than was needful to procure necessaries for his journey; he therefore took the Chester coach, and in the course of a week was enabled to reach the Irish capital, where his fame having arrived before, he was looked upon with such an eye of suspicion, that he was shortly apprehended for picking the pocket of an Irish nobleman of a gold watch and his money at one of the theatres, and was soon after committed to the New Jail to be tried upon the charge, but was acquitted for want of evidence.

Though he was acquitted on this occasion, he

was perfectly convinced the Irish capital would be too warm to retain him. He quickly determined to leave Ireland, and accordingly removed to the northern part of that kingdom, through which he took his way to Edinburgh, where he concluded that he might, for some time at least, commit his depredations with greater safety and facility than he could do either in London or Dublin.

But, in the opinion which he had formed of the character of the Scots, he soon learned by experience that he was grossly mistaken; for he was quickly observed in the capital of Scotland, where the police is more vigilant and severe than in most other parts of the British dominions. He therefore thought it prudent to depart from Edinburgh, where his gleanings were comparatively small.

However, being determined to return to London, he took Chester in his way, and it being fair time there, he is said to have contrived to get possession of the amount of six hundred pounds in cash and bank notes, with which he got clear off.

Such are the delusions of vice and the fatal sweets of ill gotten wealth, that, though additional danger attended his public appearance, from the infraction of the terms on which he was liberated from his confinement on board the hulks, (which were those of his leaving the kingdom and never more returning to it,) still he frequented the theatres, the Opera House, and the Pantheon, with tolerable success. But he was now too notorious to be long secure: he was closely watched and well nigh detected at the latter of these places; at least, such strong suspicions were entertained by the magistrates of his conduct on the occasion, that he was taken into custody, and committed to Newgate.

Here again, for want of evidence, he got clear of the charge brought against him; but, notwithstanding this, he was unexpectedly detained at the instance of Mr. Duncan Campbell, the superintendent of the convicts, for having returned to England in violation of the condition on which his majesty was pleased to grant him a remission of the punishment which he was sentenced to undergo on board the hulks; and the consequence of the detainer was, that he was made what is called a *fine* at Newgate, during the unexpired part of the time that he was originally to have served on the Thames. When the period of his captivity in this prison expired, he was, as a matter of course, set a liberty, when he returned to his former practices. He, however, was now more cautious; and being connected with some accomplices of his own cast, he was not so easily detected as he might have been with others less experienced.

In a state of alarm and anxiety, he lived a considerable time in the society of the most profligate and abandoned characters of the metropolis, when he was seen to pick the pocket of Mr. Le Mesurier, of Drury-lane theatre, and was immediately apprehended. Charge of him was given to one Blandy, a constable, who, through negligence or corruption, suffered him to make his escape. The proceedings against him were carried on to an outlawry, and various methods were made use of to detect him, for nearly two years, without effect.

But while the lawyers were outlawing him, and the constables endeavouring to take him, he was travelling in various disguises and characters through the northern counties of this kingdom.

He visited the great towns in those parts as a quack doctor, or as a clergyman; sometimes he went with an E. O. table, and sometimes he pretended to be a rider to a manufacturing house at Birmingham or Manchester; and travelling on horseback, with a decent deportment and grave appearance, the account which he thought proper to give of himself was credited, without any difficulty by those who questioned him.

But in spite of all these precautions, it sometimes happened that he was known by gentlemen whom he met, once particularly in Lincolnshire; yet not one offered to intercept or molest him, until he arrived at Newcastle upon-Tyne, where, on being recognised, he was suspected of picking pockets, and on inquiry was disdovered to be an outlaw: upon which he was removed by a writ of habeas corpus to London, and imprisoned in Newgate, where he arrived very miserable and so dejected, that on learning his circumstances, some of his friends made a subscription for him, by which he was enabled to employ counsel, and to take legal measures to have the outlawry against him reversed.

This being effected, he was tried for the original offence, that of stealing Mr. Le Mesurier's purse; but, through the absence of the Rev. Mr. Adeane, a material witness for the prosecution, he was acquitted. Being once more enlarged, he again set off for Ireland, in company with a young man of the name of Hubert, well known in the town for his fraud on the Duke of York. With this accomplice, he was so infatuated as to endeavour to carry on

T

his depredations in Dublin, where it was never his fortune to carry on his depredations for any length of time undetected ; for, Hubert being taken in the act of picking a gentleman's pocket, and handing the money to Barrington, he with great difficulty made his escape to England, where he rambled about for some time previous to his arrival in the capital, which he had scarcely entered, when he was taken into custody, for picking Mr. Henry Hare Townsend's pocket of a gold watch.

Hubert, his accomplice, was tried at Dublin, and sentenced to transportation for seven years ; but he afterwards contrived to make his escape.

On Wednesday morning, September 15, 1790, Barrington was put to the bar to be arraigned on an indictment, charging him with stealing, on the 1st of September, 1790, in the parish of Enfield, a gold watch, chain, and seals, the property of Henry Hare Townsend, Esq. Upon this occasion Barrington displayed all the talents which it has been universally allowed he possessed; but in spite of a long speech, which professed, whether sincere or assumed, great contrition for his past offences, and a determination to amend his life for the future, he was convicted, and sentenced by the judge to seven years' transportation.

During the voyage to Port Jackson, Barrington rendered an essential service in quelling a mutiny in the vessel. Upon this occasion the captain evinced his gratitude for the services he had performed, and when they had reached the Cape, at the recommendation of the former, he received a hundred dollars reward for his zeal and activity. On their arrival at Port Jackson, Barrington having been

recommended to the governor, was placed in the first
instance in Tamgabbe as a subordinate, and was
soon advanced to be a principal watchman, in which
situation he acquitted himself as a useful and active officer; insomuch that the governor determined
to withdraw him from the convicts; and at the
same time that he received his instrument of eman-
cipation, he was presented with the grant of thirty
acres of land at Paramatta. He was subsequently
appointed superintendent of the convicts; and although not permitted to return to England, he was
invested with all the immunities of a freeman, a set-
tler, and a civil officer, and had the satisfaction to
know that his diligence and activity were not only
without suspicion, but were fully appreciated.

It was here that Barrington resolved to revise
the notes he had taken during the voyage, and of
describing more fully the places they had touched at.
He has accordingly produced a very useful and in-
structive work.

In addition to this performance, he compiled a
complete history of the country itself, from its first
discovery, which included an account of its original
inhabitants, their customs and manners, with an
historical detail of the proceedings of the colony
from its foundation to his own time. He continued
in the situation in which the governor had placed
him till his death : and performed the duties of his
office with an unwearied assiduity, which at last su-
perinduced a general decay of nature, of which he
died in the year 1811.

WOLFE.

PASSING through Germany on my tour over Europe, I arrived at the village of Stutgard, in the summer of 1779, about three or four years before an execution was to take place, the wretched victims whereof were the topic of every one's conversation, who, at the same time as they condemned their actions, felt for the agonizing pangs which they were doomed to suffer.

The parish church having been broken open, and robbed of every thing valuable about three months previous to my arrival, several persons had been apprehended on suspicion, many of whom had been put to the rack, in order to extort a confession, but without any success ; in consequence of which, the magistrates had been obliged to release them for want of sufficient evidence to condemn them, and to give up all farther inquiry, till chance should bring the matter to light.

Many weeks had now elapsed before the enraged and disappointed priests, aided by the eagle-eyed assistance of the justice, were able to trace out the sacrilegious robbers of the sacred treasures, and feast their savage vengeance on the struggles of the victims of their remorseless fury expiring on the fatal pile, when at length an accident effected what all the tortures of the rack, their advertisements, and large promises of reward, were not able to do, and delivered into their holy fangs the perpetrators of that horrid action.

There lived in the outskirts of the village an old man named Peter, unsuspected by any one, and a great favourite with the children of the place, whom he often treated with sweetmeats and nicknacks, frequently amusing them also with little stories of his own invention; but he was universally feared by the aged, whose credulity went so far as to persuade them that he had dealings with the infernal monarch of the lower regions, and for no other reason than because, when he was in a good humour, he would show them some proof of the skill he had in the art of legerdemain.

This hoary headed man, who lived in an almost ruined cottage, with every appearance of the most extreme indigence, and could not be supposed to possess any ill gotten wealth, went frequently abroad, but for what purpose the neighbours, with all their prying curiosity, were never able to discover, though some ventured to affirm that he went a begging: others, still more superstitious, asserted that they had seen him through the chinks of the window shutters, laying seemingly deprived of life; while some again declared, in the most positive manner, that they had seen him flying through the air on a broomstick, to pay a visit, as they pretended, to his infernal master, to whom it was said he had sold both his body and soul.

Luckily for him, this man was absent from the village at the time this church robbery was committed, to the infinite satisfaction of some who thought him to be a harmless being, and to the vexation of those who pretended to have been considerable sufferers by the malicious tricks of his reputed sorcery; since, if he had not, the latter would have found

some pretext to deliver him into the hands of the
civil power, as a suspicious person, because he
never went to church, although he was reputed to
be a Roman Catholic.

Some weeks after the above mentioned prisoners
had been discharged, Peter returned to the village
on a holiday after sunset. The children no sooner
saw him approach than they left off their play, and
ran toward him, hailing their hoary friend with loud
acclamations of joy, searching his pockets for sweet
meats, and teazing the poor man so unmercifully,
that he lost all patience, and threatened to chastise
his clamorous followers with a staff that he used
commonly to walk with. The threat only served to make them more boisterous than before ; and
some of them, being more mischievous than the
rest, began to prick him with pins ; which exasperated him to such a degree as to induce him to put
his threat actually into execution ; which was no
sooner perceived by the mothers of these unmannerly
boys, than they flew on him like so many harpies,
in order to revenge the outrage he had committed
on their darling offspring, and his profanation of the
holiday ; and at the same time alarmed the whole
neighbourhood with the loudness of their vociferation, which soon brought the husbands of these female viragoes to their assistance, while the children
made the uproar still greater with their cries, upon
seeing their old benefactor thus exposed to the fury
of their enraged parents.

As for poor Peter, he with much difficulty made
all possible haste out of the crowd, in order to free
himself from the clutches of his merciless persecutors, but not without receiving many a hard blow

from the infatuated vindicators of juvenile imperti-
nence, and at length sheltered himself from farther
persecution under the roof of his own humble dwelling.

As soon as he had removed in some measure
from the flurry which this unexpected attack had
thrown him into, he, to his inexpressible terror, discovered that he had left his wallet behind him in
the scuffle, and rushed forth like a madman, in order to use his endeavours to recover his lost property; which upon his arrival at the former scene
of action, he discovered the victorious party carrying off in triumphant exaltation. In vain did he
exert all the rhetoric he was master of; it was all
to no purpose, although he entreated, whined, and
at length, almost driven to madness, called down a
thousand curses on them for their treachery; since,
to his no small misfortune, the hearts of his enemies were as void of penetration as the adamantine
rock; and when, in a paroxysm of rage and chagrin,
he attempted to regain it by force they drove him
back to his humble dwelling amid a violent shower
of stones.

On searching the wallet, the first objects that
presented themselves were a tattered pair of breeches,
an old ragged shirt, and several odd stockings.
Next a large book, and a few curious instruments;
at last they found a leathern bag at the bottom, tied
with cord in such a manner as completely baffled
all their efforts to untie it: but at length they succeeded in gratifying their curiosity, by cutting the
bag; when to the amazement of the gaping assembly, a vast quantity of gold and silver pieces fell
from the hole they had made upon the ground. A

long silence now ensued, which at length was interrupted by a voice exclaiming, 'thanks to St.
Nicholas! the mystery is unravelled, and we have
now found out the sacrilegious robber of our church.'
There was no more wanting to make the enraged
multitude resolve on his destruction, who went immediately in a body to the justice roaring out with
one voice, that they had at length found out
the vile despoiler of the church. The justice,
amazed at the unusual uproar, felt a strong inclination to inquire into the real cause of it, and accordingly ordered some of the principals to be admitted: but his astonishment was considerably increased when they showed him the vast quantity of
money they had found in the wallet of father Peter.
In the mean time, such of the mob as had not been
admitted, made the best of their way to the mean
hovel of their victim, whom they, with relentless
fury pulled forth, and hurried him to the justice's
house amid innumerable blows and insults, where
he was immediately delivered into the hands of
the officers of justice, who instantly conveyed him
to the town-house, and the next day was brought to
trial, when he was commanded to give an account of
himself and by what means he became possessed of
such a sum of money; which he, however refused
to make any answer to, except he became possessed
of it in an honest manner; and, even when he had
been put to the rack, he still persisted in his first
assertion; through which the justice, being unable
to convict him of what was laid to his charge, was
obliged to set him at liberty, but refused to restore
the money until he should have brought some
person to prove that he had obtained his money by

lawful means. Father Peter promised the justice
that he would produce a satisfactory account of his
accumulated wealth ; and taking his leave, made
the best of his way to his humble dwelling : which,
upon his arrival, he found had been closely inspect-
ed by his neighbours, who, upon being unable to
discover any other articles than a few tattered
clothes and some broken remnants of furniture, retired greatly disappointed, after having thrown every
thing about the place ; which, however, father Peter consoled himself for, by reflecting that, although
he had lost his money, he had, by perseverance and
fortitude, regained his liberty.

In the mean time the justice, who was what the
world terms a very prudent man, pretended to drop
all farther inquiry ; but under this mask of indolent
security, he secretly set some of his most trusty
followers to watch the motions of father Peter,
which for some time seemed of no avail. However he was seen at last by one of his neighbours
leave his house one morning by the break of day,
and set of with a wallet on his back and a staff in
his hand, full speed. This good-natured neighbour,
proud of the opportunity, fled to the officers of
Justice, in order to inform them of what he had
seen, who no sooner received this intelligence, than
they set off after him in disguise ; and after a sharp
walk of several hours succeeded in getting sight of
him about noon, whom they followed at a distance,
until they saw him enter a lonely alehouse ; when,
having waited a long time for his coming out to no
purpose, they began to entertain suspicions of an
unfavourable kind, and accordingly hid themselves
behind an adjacent hedge, where they continued

waiting his re appearance until the twilight set in.
The sable queen of night had scarcely spread her
dun mantle over the terrestrial globe, when the
trampling of distant horses assailed their ears, and
seemed to approach nearer and nearer. Nor were
they at all out of their opinion, for soon after a
troop of horsemen alighted, and entered the same
house as father Peter had done before them ; which
the spies no sooner saw than they ventured from
their hiding places, and crept along softly to the
windows, where they had not listened long before
they heard the jingling of money, and upon peeping
through one of the cracks of the window shutters,
discovered a number of armed men sitting round a
table nearly covered with dollars, and father Peter
at the head, feasting his eyes, with the delicious
prospect before him. The officers, having now got
sufficient information, seized each of them one of
the robber's horses, and mounting them, rode-back
to the town with all possible speed.

As the public house was situated at a distance
only two leagues from the village, it did not take
them more than an hour riding thither; when, upon
informing the justice of all they had heard and
seen, they were immediately sent back with a large
party of the town guard, well armed, and mounted
on the fleetest horse they could procure. The
whole party arrived at the scene of action a few
hours before midnight, where they actually found
the robbers still seated round the table, drinking and
carousing in the utmost security. It is impossible
for words to describe the horror of the robbers, who
all started up as if they had been awaked by a sudden clap of thunder upon the town's guard rushing

into the room, who seizing their arms, threatened
to blow their brains out, if they offered to make any
resistance; upon which the robbers, giving way to
despair, patiently submitted to have their hands
tied. This done, father Peter, the servants of the
house, and the landlord, whom they found concealed under the bed, were seized, and as soon as they
were properly secured, borne off in triumph with
their vile associates. The robbers who were ten in
number, were dressed in hunting coats, and their
purses filled with both gold and silver. The whole
cavalcade moved on slowly with lighted torches,
and arrived at the village before day-break; when,
owing to the lateness of the hour the prisoners were
lodged in separate dungeons. Early in the ensuing
morning they were had up for trial; and the youngest of the robbers being questioned first, refused to
make the smallest confession; upon which he was
put to the rack, which soon made his stubbornness
to give way; and unable to bear the torture, he
screamed out for mercy; and upon being let down,
made an ample discovery of all that he knew, namely,
that their gang consisted of fifty three in number,
and was scattered all over the country; they had
secret places under ground, but their principal resort or head quarter, was an old castle, on the bor-
ders of the black forest, which was also the grand
magazine of their ill got treasure.

He also confessed that father Peter was in close
connexion with them, and that he never had any
settled place of abode, but took up his residence
sometimes in that village, and at other times in the
adjacent ones, that he was also possessed of the
burghership in several cities, in which he had both

houses and estates. The robber concluded with a solemn denial of having any hand in the robbery committed in the church, but at the same time pointed out three of the prisoners, whom he said had been concerned in it, adding, that he could not tell whether father Peter had been accessory in that affair or not. The day being now far advanced, they were remanded back to prison; and the next morning, the three robbers, who had been charged with the sacrilege by their companion, were brought to the bar, but all of them refused to plead guilty: upon which they were put to the rack, when the first of them, who was an aged man, bore the three degrees with the utmost fortitude, and died a few hours after, without ever divulging the secret. The second confessed, at the third degree, that he had been concerned in the above robbery, at the same time declaring, in the most solemn manner, that his surviving companion was innocent, and that he himself had been persuaded by father Peter to commit the sacrilege. The hoary hypocrite was next called to the bar, who listened to the charges laid against him with the utmost composure, and then made an ample confession of his guilt in the following words :—

Yes, exclaimed he, his whole frame trembling with the violence of his emotions, I am guilty; and would to God, that I had no other crime to answer for but this. The monks who are the votaries of luxuriousness and debauchery, and who, in honour of an image of stone, have with a savage fury, ruined and drove from their native land an innocent family, who, in consequence of their cruelty have been forced to beg for their bread in the streets of this village, these obdurate villains are far greater felons than myself; and I therefore rejoice at having been chose out by Providence as an humble instrument in its hands to avenge the wrongs of those innocent sufferers, and in having been enabled to restore to the hapless objects of their rapacity, in some measure, their lost property. If this action of mine appears in your eyes deserving of punishment, you may tear these old limbs asunder; but, although you may break those withered bones, and reduce my worn out frame to original nonentity, you shall not hear me groan, nor utter a single complaint, conscious of the rectitude of my own action.

Here he paused, and the judge and the sheriffs gazed at each other in silent astonishment, not daring to question him any farther; which he perceiving, proceeded voluntarily to inform them of every occurrence respecting the sacrilege, the family he had before alluded to, and how the jewels, gold and silver furniture, which had been taken out of the church and convent, had been converted into money, and forwarded to the injured parties, whom he had discovered by means of an original will, which the monks had secreted at the time when they forged another, in which it was pretended that the testator had left the whole of his possessions to religious uses, and that the whole had been carried on in so secret a manner, that they were not even acquainted with the names of their benefactors.

The astonishment of those who were present, increased with every word he uttered; and as soon as he ceased to speak, a general buz of admiration was heard throughout the court: while the generous motives attending the sacrilege, and the frankness of his confession, operated so strongly in favour with his judges, that they resolved unanimously to miti-gate his sentence if possible; in consequence of which resolution, father Peter and his associate were put to the bar, in order to have sentence pronounced against them.　According to the laws of this coun-try, which in these cases exert their utmost rigour, the two culprits should have been burnt alive ; but the judge giving way to the dictates of his heart, doomed them to be first beheaded and then burnt; during which awful period, father Peter displayed the greatest firmness of mind, at the same time comforting his companion, although he had betray-ed him.　As soon as the sentence was passed, he thanked the judges for their clemency, and then left the court, supporting with his arm his confede-rate, who, possessed of less fortitude than himself, presented to view a ghastly portraiture of despair and despondency.　The next day was appointed for their execution.　I left the court overwhelmed with misery, and retired to my inn, where I passed the night in broken slumbers, so much was my mind taken up with the occurrences of the preceding day ; from which I was awakened the next morning by the solemn tolling of bells, which announced the ap-proaching execution.　I immediately arose; and set out with trembling steps, where father Peter was to atone for his past crimes.　The streets were crowd-ed by the gaping multitude, who seemed to await with savage curiosity the approaching spectacle.—

Struck with secret awe, I approached the place of execution, and my blood chilled with horror on beholding the fatal pile that was soon to terminate the lives of my fellow creatures.　I had not, however, been long in that situation, before a sudden noise awoke me from my reverie; and, upon raising my eyes, I beheld the solemn procession advancing slowly toward the scaffold. Father Peter marched foremost with firm and manly steps, followed by his fellow sufferer who, if possible, looked ten times more dejected than before. Already the sword of the executioner was lifted in the air, and glistened in the sun, waiting the appointed signal to give the fatal blow. Every eye appeared fixed on the place of execution; and it was not until father Peter had expiated for his former crimes, that they seemed sensible of any other object.

Upon hearing that the captain of the robbers was to be tried the next day, I suffered curiosity once more to get the better of my prejudice, and resolved to stay one day longer.

The trial began at six in the morning. I took care to secure a good place before the arrival of the terrible leader of the robbers, who no sooner appeared at the bar, than an universal terror seemed to pervade the whole assembly, on beholding him. He was of a gigantic make, near seven feet high, his robust limbs corresponding with his extraordinary size. His black and bushy hair covered part of his sun burnt face, which was disfigured by two large scars across his left cheek. His eye (for he had but one left,) flashed like lightning when he beheld the dread arbiters of life and death eager to pronounce his doom. The judge exhorted him to speak the truth, and not to aggravate his guilt by stubbornness. However, nobody expected that a wretch of his appearance would pay the least regard to gentle admonitions, and perhaps remain silent under the tortures of the rack. His savage look and lofty mien seemed to betoken an haughty spirit not easy to be subdued. Imagine, therefore, my astonishment, when contrary to all expectation, he began as follows :—

My Lord and Gentlemen,—I am in your power, and well aware that nothing can avert my impending doom. I scorn the tortures of the rack, and defiance to every human effort, to force me to a confession of my crimes. You might tear my limbs asunder and kill me by inches, and yet you would never extort a single word from my lips, if I had no other reasons to deal candidly with you. However, I will spare you that trouble, and openly confess my crimes, their origin, and their progress, by being firmly persuaded that the history of my life will afford a useful lesson to judges, and teach the guardians of the people to be careful how they inflict punishments, if they will not make a complete rogue of a hapless wretch, who would have been recalled to his duty, and preserved to human society, by gentle treatment. I never should have become a robber, had not the too great severity of the laws made me an enemy to mankind, and hurried me to the brink of despair. I know my doom is fixed. However, if your heart is no stranger to pity, you will at least not refuse a tear of humanity to a poor unhappy man who has been dragged by dire fatality into the path of vice, and forced to commit deeds his soul abhors.

Here he stopped. Awful silence swayed around, and my curiosity was harrowed up to the highest degree, when he proceeded in nearly the following strain:

'I am the son of an innkeeper at A——, whose name was Wolfe, and who died when I reached my twenty-fourth year. I succeeded him in his business, which, being but indifferent, afforded me a deal of leisure time. Being an only son, I had been spoiled by my parents, who were delighted with my wanton pranks, and indulged me in the most foolish fond manner. Grown up girls complained of my impudence when I was but twelve years old, and the boys all paid homage to my inventive genius. Nature had not been at all deficient with me in respect of bodily endowments; but an unfortunate kick from a horse so disfigured my face, that the girls of the village shunned me, and my playfellows took every opportunity to make me an object of their ridicule. The more my female acquaintances avoided me, the stronger grew my desire of pleasing. As I grew up, I was given to sensuality, and at last persuaded myself to be in love. The object of my attachment treated me with scorn, and I had reason to apprehend that my rivals were more successful than myself; but the girl being poor, I flattered myself that her heart, which was inaccessible to my vows and prayers, would yield to presents, which I knew not how to procure, the small income of my business being scarce sufficient to defray the expences I was at in vainly endeavouring to render my person less disgusting. Naturally addicted to idleness, and too proud to retrench my expensive mode of life, I had only one resource left to better my fortune—a desperate one, though thousands have often tried it with success. The village in which I lived gave me frequent opportunities of committing depredations on the game, and the money I raised in that way wandered regularly into the hands of my mistress. Robert, a game keeper to the lord of the manor, was one of the admirers of Jenny, which was the name of my paramour, he soon observed the advantage which my presents procured me over him, and being spurred by envy and jealousy, he watched me closely. By degrees he resorted to the Sun, which was the sign of my inn, more frequently than ever, and his prying eye soon detected the source of my liberal gifts.

I was thrice detected, and thrice punished, by the instrumentality of the game keeper Robert; but on obtaining my liberty I had recourse to my old practices.

This mode of life I continued several months without being detected. One morning I was rambling through the forest, pursuing the traces of a deer. Having hunted without success two tedious hours, I began to give up every hope of coming at my prey. when I saw it once more within the reach of my gun. I took my aim, and was going to fire, but started suddenly back, when I saw a hat upon the ground not far from me. I looked around with great circumspection, and beheld Robert, the gamekeeper, standing behind the trunk of an oak, and aiming at the same deer which I intended to kill. My blood froze within my veins, as I beheld the author of all my misfortunes: and this very man, whom I hated most among the whole human race, was within the use of my fusee.

An infernal joy thrilled my whole frame. I would not have exchanged my gun for the universe; the burning revenge, which till then had been rankling

in my bosom, rose up into my fingers' ends, which
was going to put an end to my adversaries, life, when
an invisible hand seemed to retain my arm to prevent the horrid deed. I trembled violently, as I
directed my gun against my foe; a chilly sweat be-
dewed my face; my teeth began to chatter, as if a
frost had seized my frame; methought I felt the
icy fang of death upon my heart, and every nerve
was quivering. I hesitated a minute—one minute
more elapsed—and now a third. Revenge and conscience were struggling violently for victory. The
former gained, and Robert lay weltering in his
blood. My gun dropped on the ground when he
fell. Murderer! I exclaimed in quivering lips.
Advancing nearer to the spot where my enemy was
swimming in his blood, I saw him just expire.
Petrified with horror I stood motionless before my
murdered foe. At length, a yelling laughter restored me to the use of my senses. Wilt thou any
more tell tales, good friend? said I, stepping boldly
nearer, and turning him upon his back. For six
hours I fled through the forest; as I entered a narrow footpath, which led through the darkest thicket,
suddenly a rough commanding voice ordered me to
stop. The voice was not far off: agony and the
horrors of despair, which had assumed their dreadful sway over me, had made me entirely regardless
to the objects around me; my eyes were cast to the
ground, and I had covered part of my face with my
hat, as if that could have hidden me from the eye
of the lifeless creation. Starting and lifting up my
eyes, I saw a savage looking man coming towards
me. He was armed with a tremendous club, his
figure was of a monstrous size (my first surprise,

at least, had made me think so,) and the colour of his face was of the mulatto hue, which gave to the white of a squinting eye additional terrors. Instead of a girdle, he had a buttonless coat, tied with a thick cord, to which an enormous knife and a brace of pistols were fastened. I had quickened my steps when his terrible voice assailed my ears, but he soon came up with me, and stopped me with a powerful arm. The sound of a human voice filled my soul with terror; however, the sight of a ruffian raised my spirits. In my miserable situation, I had reason to tremble at the sight of an honest man, but none at all at a robber.

Who art thou? thundered the frightful figure in my ear. Thy equal, I replied, if thou art really what thy appearance bespeaks?—This is not the right way. What business hast thou here?—And what right hast thou to question me? I replied in a determined accent.

The terrible man surveyed me from top to toe. He seemed to compare my haughty answer with my defenceless situation. Thou art an impudent beggar, he resumed at length. Very possible, I have been one but yesterday. He laughed, exclaiming, with a horrid grin, my honest friend, I hope thou dost not presume to be thought any thing better.— That is nothing to thee. So saying, I wanted to pursue my way.

Fairly and softly my dear boy, why in such a hurry? What weighty business is it which makes thee run so fast? I mused a moment, and cannot conceive what prompted me to reply, in a slow accent, Life is short, and hell is everlasting. He started at me with a ghastly look. I will be d—d, he resumed at length, if thou hast not stumbled against a gallows on thy way. It may come to that some time. Farewell, comrade.—Stay a moment longer, he exclaimed, taking a tin bottle from his hunting pouch, and offering it to me after he had swallowed a large draught. I swallowed greedily the contents of the bottle, and new strength animated my whole frame.

Meanwhile my new companion had stretched himself upon the grass, and I followed his example. Thy brandy has given me new life, said I; we must be better acquainted with each other, he made no reply, but struck fire and lighted his pipe. Is it long since thou hast carried on this trade? He stared at me, and said, what means that question? I took the knife from his girdle, being now grown bolder, and continuing my discourse—has this instrument done much execution?—Who art thou? he roared out in a terrible accent at the same time flinging his pipe on the grass and starting up? A murderer, like thyself, but only a beginner. He gazed at me very earnestly and took up his pipe. Thou art no inhabitant of these districts, he resumed at length. I am; hast thou never heard of Wolfe, the inn-keeper, at A—? He started up, as though frantic, exclaiming, in a rapturous accent, Wolfe the inn-keeper, who has been so severely punished for game stealing! That very man I am. Welcome, comrade, a thousand times welcome! he exclaimed, shaking me joyfully by the hand, how glad I am that I have found thee at last! Come along, brother, he said, now thou art ripe, thou art the man I wanted for my purpose. I shall acquire great honour by introducing thee to our common-

wealth. Make haste, and follow me. Whither art
thou going to conduct me? Don't ask questions,
but come and see. So saying, he dragged me for-
cibly after him.

As we proceeded, the forest grew more and more
intricate, and impenetrable, and gloomy. Neither
of us spoke a word until I was suddenly roused
from my apathy by the whistle of my leader. I looked around, and beheld myself at the declivity of a
steep rock projecting over a deep cavern, and a ladder rose slowly from the abyss, a thundering voice
halloed from the deep, and the winding cavern
echoed to the sound. My leader descended, first
bidding me to wait till he should return. I must
first secure the mastiff which guards the entrance to
our abode, he said, thou art a stranger, and the
ferocious beast will tear thee to pieces. So saying
he disappeared. My leader soon re-appeared, bidding me descend into the cavern. I had no other
choice left but to submit to necessity, and went
down. Having advanced a few steps under the excavated rock, our passage grew larger, and I beheld some huts at a distance; and, as I approached
nearer, a round spot covered with grass appeared to
my view. About twenty people were sitting round
a blazing fire. Here, my leader exclaimed, here I
bring you a new member of our society, whose
name is not unknown to you. Rise and welcome
the celebrated Wolfe, of A——. Wolfe! they all exclaimed with one voice, forming a circle around me,
men, women, and children. Their joy was un-
feigned and cordial; confidence, and even respect,
was marked in their looks. My unexpected arrival
had interrupted their dinner; they retook their

seats, and pressed me to partake of their inviting meal, which consisted of venison of all kinds, and stewed fruits. The goblet filled with delicious wine wandered from hand to hand, and spread merriment and joviality around. You see, brother, said the man who had introduced me, how we live here : every day passes like the present. Is it not true, comrades? Yes, every day passes like the present, the whole crew exclaimed. If, therefore, you think you can accustom yourself to our manner of life, then stay with us, and be our captain. Do you consent to it. comrades? An unanimous yes rent the air. I then exclaimed, after a moment's consideration, I will stay with you, comrades.

By means of house-breaking, and some highway robberies, we soon got possession of a large sum of money, with which we dispatched one of our associates to a distant town to buy four horses, fire arms, powder and ball. Thus furnished, the first tempestuous night the houses of the hated judges were pillaged ; and whenever the face of the earth was covered with midnight darkness, we sallied forth from our den to destroy the game in those parts where my misfortunes had commenced, and I always took care to let my persecutors know that it was Wolfe who committed these depredations.

The terror of my name soon spread itself all over the country, and the neighbouring magistrates tried every means to get me into their power, a great reward was promised to him who should take me dead or alive, and, if one of my associates, a full pardon: notwithstanding which, I was so fortunate as to elude the watchfulness of my pursuers for a considerable time, and to frustrate every attempt on my liberty.

I had carried on this infernal trade a whole year, when I began to be tired of it. The gang, whose leader I was, having disappointed my sanguine hopes, I soon perceived, with terror, how much my fancy, heated by wine and loose desires, had been imposed upon, when I consented to become the captain of these robbers. Hunger and want frequently supplied the place of luxury and ease, which I had expected, and I was necessitated many a time to risk my life in order to procure a scanty meal, which hardly sufficed to appease the violent cravings of my empty stomach.

The visionary image of brotherly concord disappeared, and envy, suspicion, and jealousy stepped into its place, loosening the ties of society. The solemn promise of a full pardon to him who should deliver me into the hands of justice, was a powerful temptation to lawless robbers, and I was well aware of the dangers which surrounded me. I became a stranger to sleep, and a victim to never ceasing apprehensions; the phantom of suspicion pursued me every where, tormented me when awake, lay down with me upon my couch, and created frightful dreams, when my weary eyes were now and then closed by the hand of slumber.

About this time a war broke out in Germany, and recruits were raising every where, which gave me some hopes to retreat in an honourable manner from my associates, and turn a useful member of society. I accordingly wrote a letter to my prince, humbly entreating his pardon, and desiring to enlist in his service.

This petition was not taken the least notice of, as were neither a second and a third; when, not having the least hope of being pardoned left, I detemined to leave the country, and die in the service of the king of Prussia, as a soldier. I gave my gang the slip and began my journey. My road led me through a small country town, where I intended to stay that night.

A few weeks ago a proclamation had been published through the whole country, commanding a strict examination of every traveller, because the prince had taken a part in the war as a member of the German empire. The gate keeper of the town I was going to enter, was sitting on a bench before his house as I rode by ; my forbidding countenance and motley dress raised his suspicion, and as soon as I had entered the gate he shut it, and demanded my passport, after he had first secured the bridle of my horse. I was prepared for accidents of this sort, having provided myself with a passport, which I had taken from a merchant whom I had robbed. However, this testimony would not satisfy the eagle eyed gate keeper, my physiognomy being in direct contradiction to it, and I was obliged to follow him to the bailiff's house. He ordered me to wait his return at the door.

The passport was examined, and mean while a rabble began to assemble around me, attracted by my strange figure ; a whispering arose among the multitude, and some of the crowd were pointing alternately at me and my horse : the latter having been stolen by one of my former associates, my conscience gave the alarm. The gate keeper returned with the passport, and told me, that the bailiff, understanding that I came from the seat of war, would be glad to have half an hour's conversation with me, and to get some information of our army. This message increased my apprehensions of being known; and fearing the invitation of the bailiff to be a snare to get me in his power without any resistance, I clapped spurs to my horse without returning an answer.

My sudden flight gave the signal to an universal hue and cry. A thief! a thief! exclaimed the whole multitude, pursuing me with all possible speed. I therefore redoubled the swiftness of my flight, goading the sides of my horse without mercy. My pursuers were soon far behind me, panting for breath, and liberty promised to gladden my heart again, when the fleetness of my flight was suddenly stopped by a dead wall. My pursuers gave a loud shout when they saw me entrapped, and I had given over every hope of effecting my escape, when a sudden thought struck me that the wall might be the city wall, and that perhaps I might regain my liberty through a window of one of the houses at the bottom of the street. The door of that on the left side was open. I jumped from my horse, and entered it with a pistol in each hand, bolting the door after me, and hastening up stairs without being seen by any of the inhabitants. My pursuers were close at my heels, and thundered at the door when I was rushing into a room where nobody was but an old woman. Seeing a man with a brace of pistols terror fettered her tongue, and she fell down in a swoon. I opened the window, and imagine my joy, when the open fields met my anxious eye. I bolted the door, placed chairs and tables against it, threw the bed out of the window, and concealed

myself in the chimney, to await there the setting in
of night.   This was the work of a few moments:
and I was safely housed in my hiding place, when
the door was forced open with a thundering noise.
My calculations had not deceived me, and my plan
succeeded as well as I could expect it.   My pursuers, seeing the window open, and the feather bed
lying in the field, believed firmly that I had effected
my escape.   Some young men jumped boldly down
and others went on horseback to pursue me: the
old woman, who could tell no tales, was carried to
another part of the house, and I was left alone to
muse on my awkward situation.

At length the feather bed was brought back, but
nobody came to sleep on it that night, and the room
remained unoccupied.   As soon as midnight silence announced to me that every body was gone to
rest, I slided softly down the chimney, tore one of
the bed sheets, and twisted it in a line, to make use
of it in getting into the field.   No sooner had I
touched the ground than I took to my heels, to
reach before daybreak the Black Forest, which I
knew was only two miles distant, being well aware
that the whole country would be in a hue and cry
after me as soon as my nocturnal escape should be
known.

I now resolved to enlist in the Prussian service,
and soon found my way to the highroad, and directed my steps to F——.   I determined not to enter
any inhabited place before I should be obliged by
necessity to do it, lest some new misfortune might
cross my military scheme.   With that view I left
the high road whenever it led through a village,
walking all night long, and slept in the day time,

Thus I travelled onward two nights without having
met with any accident, when, at the close of the
third day, I was obliged to direct my course to a
small hamlet, in order to provide myself with provisions. As soon as it was dark, I went with fearful steps to a baker's shop to purchase some bread,
but great was my terror when I wanted to pay for
the small loaf of coarse bread I had bought, and
could not find my purse.

Being entirely destitute of money, I offered one
of my pistols, which I took out of my pocket in lieu
of payment. The baker viewed me from top to toe,
and after some hesitation agreed to the bargain.
Unfortunately, the house of this man had been robbed some time ago by a body of thieves, and my savage look. joined with my singular appearance, rendered me suspicious to the baker, who, ever since
the robbery, took every ill-looking stranger for a
thief. Prompted by that notion, he ordered one of
his people to follow me at some distance as soon as
I had left the house. and went instantly to the bailiff to inform him of his suspicions, and the strange
substitute for money which he had accepted from
me. The magistrate, who had been indefatigable in
his researches after the daring robbers, without succeeding in his endeavours to find them out, soon
fell in with his opinion, and ordered some stout fellows to follow the suspected thief, and to secure him.

In the mean time I had struck again into the
forest, seated myself behind some bushes on the
bank of a rivulet, and began to appease the demand
of hunger. not observing that I was followed, when
suddenly four sinewy arms seized me from behind.
The unexpected surprise, the continual fatigues I

had undergone, and the strength of my adversaries, rendered it impossible to separate myself from their powerful grasps, and I was taken before the magistrate, who demanded my passport. Having been obliged to leave it behind, when my alarmed conscience had drawn upon me my late disaster, I had no other choice but to pretend to be an Austrian deserter, who wanted to go into the Prussian service. The magistrate, mistrusting my veracity, ordered me to be searched, when a loaded pistol and a large knife were found upon me. This increased the suspicion of the zealous magistrate, who, without further ado, sent me to prison. New apprehensions of a dreadful nature assailed now my unhappy soul. The fear that all my former crimes would be detected, filled my desponding soul with black despair; however my lamentable situation soon took a turn more favourable that I could expect. A transport of Prussian recruits passing through the village in the afternoon, the magistrate ordered me to be delivered to the commanding officer, thinking this to be the most commodious way to rid the country of a fellow, whose whole appearance bore evident marks of his thievish profession, and to save himself the trouble of a tedious examination. My size, and the robust make of my limbs, rendered me a very acceptable acquisition to the recruiting officer, and I was then enrolled as a Prussian soldier, to my unutterable joy.

Thus, from a robber, was I at once appointed to fight the battles of Frederick the Great, and made a solemn vow to fulfil cheerfully the duties of my honourable calling. Our transport arrived safe at Magdeburg, where, with the rest of my companions

I was instructed in the military art. The corporal that was appointed to teach me the manual exercise, was famous for his severity, conforming to the principles of his royal master, who, as it is universally known, had laid it down as a rule to inspire his martial bands with heroism by the frequent application of wooden arguments. I was not in the least partial to that sort of reasoning, and found it very difficult to brook the brutality of my drilling master, who seemed to have a secret predilection for me, by his plying my back so frequently and severely.

Nevertheless, I exerted myself to the utmost of my ability to please this rigorous corporal, and to shelter myself against the frequent heavy showers of blows and cuffs; but not being able to accomplish my object, resentment and hatred began at last to rankle in my heart; my whole stock of patience was exhausted, and I began to have frequent recourse to drinking, in order to dispel the gloominess of mind which haunted me incessantly, and to drown the recollection of my forlorn situation. One day, coming half intoxicated to the parade, I acquitted myself so badly, that my military mentor plied my back most unmercifully. My anger was roused, my blood was boiling, and I called my chastiser a savage beast, a blood hound, and many other names of the same description. The fury of my tyrant being raised to the highest degree by that language, he inflicted his blows with such violence, that I, in a fit of despair, struck him to the ground with the but end of my gun. I was seized, carried to prison, and sentenced by a court martial to run the gauntlet. The day of execution arrived, the soldiers were drawn up, and my back was bared; when lo! the mark of my ignominy was seen between my shoulders. It being evident that the sign of the gallows was there marked, and that I had been under the hands of a common hangman, I was thereupon declared unworthy to receive military punishment, and was sentenced to work in the fortification.

Confined with the dregs of the human kind, and ever in company with the basest villains, my weak virtuous resolutions began gradually to wear way; and I concerted plans of effecting my escape. One of my fellow prisoners joined with me in devising the means of regaining our liberty, and after many fruitless efforts we at length effected our escape assisted by an impenetrable fog, which covered our flight. As soon as our escape was made known in the fortress, the cannons were fired and the country roused. Notwithstanding which, we happily eluded our pursuers, and reached at the close of day a wood, where we resolved to conceal ourselves in the tops of the trees till the heat of the pursuit should abate. In this uncomfortable situation we remained as long as our small stock of provisions lasted, consulting with each other by what means we could procure an independent livelihood, and at last agreed to resort to the Haunted Castle in the Black Forest, and there commence robbers. After many fatiguing rambles and alarming fears, we arrived at length at the wished for asylum.

My inventive genius soon suggested to me a scheme for rendering that desolated fabric more secure and guarded against the intrusion of unwelcome visitors, by raising an idea in the minds of the neighbouring villagers of its being haunted by evil spirits. In order to accomplish our design, we set up a most dreadful howling and doleful lamentation, whenever we perceived any of the villagers near the environs of the castle. We now committed numberless robberies, and, as our numbers increased, became more daring, till, after a series of thirty years, our infernal society sustained a deadly blow by the nocturnal surprise which delivered us into the hands of punishing justice.

Thus my lords and gentlemen, I have related the leading particulars of my unhappy life. I have not wilfully omitted any circumstance. I throw myself entirely on your mercy; and whatever sentence you may deem proper to inflict, I shall cheerfully, and with resignation, submit to it.

Wolfe's life will be spared on account of this faithful confession, and the great assistance he has afforded his judges in putting a final stop to the depredations which have been so long committed near the Black Forest. He is to be committed for life to the house of correction, where he will have sufficient leisure to reflect on his past life, and to prepare to meet that eternal judge who sooner or later overtakes the wicked in their vile pursuits.

J. S. Pratt, Printer, Stokesley, Yorkshire.